IT'S NOT A DATE

What Reviewers Say About
Heather Blackmore's Work

Like Jazz

"This book is a top of the line winner that grabbed me, held me, and more than entertained me from start to finish! ...I totally recommend this book; it is capable of being enjoyed on many levels, from different angles, and in its totality. Please do not miss this thoroughly satisfying book!"—*Rainbow Book Reviews*

"An excellent debut and an excellent book: well-developed, engaging characters, good plot, great setting."—*Rainbow Awards 2014*

For Money or Love

"As it progresses the characters deepen, the plot thickens and it becomes so much more than 'just' a romance. The story pulls you along on a whole series of levels, with several interesting sub-plots and entertaining characters to follow...by half way through [I] literally couldn't put it down...I loved it."—*The Lesbian Reading Room*

Visit us at www.boldstrokesbooks.com

By the Author

Like Jazz

For Money or Love

It's Not a Date

IT'S NOT A DATE

by

Heather Blackmore

2018

IT'S NOT A DATE

ISBN 13: 978-1-63555-149-5

THIS TRADE PAPERBACK ORIGINAL IS PUBLISHED BY
BOLD STROKES BOOKS, INC.
P.O. BOX 249
VALLEY FALLS, NY 12185

FIRST EDITION: MARCH 2018

CREDITS
EDITOR: SHELLEY THRASHER
PRODUCTION DESIGN: SUSAN RAMUNDO
COVER DESIGN BY TAMMY SEIDICK

Acknowledgments

My thanks to the many Bold Strokes Books staffers, authors, and volunteers who helped with the publication of this novel and provided a fun and supportive environment along the way. To friends and authors Kathy Chetkovich and Cindy Rizzo: I greatly appreciate your thoughtful feedback on an early draft. Your keen insights and suggestions undoubtedly improved the end result. Shelley Thrasher, editor extraordinaire: I have been so fortunate to work with you on all three of my novels. If you ever leave me, I will hunt you down and read accounting textbooks to you. Shelly Lampe, my love and heart, thank you for your humor, love, and kindness, and for the title of this book. I am incredibly lucky to be sharing my life with you.

I wrote much of this novel on the peaceful grounds of Vajrapani Institute, a special, spiritual place in the Santa Cruz mountains that values wisdom and compassion. I was surrounded by nature's beauty and silent, truth-seeking strangers. In today's chaotic, technology-driven, limited-attention-span culture, rare havens such as Vajrapani encourage the rejuvenation of one's soul and prove that kind forces exist to more than offset the greed and short-sightedness of many of those in power. Thank you, Vajrapani, for reminding me that Kindness is everlasting.

Dedication

To forgive a loved one for something deeply hurtful is as crucial as it is difficult, for it is only through forgiveness that we open ourselves to the infinite beauty and love that an unencumbered heart can experience. This book is for everyone brave enough to grant themselves such freedom.

Chapter One

The plane pulled into the gate at Maui's Kahului airport five minutes early, which suited Kadrienne Davenport perfectly. She preferred to run on schedule, but early was better than late. Her keynote speech was slotted at the bizarre time of ten a.m., and if everything kept going according to plan, she could find her driver, check in to the hotel, get at least six hours of sleep, hit the stationary bike, shower and change for the conference, and enjoy a sit-down breakfast while she read an honest-to-God paper version of *The Wall Street Journal*, all before having to walk onstage. She hoped the gym inside her Kapalua hotel wouldn't disappoint in the way such facilities frequently did, with equipment so in need of maintenance it was surprising guests weren't issued a can of WD-40 at check-in.

It had been a few years since she'd flown via commercial airline, and as she retrieved her laptop, Kade pondered the rule about having to stow larger electronics during the initial and final minutes of the flight. The waste was staggering. With half a billion business trips taken in the US annually, she estimated the loss equated to over 16 million hours of productivity in the US alone. Surely some safety device such as a short cable that could secure one's laptop to the seat or tray table could be designed. She decided she'd either invest in a startup that figured out a safe way around the problem, or she'd start one herself.

Since she was in the second row, Kade's turn to exit came quickly. Carry-on strapped over her shoulder, she followed the initial passengers off the Jetway and into the terminal. She headed toward Ground Transportation and smiled upon seeing her middle name on a placard held by a man in a suit, wearing a chauffeur's hat. Kade approached her driver.

"I'm Kade Delaney." Kade typically opted to use her middle name when she traveled commercially in order to avoid having to engage in polite conversation on the rare chance someone recognized the name Kadrienne Davenport.

The man nodded and slid a hand into his breast pocket. "Pleasure to meet you, Ms. Delaney. I have a message for you." He extended an envelope to Kade.

Confused, Kade pulled a sheet of paper from the envelope and read its contents.

Don't be mad. –H

She leveled the man with an icy stare. "You're not my driver?"
"No, ma'am."
"Are you from a limousine service?"
"No, ma'am."
"Did Holly put you up to this?"
"I'm only a messenger, ma'am." He tipped his hat. "Have a good night, Ms. Delaney." He turned to leave.
"Wait. Can I catch a ride with you to my hotel? I'll pay you."
"Sorry, ma'am. I'm not allowed to take passengers."
"Of course not," Kade muttered. Holly, her assistant, would have seen to that as part of this little…whatever-this-was…adventure to force her to interact with people who weren't on the agenda. Alterations to the plan didn't make sense, given Kade's packed schedule tomorrow. It wasn't as if she could cram in an excursion. As she watched him walk away, she pulled out her mobile phone and dialed Holly's number, which kicked over to voice mail. "Not funny, Holly. Call me as soon as you get this." She ended the call and stormed through the tiny terminal toward the taxi stand.

The airport was like a tiny replica of a big-city version, as if it wanted to be a life-size airport when it grew up. But that would require air-conditioning, Kade thought unkindly, as the humidity hit her like a noodle thrown at the wall to see if it would stick. There were only two terminals, which could be navigated end-to-end within minutes. Photographs of Hawaiian dancers in traditional Polynesian dress lined the walls. Kade imagined the male dancers smiling at all the deplaning passengers wearing jeans or other heavy materials while they hulaed to the off-camera ukulele in only their loincloths.

The word taxi stand was generous for what was a faded yellow curb, which at present was empty. In fact, the entire airport seemed deserted except for the folks who had been on her flight. It was only eleven p.m. local time. This was an international airport. Shouldn't more people be here?

Kade waited. She was the only person trying to hail a taxi, and the longer she stood alone, the more certain she became that no cabs were forthcoming. She could call for one, but this was the land of "driving with aloha." Rush wasn't the operative word of the islands. She couldn't rally behind the idea of standing around for God knew how long. Time to hit the rental-car counters. It meant losing the time she'd planned to work during the forty-minute drive to the hotel, but this taxi stand was seeing less action than an Antarctic snow-cone vendor. Holly had some major explaining to do.

Unlike at Chicago O'Hare or Boston Logan or LAX, it took her only a few minutes to arrive at the service counters. Only one car company was open, staffed by two tired-looking fifty-somethings. Hearing dot-matrix printers spewing forth contracts, Kade hoped the vehicles offered were newer than the office technology and mentally confirmed that she was current on her automobile-club membership.

At least the view was inviting. Kade noticed the blonde as soon as she entered the rental-car area. Any woman who could capture Kade's attention while standing under the appalling fluorescent ceiling lights of a rental-car center after having spent the duration of the evening on an airplane deserved Kade's admiration. At first it was because, aside from the two people presently being served, she was the only person waiting in line. And then it was because the woman turned around and unleashed a warm smile that could have melted Kade on the spot, had she not already liquefied from the humidity.

Kade had seen that smile before. A different woman, a different time, a different circumstance, a lifetime ago. But God, it was the same smile. Kade had come across two perfect things in life—well, in the life of her youth: her friend's smiles and her friend's hugs. Cassie's smiles bested any chocolate, drug, compliment, sunny day, test score, promotion, or pardon. They had a transformative power that could boost Kade's spirits in a heartbeat and alter for the better any mood Kade was in.

And her hugs. When Cassie hugged her, Kade felt the world dissolve around them. Kade would forgo food, water, sleep, and sunlight if she could feel Cassie's arms around her again.

Given the less-than-ideal circumstances in which Kade now found herself, she was piqued that the blonde had captured her attention, and she wished she had someone like Cassie at her side, encouraging her to initiate conversation and possibly ask her on a date.

But reality was a harsh and unforgiving mistress, and Kade was stuck in her own skin, which meant squelching her desire to meet the woman with the engaging smile. She wasn't here to socialize. She slowed her pace and pretended to study something on her phone, simultaneously relieved and disappointed when the woman was called to the counter.

Jennifer Spencer was surprised by the last entrant to the rental-car queue and somewhat frustrated she'd been called forward. She definitely would have struck up a conversation. She'd seen the brunette heading toward the taxi area earlier and was a bit envious of whichever driver would be lucky enough to get the fare, though it probably wouldn't be the safest of rides with the driver focusing on the passenger via the rearview mirror instead of the road. At least that's what Jen would be doing.

The woman walked with confidence and a take-no-prisoners attitude, the kind of stride that could carry her down the streets of New York City at two a.m., assured that no one would dare approach.

She wore her silky brown hair in a low ponytail, likely for comfort during the flight as well as on the ground, considering the humidity. Her pantsuit was probably custom, given the tapered waist and extra length required in the leg. The flared hem offered glimpses of the stylish mid-heeled boots she looked like she could run in. She had a little ski-slope nose that Jen wanted to run her finger down, and her serious eyes were an interesting hazel. She wore either lip gloss or a lipstick shade that faintly accentuated the natural color of her lovely mouth, which Jen found oddly inviting, given the frown occupying it. Jen could imagine that mouth making its way down her naked body until it—

"Miss? Miss?" A voice pulled her back to reality like some vaudeville hook.

"I'm sorry. What?" Jen wrenched her gaze from the woman and returned her focus to the representative trying to issue her a vehicle.

"The supplemental insurance coverage. Do you wish to purchase or decline?"

"Oh. Decline. Thanks."

With his ballpoint pen, the man marked a number of areas on the form with Xs. "Please initial here, here, here, here, here, sign here, and initial here."

As she signed where indicated and tried to take in the rest of his instructions, Jen heard snippets of the brunette's increasingly voluble conversation with the other clerk. She gleaned that this was the last inbound flight of the night, no cars were available without a reservation, and that, yes, the woman could speak with her manager, but she'd have to return in the morning when he was on duty. The brunette said something about taxis and bum-fucked Egypt, then sliced her palm through the air as if to strike her outburst from the record. She left with a curt "thank you" and marched back toward the terminal.

Jen grabbed the proffered key and tugged her roller bag, practically running to catch up to the woman. "Excuse me," she called twice, louder the second time, and the woman stopped and looked up from her phone.

"Yes?"

Oh, those eyes up close—intelligent and appraising, sparkling with flecks of forest and autumn. Jen struggled to catch her breath and blamed it on the forty-foot dash. "Would you like a ride?" Jen seemed to catch the woman off guard because she studied Jen as if she were trying to complete a puzzle. Jen replayed the past few moments and knew the woman spoke English, so she tried again. She dangled the key fob. "I'm happy to take you wherever you're going, or at least drop you at a hotel where you can call a cab or have one meet you."

"Why would you do that?"

It was Jen's turn to be confused. "Why wouldn't I?"

"I'm a stranger you just met in an airport. I could be anyone," the woman said, seeming aghast.

Jen laughed. "What are you going to do? Steal my underwear?"

The woman again looked perplexed. Then something shifted, and she smiled. "What kind of underwear?"

Oh my God. Jen wasn't expecting that. Her cheeks heated. The woman could be playing off the idea of filching some fancy name-brand lingerie, or she could be flirting big-time. Jen extended her hand. "Jen Spencer." They were similar in stature, and Jen realized it was the woman's carriage that made her seem taller than her own five-nine.

The woman hiked her carry-on bag up on her shoulder before taking Jen's hand. "Kade Delaney. And a ride would be great, thank you." The greeting lasted several seconds longer than was customary, neither interested in ending the contact.

"You're welcome. We're this way." Jen led them to the designated car.

As Jen adjusted the seat and mirrors, she asked, "Where to?"

Kade removed her laptop from its protective sleeve and flipped it open. "I'm at the Ritz-Carlton, but I'm happy to be dropped off wherever you're going."

"You're not attending the Women in Tech conference there, are you?"

"I am. I take it you are too?"

"Which panel are you on?" With the confidence Kade projected, she probably wasn't merely an attendee.

Kade turned her head and met Jen's gaze. "I'm not on one. Are you?"

Jen put the car in drive. "Yes, and I'm trying not to freak out about it."

"You'll be fine."

"Miranda McArthur's on my panel."

Kade eyed Jen and waited.

Jen filled her in. "CEO of HipSpot."

"Right. And?"

"The fastest-growing online travel company in the world?"

"I know who she is, but I don't see why that should freak you out."

"She's amazing."

"And you're not?"

"You don't even know me."

"Not true, Jen Spencer. I know you show kindness to strangers in airports, you're in high tech, and you wear underwear. Or at least you pack it. Of course, I'd have to…see it, to know for sure."

"On?" Jen posed the question to get a better idea of the signals she was reading.

"You're in the driver's seat."

Jen stopped the car before they exited the parking lot. "You're flirting with me."

Kade raised her hands as if in surrender. "You're the one who mentioned underwear. I was merely staying on theme."

"Totally flirting."

"Sorry. I'm not trying to make you uncomfortable." Kade's expression shuttered, returning to that of the woman who was told no cars were available.

Jen reached over and closed the lid of the laptop. "I rather prefer it." She gently laid the device on the floor behind Kade.

The glint of playfulness immediately returned to Kade's eyes. "I *had* planned on working during the ride."

Jen grinned and turned onto the road. "How's that working out for you?" Jen was pleased to see that Kade's harrumph was for effect. Kade didn't seem to be in any hurry to retake the computer.

"What's the panel on?" Kade asked.

"Raising venture capital."

Kade smiled wryly. "I hope they'll be serving coffee beforehand."

"I know, right? I'm only on it because I recently landed seed financing for my company and one of my investors recommended me. The panelists run the gamut of fund-raising experience, and I'm the newbie."

"What time's your panel?"

"Right before the keynote speech tomorrow. Seven, I think?"

"P.M.?"

Jen laughed at the surprise in Kade's voice. "Yes. P.M. The agenda's in my purse, if you want to grab it. Why?"

Kade snatched Jen's purse from the backseat and immediately found the folded pamphlet. She indicated the light above her seat. "Will it bother you if I turn this on?"

"Not at all."

Kade scanned the document. Then she started to shake her head. She returned the pages to Jen's purse and turned off the light.

Jen could still see her shaking her head, her silhouette outlined by the streetlights. "What's wrong?"

"My assistant misled me about the timing of some of these panels. I thought the main networking and conference events were in the morning, followed by breakout sessions. I thought I'd be on a plane by afternoon."

"Time for a new assistant?" Jen suggested.

Kade laughed. "It's complicated."

"Isn't accurate calendaring one of the basics of the job?"

"She thinks she's looking out for me."

"By screwing with your schedule?"

"By forcing me to take a day off. Now I have nothing on my plate until tomorrow night, my colleagues think I'm out-of-pocket so they won't be pinging me, and I can't turn around and go home in the meantime. Who knows? Maybe she thought I'd share a hotel shuttle and meet a new friend, or rent a car and go on an excursion. Make me wing it to see what shakes loose."

"In her defense, it is Maui." Jen heard Kade take a deep breath and let it out slowly. "Is it really so bad, having a day to enjoy one of the most beautiful places on earth?"

"I like routine. Schedules. I'm not much of a fly-by-the-seat-of-your-pants kind of gal."

"Well, you're in luck, because I excel at spontaneity and can work with boundaries. How about this? If you're not completely beat by the time we get to the Ritz, let's grab a seat at one of the poolside bars, enjoy a cocktail, and, so that your assistant approves, talk about anything other than work. Then tomorrow morning, if you're not already sick of me, we'll meet for breakfast at a time you designate, and we'll come up with a plan for the day that involves plenty of sunshine and beautiful women."

"You're not some sort of chaperone my assistant hired to keep me from working, are you?"

"Are you really that pathetic?"

"Guilty."

"What kind of work do you do that you have to be constantly doing it? I mean, I'm a CEO and I take time off. Whole weekends, occasionally."

"Not that I don't want to delve deeper into the incredible laziness you just copped to—because, wow, weekends—but it might color what you think of me, and I'm enjoying my status as"—here Kade punctuated the air with her hands as if reading from a news scroll—"'woman in technology who fails to use technology to read conference agenda.' And by the way, how did you get a rental car?"

"It was the craziest thing. Are you ready? It's called…" Jen took her time as if revealing a major secret. "A reservation. And nice deflection on the work question."

"Thank you."

"Do you really think it would change my mind about you if I knew what you did?"

"Does Miranda McArthur really intimidate you?"

"Oh, shit. You're not Miranda McArthur, traveling under a pseudonym, are you?"

"You think I run a company that excels at helping consumers make travel plans, yet I can't even rent a car?"

"Fair point. I don't know what any of these business leaders look like. I know a lot of names, but if they're not Mark Zuckerberg or Bill Gates, I wouldn't know them from Adam. You're making me nervous."

"And you drive like my mother."

"A woman who has obviously done a few things right, so I'll accept that as a compliment, Miss Avoid the Subject."

Kade pointed toward the pedals. "When she talks, she tends to pull her foot off the gas, like she has difficulty multitasking."

"I do not take my foot off the…Wow, I totally do that."

"That's okay. It's just that much longer until the cocktail you've promised me."

"So you're game even though having drinks with a stranger wasn't on tonight's agenda?" Jen was tempted to ask Kade for her assistant's address, so she could send a thank-you note.

"I'm taking a walk on the wild side."

Jen reached for Kade's hand and squeezed it softly. "It looks good on you."

"It'll look better once you have a few drinks."

Jen appreciated Kade's self-deprecating humor. It gave her a kind of accessibility Jen wouldn't have necessarily pegged her for when she first saw her strut to the rental-car line. "If I have a few drinks, I'll be under the table."

"Perfect. I like when people look up to me," Kade quipped.

Jen glanced at Kade. "I appreciate your covert strategy to take my mind completely off my panel tomorrow."

Kade grinned. "Let's not limit ourselves. Your mind doesn't have to be the only thing to be taken completely off. Should we return to the underwear conversation?"

Jen smiled and shook her head. "What panel?"

CHAPTER TWO

Upon arriving at the Ritz-Carlton, Jen parked in the temporary-registration zone and left her bag in the car. Kade assumed it was because she preferred to self-park close to her room, once she learned where it was. But as Kade was checking in, she saw Jen standing to the side, already out of line. Kade waved her over. "What room are you in?"

"No vacancy. Apparently the conference is pretty popular. And with the usual tourism…" Jen shrugged.

"You had a car reservation but not a hotel reservation?"

"No need. There's lots of vacancy on the west side, and I figured I'd see what struck my fancy. Since I'm here, I checked, but frankly this place is a little steep for my company's travel budget anyway. I'll stay for that drink and then head out."

Kade glanced at her watch. "But it's late. You don't want to go to hotel after hotel trying to find a room at this time of night, or drive after drinking." She spoke to the clerk who was checking her in. "Make that two keys, please." She turned to Jen and offered her the key card she'd been given. "I'm in a two-bedroom suite. Stay with me." Kade flushed. "I mean, take the other room."

Jen shook her head and lightly pushed the card away. "Thank you, but I can't foist myself on you like that. Let's have that drink and figure out when to meet in the morning."

"You're not foisting yourself on me. I'm offering. There's plenty of room. I won't even know you're there."

Jen cocked her head, unleashed a slow, sexy smile, and moved directly into Kade's personal space. Her straight, natural-blond hair fell past her shoulders and framed a face of smooth, pale skin that seemed divinely inspired to highlight her blue eyes, which were pinning Kade where she stood. With effort, Kade held her ground. Jen was making it difficult for her to appear unfazed, when half of her wanted even less distance between them, and the other half wanted to escape to somewhere emotionally safer.

"That's not a challenge, is it?" Jen asked. She took Kade's hand in both of hers, traced her palm with her thumb, and whispered outside of the clerk's earshot. "To see if I can get you to notice me?"

Kade sucked in a breath, hoping Jen couldn't feel the shiver that ran through her. Hell, the simple caress practically had Kade arching into her like an affection-starved cat. Having experienced Jen's engaging personality while they bantered throughout the long drive, Kade had been noticing far more about Jen than her good looks. She had an innate beauty that drew Kade in and an intrinsic decency all the more notable by how rarely Kade came across it during her typical workday. Kade would have to be made of ice not to notice her, but she hadn't extended the offer out of a desire to get Jen into bed. She wanted her to know how much she'd appreciated her kindness.

She pulled Jen to a standstill several feet away. "I could never be in a room with you and not notice you. So if you can accept that I'm attracted to you, the room is yours. No strings. You have my word I won't try anything." Kade once again offered Jen the key card. "And it might not be good for your reputation to be seen sharing a room with me, so I suggest waiting a minute between each of us entering."

Kade felt Jen scrutinize her at length. Finally, Jen pinched the card, but she didn't take it from Kade's hand. "I don't know who you are, Kade Delaney, but I can tell you that when I choose to spend time with someone, I don't give a damn what other people think. I'll either get my bag and valet the car and we'll walk together to the room, or we'll say good night here."

Few people spoke to Kade so authoritatively. Most deferred to her. Apparently, Jen's friendliness didn't also translate into her being some shrinking violet, and Kade's interest shot up several more degrees. Kade nodded once and let go of the card.

When Jen returned from the vehicle, they walked in silence to the room. Kade opened the door and flipped on some lights. "Take whichever room you'd like," she said. "I'm not going to get too comfortable, or I'll never make it down for that adult beverage." Jen went in one direction, Kade headed the other, and they both returned to the foyer at the same time.

The walk to the hotel lounge was also silent. Though it was too dark to see the ocean, the pool below the lounge terrace was illuminated an inviting blue, and the humidity was milder here than at the airport. They opted to sit at the lanai fire pits, which cast a warm glow amid the surrounding soft lighting. Once they ordered their drinks, Kade addressed the tension that had settled between them. "You've gone quiet on me."

"What did you mean about my reputation?"

Kade should have known her comment would disconcert Jen, if not outright concern her. "I thought that might be bothering you." Where to start? And why? It wasn't like this was going anywhere. Jen could have been on a connecting flight from God-knew-where. They probably didn't even live in the same state. "We agreed: no work talk."

"So that was about *your* reputation."

Kade shook her head. "Someone might think you're angling for special treatment."

Jen smiled. "Sexual favors?"

Kade frowned at Jen's making light of it. "I'm trying to keep your best interests in mind."

"And I appreciate it." Jen covered Kade's hand with her own. "I do. But since I'm the head of my company, I don't see how being seen together could possibly mar me professionally."

In reality, Jen was right. Kade was speaking theoretically. Kade had never heard Jen's name in conversation and didn't know the name of her company. Furthermore, Kade's sexual orientation wasn't common knowledge, so unless they pawed each other publicly, an observer wouldn't jump to the conclusion that they were more than friends. While it was still possible Kade's concern for Jen could come to fruition, it was highly unlikely.

The server set their drinks down and promptly left. Jen held up her glass. "To a nearly full day off."

Kade clinked glasses with Jen and took a sip. "You're not going to attend any of the afternoon sessions?"

"Are you?"

Kade shook her head. "No. I'm only here for the post-dinner events tomorrow."

In a faux Southern accent, Jen asked, "Then, pray tell, whatever shall we do, sugar?" She looked Kade up and down as she said this but spoke so playfully that Kade knew she wasn't suggesting they spend it naked in each other's arms. At least, Kade thought so.

"Have you been to Maui before?" Kade asked.

"No. You?"

"Not in years."

"Is there anything in particular you want to see?"

"Am I allowed to flirt again?"

Jen edged closer. "Encouraged, even."

"Then yes. You, in a bikini."

"You don't have to be on Maui to see that."

"Where do I have to be?"

"If any of these shops were open, our room."

Kade wondered if Jen purposely skirted around mentioning where she lived. "Suite. We're sharing a suite, not a room." She took a healthy sip of her drink.

"Do you want to be sharing a room?"

Kade nearly spit out the liquid. She dabbed her mouth with a napkin. Knowing she was blushing, she folded the napkin multiple ways to avoid looking at Jen. The universe was once again conspiring against her, but this time it seemed to have a good sense of humor. She was as interested as she was outmatched. She met Jen's eyes and smiled. "I'm so out of my league with you."

"Why?" Jen's expression was open and attentive.

Kade laughed. "You're intelligent. Gorgeous. Driven. Funny. Warm…" She suddenly snapped her fingers and pointed at Jen. "And married."

Jen smiled. "Single."

"Ten kids."

"Three houseplants."

Another thought occurred to Kade. She finally had her. She crossed her arms. "Player."

"Never had a one-night stand."

"I rest my case."

"What case are you making?"

"That you're too much."

"You're overthinking."

"I've been told worse."

"Breakfast tomorrow. We'll come up with a must-see list complete with timetable and dinner reservations."

"Don't you want to mingle at the conference dinner?"

"I'll have plenty of opportunity when they serve drinks after the keynote. I'd rather have dinner with you."

Kade rapped her fingers on her glass. She couldn't come up with a good reason why she shouldn't join Jen for the day, and it made her uncomfortable. A warm hand covered hers and stopped her tapping.

"Stop trying to make excuses. You're unexpectedly free. Deal with it. Breakfast. What time?"

"Nine."

"Nine it is." Jen finished her drink and stood, holding her hand out to Kade, firelight dancing in her eyes. "Let's go to bed."

Kade knew she was being baited, so she simply shook her head and gave a little snort as she accepted Jen's hand. True to her word, Jen showed no worry or hesitation in holding onto it during the entire walk back to the room.

In the suite's entryway, Jen tugged her close and held her, thanking her for the accommodations and the drink. It was the kind of tight, lingering hug that Cassie used to give, and it made Kade feel special. Only with Jen, there was more. Kade had never paid attention to the press of Cassie's breasts against hers or wished her hands would travel. But with Jen, Kade's body was attuned to a pang of arousal, reveling in the feel of Jen's body wrapped in hers and imagining where Jen's fingers could roam. A faint apricot scent from Jen's hair enticed her to nestle even closer, which she denied herself.

Although she contemplated making a move to see if Jen would be receptive to the idea of sharing a bed, she wouldn't break her promise to not take advantage of the situation. When they broke apart, Jen stretched behind Kade's head to remove her hair tie, which brought their faces tantalizingly close. She ran a hand through Kade's hair and followed it with her eyes, as if contemplating the same idea Kade had. As she reached the end of the long strands, she toyed with them and shifted her gaze back to Kade.

"You're very difficult to say good night to," Jen said.

"You're making it hard for me to keep my word." Kade steadied herself by holding onto Jen's hips.

"I didn't make the same promise you did." Jen smoothed the back of two fingers down Kade's cheek.

"No, you didn't."

Jen cupped Kade's chin and kissed her softly on the mouth. "Sweet dreams, Kade." Then she walked into her bedroom.

Kade felt bereft. Certain only that whatever she dreamed tonight would be far more racy than sweet, she headed for the shower. She always felt like she needed a full-body disinfectant each time she sat in an airplane seat, and now she also needed to channel her arousal. She quickly stripped out of her clothes and stepped into the hot spray. As she lathered herself, she let her hands move slowly and caress her body in a much more sensual way than during a typical shower. The reason was maybe thirty feet away.

In her mind, Jen was touching her, Jen was bringing every nerve ending to attention, Jen's seductive smile was tearing at her defenses and self-discipline. Good Lord. With one simple kiss, one fleeting sampling of her marvelous mouth, Jen had reduced Kade to a whimpering puddle of need.

Kade pinched her erect nipple and bit her lip, trying to remain quiet even though the water and walls would shield her sounds. The film from the soap bubbles helped her palms and fingers glide easily along her skin. She imagined Jen's mouth on her breast—sucking, teasing, nipping. She twisted the showerhead to its pulsation setting. She let her fingers venture lower, through the curls at the apex of her thighs, until they met her swollen center. And then she stilled her movements. No way could she orgasm to thoughts of Jen and expect to calmly spend the next day with her. She shouldn't have riled herself up like this. The moment called for release or a cold shower, but she couldn't manage either. She flipped the setting back to its normal spray and rinsed.

As she toweled off, she barely dried between her legs, needing time to come down from the stimulation. In her tank top and shorts, she headed to the kitchenette for a glass of water. And ice. Lots of ice.

Light from the outdoor fixtures came through the glass doors of the lanai, allowing her to see. She twisted an ice-cube tray above a glass and filled it with water. She took a healthy drink and walked to the lanai. Sliding aside the door, Kade stepped out and set down the beverage.

Waves crashed over the sand in a melody that settled her mind and relaxed her body.

For some reason, she wasn't startled when she heard the stool being dragged directly behind her. Nor was she surprised by the touch of warm hands on her upper arms or the legs enveloping her and pressing against her thighs. Fingers softly caressed her neck, her clavicle, her shoulders. They wove into her damp hair and came out again, slowly sliding over her chin and throat. Kade arched into each touch, reveling in the attention of this woman.

Soft lips followed a similar path, lightly brushing her skin and affecting the rhythm of her breathing, more erratic now. When that warm mouth closed over her earlobe, Kade whimpered. Oh, God. She should have let herself come because she might very well do so if Jen continued her maddening, gentle exploration.

But the hands didn't stray farther south, and soon they were brushing Kade's hair off her shoulders. "I wanted to say good night," Jen said quietly, planting feather-light kisses along Kade's neck.

"You…did," Kade managed to say.

"Not the way I wanted to."

"How…" Jen's lips along her skin diminished Kade's capacity for speech. Kade heard her own exhale. "How did you want to?"

Without taking her hands off Kade, Jen slid off the stool and pushed it away with her foot. She turned Kade around to face her. "Like this," Jen said. As if looking for something, she searched every inch of Kade's face. Fingers followed her gaze, tracing Kade's eyebrows, cheeks, nose, and chin. "Beautiful," she said as lips supplanted fingers, kissing each area with equal devotion. When she arrived at Kade's mouth, she gazed into Kade's eyes and smiled, a magnificent, radiant thing that breathed life into the farthest depths of Kade's soul. Jen stopped a razor's edge away, giving Kade the final say.

But Kade had no choice. She was completely, helplessly, deliciously owned by Jen, and all she could do was surrender to her desire. Kade touched her lips to Jen's. It was a whisper of connection, the faint touch of a downy feather. She increased the pressure, nearly fainting with pleasure as Jen parted Kade's lips with her tongue, seeking entrance. Wet warmth cascaded into Kade's mouth, making her borderline delirious.

Kade gave herself over to the kiss entirely, reveling in the softness, the taste, the puzzle and its answer—all things Jen. She couldn't have imagined a more perfect moment, a more perfect kiss, a more perfect woman. She was at once grounded and exalted, confused yet absolutely clear. She wanted this, and for the first time in ages, she indulged in the experience.

Jen eased out of the kiss, and they took a minute to descend from the exquisite heights to which they'd climbed. "Good night," she murmured as she slowly stepped away, not letting go of Kade's hand until she could grasp it no more.

Far better than good, Kade thought. Sublime.

CHAPTER THREE

Beyond tired from the time-zone change and the flight, Kade didn't bother to set the alarm early enough to sneak in a trip to the gym. She dragged a brush through her hair and opted for another ponytail, lest Jen think small animals took up residence there in the night. The bathroom mirror was being particularly unkind this morning, and Kade considered putting on some makeup before going in search of coffee. But chances were good she and Jen would be hitting the pool or beach today, where all hell would break loose in the looks department anyway.

Upon entering the kitchen, Kade spied the coffee machine and brewed a cup. She noticed Jen on the lanai and joined her.

Jen's hair was also in a ponytail, but of course she was fresh-faced and welcoming, whereas Kade wasn't usually welcoming of anything before two cups of java. A bowl of fresh fruit, a pitcher of orange juice, a mug of coffee, and *The Wall Street Journal* surrounded Jen at the outdoor table, which overlooked the Pacific Ocean in the distance.

"Good morning," Jen said brightly.

"Morning." Kade plunked herself into a chair. "Let me guess. Morning person?"

"Not especially. Every day I wake up is a good day, considering the alternative."

This comment got Kade's attention. She edged forward in her seat and grabbed Jen's arm. "Jen, you're not...sick, are you?"

Jen offered an amused smile. "Overindulging in tragic romance novels again, honey?"

"I worry about you. Too much perk. It's unhealthy." Kade popped a grape into her mouth and grabbed a section of the paper. "Aside from that, you're fantasy material right now. Coffee, OJ, fruit, the *Journal*." She pointed under the table to Jen's crossed legs. "Killer legs." She jutted her chin in Jen's direction. "Toned arms. Amazing smile. Arresting blue eyes. Maybe I'm the one who was sick and this is heaven."

Jen set the paper down. "You know, for someone who claims to be uptight about schedules and timetables, you're pretty relaxed and awesome in the morning."

Kade grinned. "That's because I'm not myself today."

"No? Then who are you? Because I like her."

Kade chewed another grape and gave the question some thought. "It's you. Well, you and this unplanned day. Something about the combination is liberating." Suddenly the buoyant feeling she'd been experiencing in Jen's company flagged at the notion this was all temporary. "At the stroke of midnight, I'll be a rat again." Though the idea saddened her, Kade understood its truth.

"Don't you have other friends who bring out this side of you?"

No sense denying it. Kade had known as soon as she first caught Jen smiling at her in the rental-car line that she was Cassie all over again. Worse. She and Cassie had loved each other like sisters, whereas Jen, in an alternate universe, could have been so much more.

Kade looked directly at Jen so there was no mistaking it. "I did, and it didn't really work out for her." She needed to move Fantasy Woman back onto the reality plane. "I can do this for a day, Jen. I can't hurt you…no one can get hurt in one day, especially if we have a plan and stick to it. So if you're still up for it, let's come up with an itinerary. If not, you're welcome to use the suite—"

Jen covered Kade's hand with hers. "I'm up for it."

❖

Sightseeing wasn't in the cards since some of the island's best experiences, such as the Road to Hana and the Haleakala Crater, were long drives away. They settled on finishing breakfast at the hotel, stopping at a swimwear shop, taking the short drive to D.T. Fleming Beach Park, eating a light lunch at a taco stand, lazing by the pool in the afternoon, and sharing an early dinner at the hotel's restaurant.

Kade was definitely a stickler about arrival and departure times, and meticulously adhered to the schedule they established. But she was fine creating whole blocks of time for a broad purpose, such as "pool" or "beach." Much to Jen's amusement, Kade showed Jen the calendar on her phone, quickly scrolling through the next thirty days, multicolored blocks filling morning, noon, and night. Then she made a face when she hit five weeks out and the schedule was empty except for the odd event. "All that white space. Hate that," she'd said, making Jen laugh.

When Jen parked in front of the beachwear boutique and saw the outfits in the window display, she said, "We may need more time here."

Kade frowned and swiped at her phone. "You get twenty minutes. We're not spending this beautiful day indoors, trying on outfits. Whatever you buy will look fabulous on you."

"When's the last time you went swimsuit shopping?"

Kade's eyes swung skyward as if to give some thought to the question. Seconds passed with no response.

"A while, then," Jen surmised.

"Years."

"And did you just grab something and go?"

"I did what any twenty-something American woman would do. Tried on a bikini, immediately moved to one-pieces, littered the fitting room with rejects, settled on something in slimming black, scored a fantastic cover-up, and successfully declined all subsequent pool-party invitations."

Jen laughed. "Okay. Points for honesty. Here's my thinking. First, we agree that sunscreen is our friend and pasty-white means healthy. Second, no snickering at the other's farmer tan. Third, we rip this off like a Band-Aid. I'll choose four swimsuits for you, and vice versa. We decide from those."

"Bikinis or one-pieces?"

Jen considered this issue, knowing she'd prefer Kade in a bikini but allowing for comfort. "Two each."

Kade offered her hand, which Jen shook. "Deal."

But all that planning flew out the window as soon as Jen saw Kade hesitantly step out from behind the fitting curtain, wearing the jade bikini Jen had selected for her. Jen's pulse beat faster, and she couldn't focus on whatever she'd pulled from a rack. Without taking her eyes from Kade, she managed to hang the item back in place before striding over to her, corralling her into the tiny fitting area, and feeling haphazardly behind her to pull the curtain closed around them. There was barely standing room for two people, but all Jen noticed was her desperation to touch Kade.

Kade's startled, confused face was mere inches away, but Jen dropped her gaze. The green material barely covered Kade's cleavage, and her chest rose and fell with each increasingly ragged breath. They both watched Jen reach up to caress Kade's breast, her thumb gliding across the bra to Kade's nipple, which strained against the material. Kade's head snapped up as her mouth parted in a gasp that Jen swallowed in a searing kiss. It wasn't gentle or sweet or teasing. Kade's lips parted as Jen sought entrance with her tongue, yielding to Jen's overpowering need to own her in that moment.

Jen broke the kiss, fighting for breath, stumbling for control. Her behavior shocked her. To the questions evident in Kade's surprised hazel eyes, all Jen could say was, "This one." Jen blindly felt behind her, flicked open the curtain, stepped out of the fitting room, and snapped it closed. She darted out the door and took a number of calming breaths, trying to come down from her arousal, trying to regain herself. Her actions were completely antithetical to her usually grounded self, and she didn't know what to make of them.

Jen sat on the curb in front of an empty parking space, hands in her lap. She didn't want to apologize, but she'd do whatever it took to ensure Kade didn't change her mind about spending the day together. If it meant having her hands tied behind her back to prevent further misbehavior, she'd do it. (Though as soon as she thought about who might do the tying, she realized it was not the best choice of images.) Minutes later, she heard footsteps and, in her peripheral vision, noticed Kade sit next to her, plastic shopping bag in tow. Jen steeled herself with a deep breath before daring to look over at Kade, whose eyes focused on the parking lot, hidden behind sunglasses.

"Well, bathing-suit shopping will never be the same," Kade said before sliding her eyes to Jen. "How was your day?"

Jen chewed on Kade's comments before bursting with laughter.

Kade pointed to the convenience store next door. "If it's all the same to you, I'm going to grab some sunscreen. I trust you'll find something."

Once they concluded their shopping, Kade navigated them to the beach park, known more for boogie-boarding and body-surfing, but which was close and clean, offering lifeguards and shade. They changed in the public restrooms before heading onto the sand to scope out a spot, where they laid out their mats and towels.

Jen found the view nearly as breathtaking as the woman next to her.

As they applied sunscreen, Kade said, "You know, in the movies, whenever the star-crossed lovers reach the beach scene, they're never glistening with sweat. I'm drenched, and we just got here." She scooched to the edge of her mat and presented her back to Jen, along with the bottle of lotion. "And with that lead-in, I'm sure you can't wait to do me."

Jen poured some into her hand before bending to Kade's ear. "Slip of the tongue?"

"I thought that was earlier," Kade said, her voice lower than usual as she gathered her hair in her hands and held it off her shoulder.

The sexy tone catapulted Jen's attraction ever higher. Jen warmed the lotion between her hands and laid her right palm on Kade's back, a touch below the bra line. She moved down to the bikini bottoms, then up to where she'd started. She slid her thumb under the bikini top.

"The uncovered parts, darling," Kade said good-naturedly, though Jen noticed a small hitch in her breath.

Jen moved her hand along Kade's side, then slowly forward, until she spread her palm across Kade's stomach. She shifted to her knees while she inched her thumb below the center of Kade's top. Mouth at Kade's ear, she softly asked, "Did you get this...area?"

"I...did, thank you," Kade said breathily.

"Good, because I want to make sure I *do you* right. Darling." The endearment was so foreign, her words and actions so atypical, she froze. What was she thinking? She was on a public beach, for God's sake, not making some soft-porno film. The woman beneath her touch was someone to be respected, someone she did respect. Why did she lose her ability to reason whenever Kade was near? Twice today, she'd reacted to Kade's proximity like a cat in heat, and she wasn't proud of herself.

She removed her hand and scooted back several inches. She rubbed sunscreen across Kade's back and shoulders, covering the area with wide, clumsy swaths, eager to finish the job. Tossing the bottle onto Kade's mat before dropping onto her back, she slid her sunglasses into her hair and hid her face in the crook of her arm.

The sand next to her gave way a little as Kade sidled up to her, giving Jen a tiny shove to move over to share the mat. "Hey," Kade said.

Jen lifted her arm, offered Kade an apologetic look, and mumbled, "Hey," before ducking back into hiding. Kade pushed against her again, silently asking for Jen's attention. Jen rose onto her elbows and donned her sunglasses. "I'm not like this, you know. This...lust-filled letch who can't keep her hands to herself. I'm so sorry." Jen dropped onto her back and gazed at Kade. She traced her fingers over Kade's cheek. "You're just so beautiful. I'm defenseless against you."

Kade brushed her lips across Jen's fingers. "Then I'm in good company."

"Don't be nice to me."

Kade shifted onto her back and rested her head on Jen's stomach. She took Jen's closest hand and entwined it with hers. "Few people accuse me of being nice."

Jen played with strands of Kade's hair with her other hand. "Why is that? You're lovely."

"Male-dominated industry. Over-compensation. Inflexibility. Set in my ways. You name it."

Jen chuckled. "You sound like a seventy-year-old, not a…how old are you?"

"Thirty-two."

"Not a thirty-two-year-old."

"You?"

"Twenty-seven."

"Whippersnapper."

Minutes passed in relative quiet. Small waves lapped at the shore, children shouted in the distance, beachgoers lazed in the sun. Jen was content. She felt like she was away at camp, with spending money and no chaperones. Her grandmother was in good hands, Jeremy had everything under control at work, and she'd stumbled upon a woman who was quickly becoming important to her.

Continuing to gently play with Kade's hair, Jen said softly, "Kade?"

"Hmm."

"I'm glad you took the day off."

"Mmm. Me too."

The hum of a helicopter grew steadily closer, invading the peacefulness with its noise, then faded into the distance.

"Kade?"

"Hmm."

"You're going to drown in the sweat that's pooling on my stomach from your hot head if you don't get off me."

Kade's laughter rippled against her. "Hot-headed. A much more apt accusation."

Over dinner, they broached the subject of family. Jen's parents were on the East Coast taking care of Jen's maternal grandparents, leaving Jen as the primary caretaker of her paternal grandmother.

Jen didn't mind, since she was close to her grandma Edna, but with Edna's worsening dementia and Jen in a demanding job, she often found herself pulled in competing directions. Those very issues had inspired her to build her company. "No work talk, I know, but finding qualified, affordable caretakers is difficult. And on short notice? Practically impossible. My company's going to change that." She sliced another piece of their shared apple turnover, making sure to add ice cream and a berry to the forkful before holding it out to Kade.

"Many of the best technologies we have today were created by an entrepreneur who personally experienced an unsatisfactory product or service and decided to make a better one." Kade took a bite and moaned. Dessert had never sounded so lovely to Jen's ears, nor had she ever wanted so few bites herself. Delighting in Kade's pleasure was proving to be her favorite way yet to end a meal—no small feat for an admitted sweet tooth.

"Is that what you've done?" Jen asked, proud of herself for being able to keep track of the conversation, since she was mostly focused on Kade's delectable mouth.

"Ah-ah-ah. No work talk. You'll have plenty of it at the networking event tonight."

"What about you? Are you close with your parents? Any siblings?"

"I'm somewhat close to my mom," Kade said as she offered Jen a bite. "My father and I are cordial at best. I inherited all his worst qualities."

"Do tell."

"Hyper-disciplined, obsessive about cleanliness. Blows a gasket if you're five seconds late. What else? Sexist. Warm as an arctic winter."

"Well, you obviously didn't inherit all those qualities."

"I'm not sexist," Kade said as she gently pulled a berry into her mouth from her fork tines. Jen sensed Kade was completely unaware of how provocative she was, which ratcheted up her sexiness tenfold.

"Oh, come on. From what I've seen, none of that describes you."

Kade shrugged. "I got lucky for a while. I had other role models. When I was eleven, we settled into a new neighborhood where I met my best friend, Cassie. I practically lived at her house, and her parents treated me like one of their own. That's who I think of as my family."

"I'm glad you had them."

Kade gazed at Jen as if she were the answer to something, and then her expression closed. She glanced at her watch and signed the bill to her room. "You need to get to your panel."

Jen took Kade's hand and interlaced their fingers. "Where did you go just now?"

Kade caressed Jen with her thumb. "You remind me of her. Of Cassie." Jen could see Kade's eyes soften in the dim light. "Same smile. Same warmth." Kade got out of her chair and squatted next to Jen's, taking Jen's hand in both of hers. The adoration and affection she looked up at Jen with stole Jen's breath. "Jen Spencer, you've been an absolute gift to me these last nineteen, twenty hours." She rose and kissed Jen's forehead. "Thank you," she whispered. She caressed Jen's cheek before softly kissing her mouth. "Thank you." Then she walked away.

The panel was a blur. Jen was thankful she'd rehearsed her brief spiel about who she was and what her company was building, because the other parts of her brain had shut down. The moderator skillfully elicited audience participation, Jen didn't make a fool of herself in front of Miranda McArthur, and she had no idea about the rest. She was completely swept up in Kade Delaney.

Wanting the keynote speech to end before it even started, Jen was currently favoring a plan that had her bailing on the meet-and-greet afterward so she could find Kade and figure out what was between them.

Then the auditorium lights went dark, and the stage lit up. The CEO of the conference sponsor was onstage, introducing the main speaker, who was apparently the author of some best-selling leadership book as well as partner of a venture capital, or VC, firm. He provided a laundry list of the speaker's accomplishments, and Jen wanted him to get on with it. When he said, "Please welcome Kadrienne Davenport," the spotlight illuminated Kade, who waved to the audience as she walked back and forth during the applause.

Jen was spellbound. Kade—her Kade—was Kadrienne Davenport? She probed her numbed mind for Kade's answer to her question about which panel she was on. *I'm not on one.* Had she really experienced the single best day of her life with a woman known for breaking CEOs and authoring a book on what it takes to be a leader in today's global economy? Good God. And here was little Jen Spencer, with her tiny startup and a puny million in seed financing, acting as Kade's equal. Worse, coming on to her!

The spell Jen was under lasted during Kade's entire speech and the audience Q&A session. Kade was mesmerizing. She'd changed clothes, put on some makeup, and arranged her hair in a clip. Her time in the sun gave her a healthy glow. She was flawless in her pantsuit, commanding on stage, and conversant on a range of topics. Amazing.

And then Kade was finished. After the applause died down, an announcer reminded everyone about the mixer getting underway. Should Jen stand among the throngs trying to get a word with Kade? Should she avoid her? Could she get her head into the game long enough to survive an evening of small talk with other attendees, which she had zero desire to engage in?

She found herself walking through the crowd, drink in hand, rudderless. She didn't want to see anyone here except Kade. And with so many participants, she couldn't spot Kade anywhere. She decided to ask. Finally, after speaking with half a dozen people, she learned that Kade wasn't attending. That was all she needed. She set her drink on a table and left the ballroom.

Upon opening the suite door, Jen immediately knew Kade was gone. She went to Kade's room and confirmed her suspicion. Kade hadn't wanted the time off that her assistant had imposed on her, so she would be on the next flight off the island, likely a private charter.

Hadn't wanted the time off. That's what kept playing in Jen's head. Kade hadn't even wanted the day that exceeded Jen's finest dreams. Jen sank onto Kade's bed and thought of how she'd acted. As an equal. As a partner to Kadrienne effing Davenport. She laughed—embarrassed, confounded. Kade *had* treated her as an equal. She'd conversed with humor and intelligence, and participated fully in kisses that Jen damn well knew were extraordinary. She hadn't sought any diversion from her original schedule, yet she'd embraced their time together completely. Well, Jen might not know much about Kadrienne Davenport, but she was confident she had learned a lot about Kade Delaney. Too bad Ms. Delaney wasn't allowed to come out and play very often.

CHAPTER FOUR

One Year Later

Kade was in the large conference room of her firm's Menlo Park office, working hard to remain in her seat. The executives of a new office-productivity software application were now several minutes over their allotted time, and she wasn't interested in hearing more. No matter how efficient a new integrated time-management system might be, she couldn't get excited at the prospect of an investment when its owners couldn't keep to a schedule. The irony was lost on the group. Usually Holly would promptly call or personally interrupt a meeting that ran long, but Holly was out on an errand.

When Kade's phone vibrated, she excused herself and headed to her office. "Charles, what a pleasant surprise. What can I do for you?" Kade asked. Charles Jameson was an angel investor who occasionally wrote large checks for companies he felt passionate about, and Kade's first foray into the tech startup world had been one such investment. Charles had been impressed by the then twenty-one-year-old CEO, and he had become a mentor to her over the years. He was one of less than a handful of advisors who had her complete respect.

"Start another company and make us both rich, Kade." It was his normal greeting, though his voice didn't carry its typical strength.

"I've done that twice now, Charles. I'm retired, remember?" Retirement was a longstanding joke between them. At thirty-three, with more money than she could ever spend as a result of selling her first two companies, Kade was no closer to retirement than she'd been in the womb. Same with Charles, who, at nearly sixty, liked to say that his marriage depended on his business ventures because his wife would divorce him if he didn't get out of the house. "You sound a little under the weather."

"Under a freight train, more like. I'm calling from the hospital. You wouldn't believe what I've had to go through to get these damn nurses to give me my phone."

Kade passed through her office doorway and shut the door. "Please tell me you're on the mend from whatever's landed you there, my friend."

"Heart attack, double bypass. All's well except for the food. And the damn drugs. If I behave myself, I'll be good as new in no time."

"If you were to behave yourself, I wouldn't recognize you."

"Two peas in a pod, eh? Look, Kade. I need a favor. I'm on the board of a few startups that might need some attention until I'm back on my feet. I know you have your hands full in prima-donna land, but there's no one I trust more. Can I count on you?"

According to Charles, venture capitalists were a bunch of divas that helped startups like sugar helped dieting. To him, most were ivory-tower-living folks who failed to understand the major execution challenges facing their portfolio companies yet rarely allowed this fact to stop them from offering advice. One of the rare times Kade hadn't heeded Charles's counsel was when she'd accepted the offer of partner in Matlock Ventures. Kade believed she could help her portfolio companies because she had direct experience running two startups, and Charles thought she was an exception among her VC colleagues.

"Of course. Have Pamela give Holly the details, and I'll have company counsel draft the paperwork to transfer your board seats to me on an interim basis. Can you e-sign?" Pamela was Charles's longtime assistant.

Charles laughed, sounding like he had marbles in his chest. "You know Pamela signs all that stuff. I haven't even signed a tax return in twenty years."

"Consider it done. And please take care of yourself and listen to your doctors."

Charles groaned his complaint. "Kade? Thank you." He ended the call.

Kade sat at her desk and typed the password to her laptop. She was about to email Holly, but Holly knocked and entered without waiting for a reply. Typical.

"How is Charles?" Holly asked. "Did he say when he'll be released?"

Kade didn't bother asking how Holly knew she was off the phone or that Charles was in the hospital. Holly had a sixth sense. And probably spyware. And webcams. Wire taps, maybe. Kade had long ago stopped wondering how Holly got her information and simply accepted her gift. In this case, odds were that Pamela and Holly were in cahoots, but Kade preferred not to be informed. She got a kick out of thinking Holly had some sort of superpower when it came to knowing things about her life, except for those times when Holly played matchmaker or otherwise insinuated herself in Kade's nonexistent love life.

"He didn't, but he sounds ornery. I imagine the nurses have their hands full. Would you send over a plant or some flowers?" Kade shook her head. "Scratch that. Send golf balls, some tees, and a gift certificate for a new putter as a recovery incentive. And a *Playboy*."

"Already done. Except it's gloves instead of tees, a certificate for eighteen holes, and a *Penthouse*."

"You rake."

Holly shrugged. "Better articles."

"Looks like I'm going to have to keep the eggs warm in his startup nest for a little while. Would you ask Pamela—"

"He's on three boards. Counsel for each company has been notified. We should see paperwork from each of them by end of day, naming you officially. One has a board meeting at ten tomorrow in Palo Alto. Pamela gave me the details, and the address is in your calendar. I've moved your ten o'clock to three and punted the three to Thursday."

"Please make sure they know—"

"Ten o'clock, sharp. They've been informed."

"Why do I even need to be here?"

"To play token female partner at the all-white-boys club."

"Oh, right."

Kade's irritation was spiraling ever higher. She'd found the Creative Care office only because of her phone's GPS. It was located on the second story of a strip mall that didn't appear to have a second floor, and it took two trips around the parking lot to find a staircase. Thankfully, Holly had provided the suite number since the company's name wasn't posted on the door. And now she sat in a windowless conference room at 10:13 a.m. and didn't bother to hide her displeasure.

Grabbing her purse, she stood and addressed the company's twenty-something co-founder, who had spent the last few minutes typing furiously on his laptop, avoiding eye contact, and probably fearing for his job. "I'm sorry, Jeremy. I don't have time for this. This meeting was supposed to start at ten. I don't know anything about Creative Care and anticipated needing the full hour to get up to speed, but clearly that's not happening. Charles is much more forgiving than I am, and I'm sure you can reschedule once he's back online. Good luck to you." She nodded and headed for the door. It opened before she reached it.

A woman rushed in and spoke while glancing down to drop her keys into her bag. "I'm so sorry I'm late. There was a multicar pileup on the freeway, with CHP and fire eng—ohmygod." Jen looked up and stopped mid-sentence as her eyes met Kade's.

Kade stepped back and let her eyes briefly roam over Jen's body. Jennifer Spencer was beautiful in a pale-blue skirt suit that accentuated her dazzling eyes, which were abnormally wide and communicating that she was as startled as Kade. Her blond hair was down, cascading over her shoulders with girl-next-door simplicity that reminded Kade of her natural approachability and warmth. Kade couldn't remember ever feeling so blindsided.

"What are you doing here?" Jen asked, clutching her purse to her chest as if shielding herself from Kade's presence.

Kade stood taller, trying to project a calm indifference she wasn't feeling. She nodded at Jen, the entirety of the greeting she could manage. "If you'll excuse me." She brushed past Jen without looking back.

❖

"What the hell was she doing here?" Jen asked Jeremy, which came out like an accusation. She raised a palm in apology and took a breath. "Sorry, Jeremy. I mean, why was Kadrienne Davenport here just now?"

"You know her?"

"Everyone in Silicon Valley knows her. Of course I know her."

"I know *of* her. Everyone knows *of* her. But you actually *know her* know her?"

Jen waved him off and shook her head. "Not really. No. She's...ugh. Are we ready to start? Is Andrew on the line? Where's Charles's stand-in?"

"I told Andrew we'd dial him in. And *that*..." Jeremy pointed out the door, "or should I say *she*, is your new boss. Hand-selected by Charles."

Jen felt the blood rush from her face. She steadied herself with a hand on the back of a chair. Jeremy quickly handed her a bottle of water as she dropped into the seat. "Jen?"

"That can't...we can't...she can't...no. Please get Andrew on the phone. Now." Jen took a swig of the water and waited for Jeremy to get through. Once the company's attorney was on speakerphone, Jen said, "Andrew, it's Jen Spencer and Jeremy Corbin. Today's meeting's been cancelled. Listen. Do we have any way of vetoing Charles's choice for his board seat?"

"No. Someone has to represent the investors, and since he's the majority preferred stockholder, it's his seat."

That wasn't the answer she'd hoped for. "What are our options?"

"To get rid of her?"

Jen looked at Jeremy as she replied, knowing she owed him an explanation. "Yes."

"They're limited, Jen. You can contact Charles, communicate your concerns, and see if he'll either keep the seat himself during his recuperation or appoint a different person to represent the investors. But as of now, the paperwork's completed. You have the common seat, Ms. Davenport has the preferred seat, and the third seat remains open."

Jen was quiet.

"Jen?" Andrew asked.

"We're still here," Jen said dejectedly.

"I want you to consider three things," Andrew said. "First, I've worked with Charles multiple times. He can't abide B players. He must hold Ms. Davenport in extremely high regard to ask her to take his board seat. So if you approach him about this issue, make sure you have your facts straight. Second, consider his health and the interim nature of the appointment. Is this something you really want to bother him with at this time, for what's probably a very limited duration? Lastly, consider Ms. Davenport's credentials. She's served on a number of boards and works for a highly respected firm in the Valley. Not only might you learn something from her, but she's very well connected. Is this a person you want to be known for trying to kick off your board?"

"Good advice, Andrew. I'll talk to Jeremy, and we'll call you back if we need you."

When the call ended, Jeremy spoke. "Mind telling me what's going on? Getting someone like Kadrienne Davenport on our team is a major coup for a company our size. Instant credibility. What's your problem with her?"

Jen rubbed her face with her hands. Jeremy was her friend and first hire, and he'd been so strong out of the gate as her chief technology officer that she'd offered him co-founder status and stock. He deserved the truth. "Don't hate me."

"Uh-oh."

"My trip to Maui last year. What comes to mind?"

Jeremy shifted his gaze to the ceiling in contemplation. "Uh... conference? Um..." He locked eyes with her and slapped the table.

"Hot woman you came on to and were mortified by once you found out who she was?"

"Bingo."

"Ho-ly shit."

Jen could only nod. "I was hoping I'd never see her again."

"Liar. She's fucking gorgeous."

"Not helpful," Jen replied in a sing-song manner.

"She's a viper. Practically made me pee my pants."

"Better." Jen appreciated Jeremy's ways of sticking up for her. "She does actually have something of a reputation as a—well, let's say hard-nose. Trust me. I binge-Googled the hell out of her after Maui. But I don't want to be one of *those* people, tearing a woman down because she's successful. She's found something that works for her. More power to her." Not that the renowned Kadrienne Davenport would ever give her the time of day anyway, but the last thing Jen needed was to be distracted at work, where she had to be constantly firing on all cylinders. Workplace inequality was alive and well in Silicon Valley, with women having to continually prove themselves capable of the C-level positions historically awarded to men, all the while juggling the imbalanced weight of their responsibilities at home.

"Does it, though?" Jeremy asked.

"Does it what?"

"Work for her. The Maui woman you fell for sounded nothing—"

"I didn't *fall*. I was…charmed. Mildly."

"O-kaaay. The *charmer* you described was nothing like the woman who was here. And the woman who was here is not your type whatsoever. I was trapped for not even fifteen minutes, and still my life flashed before my eyes."

Jen held up a palm to curb the conversation. "This is my new boss we're talking about. There will be no talk of type, charm—"

"Hotness."

"Hotness or any other factor. Clear?"

He mock-saluted. "Aye, aye, Captain." He again pointed in the direction of the door. "Your boss though. Kind of a stickler on the schedule front."

Jen smacked her forehead dramatically. "Which I completely blew. Jesus, she wrote a *book* about holding meetings on time." She touched his forearm and spoke earnestly. "Jer, I left an hour—an *hour*—earlier than normal."

"Traffic's traffic. She can't hold people responsible for things beyond their control."

"She'd say I should have left earlier."

"Probably. So what's the plan?"

Jen took a deep breath and considered her options. She didn't have to reschedule the board meeting. It was primarily for Charles's benefit, to keep him in the loop about their progress. But it was a two-way street, as sometimes Charles advised them in meaningful ways or provided a contact he thought could help in some regard. She supposed Kade could offer similar guidance. "I guess I'll try to reschedule the meeting at her office. Make it convenient for her."

"Does it make sense for you to meet with her one-on-one? Move past any awkwardness from Maui?"

"Possibly. She might not even remember me. In fact, the way she looked at me just now, you'd think I was something she'd peeled from the bottom of her shoe."

Jeremy laughed. "Yeah, if that shoe had stepped in caramel with chocolate sauce. She looked like she was about to eat you for lunch."

"Face it. This is why we're single. We haven't the slightest clue about women."

"We're not single. We're married to our jobs."

"There's that."

Kade was pissed with a capital A. No, make that P. She was so angry, she couldn't even spell. She stalked to Holly's desk and motioned her into her office, something she rarely did. She posted herself at her doorway until Holly brushed past, and she closed the door. "What in bloody hell do you think you're doing, letting me walk into the lion's den?"

"We're British now?"

"We are rankled, with a capital…Ugh. A little warning would have been nice."

"You seem upset."

"You've known since yesterday that I'm suddenly a director for *her* company!"

"Who?"

"Don't play dumb. Creative Care. Ring a bell?"

"Your ten o'clock."

"Creative Care, formerly called Care Labs, apparently. According to the conference agenda, she was CEO of Care Labs. Now she's CEO of Creative Care. Tell me you didn't know that."

"I know that a Jennifer Spencer is CEO of Creative Care, formerly called Care Labs, yes."

"Yet you didn't tell me."

"You've been to dozens of conferences. If you're this upset, you must mean Maui."

"Yes. Jen Spencer."

"You told me you'd met someone who reminded you of Cassie. You told me Cassie would have tried to set you up with this woman. You told me you thought the two of them would have become fast friends."

"Yes." Kade knew all this. Why was Holly stalling? She was the most forthcoming person in Kade's life. Why not give her a heads-up? Let her mentally prepare?

"You also told me you were happy you wouldn't be seeing her again because you could do the same to her that you did to Cassie."

"Yes." Kade was beyond exasperated.

"You never told me her name."

Kade paused. That was probably true, but she was too riled to admit defeat. "I'm sure I mentioned the CEO of Care Labs."

Holly shook her head. "CEO of a startup."

Kade took several breaths to calm down, something she should have done prior to initiating this conversation. Holly didn't deserve an upbraiding. She looked after Kade better than anyone in Kade's life, better than Kade herself did. She wrapped her arms around

Holly. "I'm sorry. Please forgive the lunatic who charged in here just now." When Holly returned the embrace, Kade felt mildly better. She hadn't yet lost *this* friend.

Kade slumped into one of her visitor chairs. "I can't...I can't."

Holly sat next to Kade. "What can't you do?"

"I need to resign from this board seat. I can't be in this woman's life. This woman cannot be in my life."

"If she has this effect on you, I disagree."

"No. No. Charles is going to have to find someone else. I'll call him." Kade stood and rounded the desk to her usual chair.

"Aren't you being a bit rash? What happened at the meeting? Did she say something to you?"

"No. She was late. I left."

"You didn't talk to her?"

"No."

"I think you owe it to Charles to at least have one conversation with her. I mean, what are you going to tell him? 'I have a crush on Jen so I can't be on her board'?"

It was a good point. What exactly was Kade's logic? "I don't have a crush on her."

"Then you should have no problem talking to her. It's business, which you excel at."

"Stroking my ego won't work."

"No?"

"Maybe."

Holly's phone buzzed, as it often did, but she ignored it and glanced at her watch instead. "You weren't expected back until eleven thirty. You have market research until one. Lunch arrives at noon. Sushi. So why don't you hit the gym? Eat when you get back."

Market research was a catch-all involving sifting through the numerous newsletters and blogs Kade received daily, as well as reading online articles, venture-capital investment summaries, stock-market bulletins, and testing product demos of her own portfolio companies as well as competitors'. She could easily fill her days with US research alone, so combined with staying current with what was happening in European, Asian, and South American markets, it was a recurring calendar item Holly often used whenever Kade wasn't saddled with a call or meeting.

"Hit the gym" was a euphemism for "chill out." Although Kade could barely carve thirty minutes of exercise out of a ninety-minute slot, given the required drive, shower, change of clothes, hair and makeup time, the infrequency of Holly's gym suggestions meant that Kade always heeded them, for both their sakes.

"Sold," Kade said, snatching her purse and following Holly out of her office. Holly's phone buzzed again, and she pointed out to Kade the caller ID of Jennifer Spencer. "Don't even think about rescheduling the board meeting. She had her chance."

"I wouldn't dream of it," Holly said as she shooed Kade away.

"Kadrienne Davenport's office," said the woman who answered Jen's call.

"Yes. May I speak with Kade please? I mean, Kadrienne."

"Who's calling, please?"

"Jennifer Spencer."

"CEO of Creative Care."

"That's right."

"She isn't available at the moment. May I take a message?"

"May I have her mobile number? She's on my board, and I'd like to be able to contact her."

"I assure you, Ms. Spencer, if she's available, you can always get ahold of her through me. Day or night."

"And if the message is private?"

"Then you would already have her number in order to deliver it."

Jen didn't have a comeback.

"Do you have a private message for Kadrienne?" the assistant asked.

"No." At this point, Jen couldn't even remember why she'd called.

"Are you still there, Ms. Spencer?"

"Yes. I'm here. And please call me Jen. With whom am I speaking, please?"

"Holly Keller."

"If you don't mind my asking, have you been with Kade—Kadrienne—long?"

"I'm the only assistant she's ever had."

"Then I should thank you. For looking out for her. She once told me you do that. So…thank you."

"You needn't thank me for looking after Kade, Ms.—Jen."

Jen noticed Holly's slip with the informal name. "Can you tell me her next available appointment? I'd be happy to meet at her office."

"Rescheduling this morning's meeting? Or something else?"

Jen could hear keystrokes in the background. Briefly surprised to learn that news of the failed meeting had already gotten back to this woman, Jen reminded herself that good assistants always knew these kinds of things. "Rescheduling."

"She has an hour at two o'clock tomorrow. Does that work?"

"Tomorrow?" Jen didn't expect anything so soon.

"Yes. No good?"

"No. That works. I'll take it."

"I suggest arriving early. We have secure Wi-Fi throughout the conference rooms, which you're welcome to use while you wait."

"Great. Thanks for your help." In less than twenty-four hours, Jen would be face-to-face with her new boss, a woman too rigid to accommodate a thirteen-minute meeting delay. A sexy-as-hell woman Jen had wet dreams about, who probably couldn't pick her out of a lineup.

She wasn't sure whether she wanted to show up in chain mail or a teddy. The only thing she knew was she wouldn't be late.

CHAPTER FIVE

Jen was prepped and ready with her A game. This wasn't anything major. She covered these topics regularly, lived and breathed them daily. Market size, competitive landscape, product roadmap, channel strategy, marketing plan, key hires, financial model. She knew it all. She'd bring Kade up to speed on everything and answer any questions she might have.

So she'd kissed the woman. So what? It's not like they'd slept together. And even if they had, it was a long time ago. She hadn't thought about Kade since Maui. Well, there was the thorough Internet research she'd done immediately afterward, but that was it. At least consciously. The woman known as Kadrienne Davenport was a high flyer in a competitive industry, with a reputation for being as sharp as a steel blade and as inflexible. Highly respected and feared. Personnel shakeups within her portfolio companies weren't uncommon under her watch, but there was no arguing with her success rates. She'd started, helmed, and sold two companies for hundreds of millions while in her twenties, and as a partner with Matlock Ventures, a venture-capital firm in Silicon Valley, several of her early investments had already borne fruit, those companies having been acquired for undisclosed sums.

Subconsciously, Jen's thoughts regularly strayed to Kade, who featured prominently in her dreams, most of which were clothing optional. None of it had bothered Jen. Why shouldn't she dream about a beautiful woman with whom she'd shared a special day? She passed her days running a company and spending time with her grandmother, not clubbing until all hours or reviewing online-dating profiles. Getting Creative Care off the ground required her complete attention, and she was passionate about its mission. She wasn't in danger of losing focus on the things that mattered simply because she now reported to a woman she was once attracted to. For a brief period. In a faraway place.

This is what she repeated to herself as she made her way to Kade's assistant's workstation.

Jen stood at Holly Keller's desk and offered her hand. From Holly's take-charge manner, Jen expected someone older than this twenty-something woman, though her professional ensemble spoke of sophistication. Her coloring resembled Jen's, her hair more of a dirty blond than Jen's natural shade. "Hi. Jen Spencer. It's nice to finally meet you."

Holly stood as well and shook Jen's hand. And held it. Jen felt so scrutinized under Holly's gaze that she quickly wiped her lips with her free hand. Did she have a crumb or something stuck to her mouth? She didn't feel anything amiss. "I'm sorry. Have we met before?"

Holly smiled warmly and her honey-brown eyes softened. "You remind me of my sister."

Okay, a little awkward, but far better than being reminded of a mean headmistress or recurring nightmare. Jen returned the smile. "I hope that's a good thing."

"It's an excellent thing. You're early. Can I get you some water? Coffee?"

"I've been holed up at the café around the corner. I think I'm sufficiently caffeinated. Water would be great, thanks."

Holly pointed down the hallway. "Second conference room on the left. I'll let her know you're here."

Jen settled in and followed a placard's instructions regarding the Wi-Fi network and password. Holly came in, arranged two coasters, set a glass of water next to Jen and the other at the adjacent seat. Jen hoped Kade would take the seat across from her instead.

A few minutes later, Jen looked up when she heard a knock on the conference room door, and Kade entered. Radiating confidence and savvy, she looked cosmopolitan in a tailored, two-button, navy wool jacket with matching leg-lengthening bootcut pants. Her dark hair was in an elegant French-twist updo that showed off an enticing amount of neck, a deliciously soft and sexy area Jen suddenly recalled with vivid clarity. It was exactly the wrong thing she should be thinking of, yet she couldn't deny that her attraction to Kade was apparently impervious to the passage of time.

She immediately felt an internal battle break out between the side of her that wanted to embrace Kade and the side that needed to maintain a professional detachment. For as much as she wanted this meeting to be solely work-related, Jen followed her feelings. Kade had an uncanny way of stirring her, and, however necessary, ignoring that allure would prove difficult. Would they acknowledge their previous acquaintance? She stood and offered her hand, which Kade took. "Thank you for seeing me. I apologize again for yesterday."

"You have an hour, Ms. Spencer. Show me why Charles believes in you." Kade snatched the water and coaster and planted them and herself on the opposite side of the table. It was what Jen had originally wished for, but now it felt like a rebuff. It stung.

Jen nodded and retook her seat. Apparently they would not address their prior association. She launched into her presentation.

In eighteen minutes from start to finish, Jen reached the end of her PowerPoint deck. Most of the time, it took much longer to deliver because people usually asked questions along the way. Kade hadn't said a word. Jen prompted her. "Questions?"

"What's your fund-raising plan?" Kade asked.

"Well, we're still programming the redesign that will streamline—"

"You said you have four months of runway," Kade said.

"Yes, but the product isn't—"

"Get it there. Yesterday. You're running out of cash."

"I know, but without—"

"Conventional wisdom is to start raising money six months beforehand."

"I know the rule of thumb, but the product needs to—"

"You have no customers."

"Yes, but our VP of sales is—"

"Without a working product and customers, you can't raise money."

"Which is why our VP of sales—"

"How long has he or she been with you?"

"He. Almost three months."

"Terminate him."

"We need sales and I'm not a salesperson."

"Apparently neither is he. Look, Jen. Can I call you Jen?" Jen was too startled by the sudden shift to a personal question to answer, and Kade didn't wait for her to. "You're a twelve-person company. You shouldn't *have* a VP of sales. You're in beta—glorified alpha. You need to close some deals yourself before you incur that kind of overhead."

"With severance, it's not like we'd save any—"

"Severance? For what? In return for a release of liability? What's he going to sue you for? He hasn't sold anything. No. Terminate him and save the money. Go with what you have, and shelve the redesign until you have customers demanding it. Do the onboarding manually if you have to. You're not trying to prove scale at this stage. You're trying to prove utility. Set up meetings with your top prospects, and get moving on closing business."

"I wouldn't feel right about not giving severance."

"But it feels right to run your company off the edge of a cliff and not be able to pay anyone?"

Jen snapped the lid of her laptop shut. "I care about my team."

"Well, then group hugs all around for the next four months, because that's all you'll get."

Jen shoved her laptop into her bag and left without another word.

❖

Instead of returning to the office and giving Jeremy the details of her lambasting, Jen went to her grandmother's house, oddly indifferent as to whether today was a good day for Nana's memory, which she usually longed for. Sometimes Nana's short-term recall was so poor she repeated the same questions over and over, which Jen used to try to answer as if for the first time. She'd subsequently learned that changing subjects proved less frustrating for both of them. Jen herself had good and bad days, sometimes infinitely patient and other times childishly the opposite. Today she wanted to vent about her new boss, and it wouldn't matter whether her grandmother could follow along.

When she arrived at the house, she was pleased to see a car in the driveway. It belonged to Doreen, one of Nana's two primary caregivers. Nana required around-the-clock care, so while it was typical for a caregiver to be there, it was always a relief because it meant Jen didn't have to struggle at the last minute to find care. Nana wished to remain in her home instead of moving to an assisted-living facility. She could get around the house with a walker and could make simple meals, but her strength and balance were poor. Plus, she was forgetful. The combination meant she needed someone to monitor her full-time. Even though she felt self-sufficient, the number of times she'd fallen or inadvertently put herself in harm's way indicated otherwise.

The house smelled of Pine Sol, mothballs, and cedar, all of which reminded Jen of the many days she'd spent here in her youth. Of late, it also smelled faintly of urine because of Nana's increasing incontinence.

Jen greeted Doreen, and when she saw the empty lounge chair in front of the TV, she went into Nana's room. A game show was on the television, and Nana's eyes and mouth were closed, which meant she was dozing. When she slept soundly, she snored with her mouth open. There was nothing shy or cute or feminine about it—the small-framed woman became a wind tunnel who could scare crows if left in a field.

Jen set about folding the few clothing articles and throws strewn about and went into the kitchen to refill Nana's water glass. Doreen was putting away dishes, and Jen took a moment to inquire about Nana.

According to Doreen, Edna was having a mixed day. She'd known who Doreen was, asked after Doreen's children, and allowed her to assist her in the bathroom. But she had no appetite. Even at Doreen's suggestion of whipping up a batch of Edna's favorite cornbread, Edna had apparently shown little enthusiasm.

Jen took out a handful of green seedless grapes from a bowl in the freezer, sliced them in two, and returned to Nana's room. Her grandma loved frozen grapes, letting them defrost in her mouth and play on her tongue. She said they reminded her of the Popsicles she ate in the summertime as a girl, and Jen adored the goofy looks her grandma made as she worked them over.

Jen set the small bowl on the nightstand and sat on the bed. She was fairly attuned to Nana's sleeping patterns and knew she was simply resting. She took Nana's hand, a small, claw-like thing that seemed of late to be made entirely of knuckle, and waited. When Nana's eyes fluttered open, she smiled at Jen. "Didn't expect you."

Jen kissed Nana's cheek. "Wanted to check on you. Make sure you were behaving."

Usually Nana would return some quip, but she only shook her head. That tripped Jen's internal concern sensor, but it was too early to really worry. Jen snatched a grape half and held it in front of Nana's lips. When Nana opened her mouth to accept the fruit, Jen's sensor quieted. After swallowing the third piece and keeping her eyes on Jen, Nana said, "Tell me."

When lucid, Nana could always ascertain when something was bothering Jen. Since those insightful moments came less and less frequently, Jen appreciated them all the more.

"Work," Jen said. Edna didn't understand most of what Jen did each day. She'd lived her life without computers and smartphones.

Nana kept working the latest grape, waiting.

"We're behind schedule. Cash is dwindling. I hired too soon."

"Says who?"

"Someone who knows." Jen fed Nana another half, and they fell into silence. Jen watched as Nana studied her.

"Then listen and learn."

"What if I'm too soft to make the hard choices managers need to make?"

"Treat your employees the way you want to be treated, and you can't go wrong."

"I can't lose this company, Nana. We can help people. I know we can."

"Then you will."

Jen hadn't known it until that moment, but that's what she needed to hear. Nana had always been in her corner. And even on days when she asked Jen ten times in a row whether the clothes were out of the dryer or if Jen had spoken with her parents recently, Nana always would be. Jen had tremendous faith in herself, but occasionally she needed to know that others had faith in her, too.

Jeremy entered the conference room with a "Whoa." Jen was brainstorming, and it was never pretty. She could feel how low her ponytail had moved, a sure sign her hair was coming loose and giving her a disheveled, sleepless aura. The whiteboards were bursting with multicolored bullet points and asterisks, and sticky notes lined the walls, though many lay crumpled on the table and littered the floor.

Jen had returned to the office and commandeered the conference room. She was in "beast mode," a phrase Jeremy had appropriated for her shortly after they started working together. She'd put him on notice to expect to work late and summoned him via instant message.

"I guess this answers how your meeting went," Jeremy said as he continued to survey the battlefield.

She was ready for him. "We're spreading ourselves too thin. We need to refocus. Instead of running tests in three markets, we need to stick with San Francisco until we've raised more money." She outlined the new marketing game plan for him. "We need to cut two people. That will allow us to boost ad spend in San Francisco and give us another month to secure funding. Longer, if you and I take a pay cut."

Jen flipped on the projector and pulled up the product roadmap. "I need your entire team on the mobile app, rolling out the original design." She walked to the screen and pointed at several rectangles, each of which identified a project. "Out of this, this, and this, what do we push out?"

❖

It took another two weeks of planning and execution, but Jen and Jeremy completed what they considered Phase One of their fund-raising strategy. In large part, it meant scaling back what they'd originally intended to accomplish by the time they set out to raise their next financing round. As was typical in a startup, they had limited personnel with which to make headway. And now, after laying off two people, they were even more resource-constrained. Six-day workweeks with twelve-hour days were luxuries of the past.

Jen had been particularly concerned about the terminations. She disagreed with Kade that their VP of sales had failed. True, he hadn't signed any deals, but all sales hires had a learning period during which they weren't expected to sign new customers. The company's sales strategy wasn't fully fleshed out, the product was still in beta, and limited leads were coming in from marketing efforts. It's not like he had a lot to work with.

She'd been less worried about laying off her product-marketing guy, who'd been fresh out of MIT with multiple job offers in hand when he'd accepted hers five months ago. The VP of sales was far more senior, with two kids and another on the way. During his hiring process, he'd expressed concern over the company's medical benefits, which were fairly vanilla and couldn't compete with the tech behemoths in the Valley. So Jen compromised. Instead of a lump-sum severance payment, she'd offered to cover up to six months of family medical coverage if he hadn't found another job during that time frame. Even if everything went south, Jen was confident the company would have enough cash in the bank to make good on that promise. She would give up her own wages if it came to that.

Jen had initially taken aim at Jeremy's engineering group, too, wanting to shave the expense of three people in total, but Jeremy had asked her to allow him to meet privately with each member of his team to see if any might volunteer to join him and Jen in deferring a portion of their compensation until they closed their funding round, after which they would be repaid. Given the risk of bankruptcy, Jen was skeptical but granted Jeremy permission. He had surprised her with the news that all of them were on board and completely confident in Jen's leadership. She was so moved by their gesture of good faith and so keen on keeping everyone motivated that she insisted they offer each person additional stock options above their current holdings. They would need to get board approval, which meant getting Kade to consent, but Jen would go to the mat for her team.

In fact, Kade was part of Phase Two of their fund-raising strategy.

Jen and Kade hadn't communicated since their abbreviated board meeting. Kade didn't seem the type to sit idly by and let one of her corporate charges go off the rails, but Jen hadn't heard from her. She hadn't heard from Andrew either, which meant that, to her knowledge, Kade was still representing the investors on Charles's behalf.

Jen was uncertain as to how best to contact Kade. She could take the easy route of sending an email, or she could call Kade's assistant and try to connect with Kade via phone.

Part of the problem was the complete lack of acknowledgment of what they'd shared on Maui. They'd spent most of a day together. They'd kissed. Not simply kissed—Jen couldn't forget how Kade had welcomed her caresses. Did Kade indulge in such a vast number of affairs she didn't even remember the names or faces of her conquests? Did Kade have any idea that it was Jen who had once caused her to shiver under her caress? What good would it do to remind her? Was Jen's ego so weak that it needed the mighty Kadrienne Davenport to boost it? Would it scratch some itch if Kade conceded she'd once enjoyed the touch of a woman who was simple and plain in every way?

The sand in her company's hourglass was the ultimate arbiter. With cash running out, time was not a luxury she had these days. She dialed Holly Keller.

"Holly, it's Jen Spencer with Creative Care. I'd like to set up a working session with Kade, sooner rather than later. Should I iron that out with her or you?"

"Is this for Creative Care?" Holly asked.

"Yes."

"Then it will have to be after hours and offsite. Unless Matlock Ventures is considering an investment?"

Jen hadn't considered this wrinkle. Kade was helping Charles, who wasn't associated with Matlock. But it hadn't been an issue when Holly scheduled their meeting in Matlock's conference room. Had one of the partners said something to Kade or Holly? Jen didn't want to put Kade in an awkward position with her firm. "Not to my knowledge, no. You're right. What do you recommend?"

"Kadrienne often has meetings at her place because it has a conference room with whiteboards, poster board, projector, markers, you name it. I suggest ordering takeout and having a working session over dinner. I'll add you to the building-security white list."

An air-raid horn sounded through Jen's skull. Dinner at Kade's sounded far too intimate for what she had in mind. "Sorry. To be clear, I'm not bringing my team. It would only be Kade and me."

"Then it shouldn't take long to decide on takeout. Is there a problem?"

Was this how these things were normally handled? What if Kade were a man? Would his assistant really be suggesting a tête-à-tête over dinner at his home? Of course, there was nothing romantic about the boardroom-like setting Holly had described. And Holly probably set up such meetings routinely. If others didn't make it an issue, why should she?

"No. That sounds fine. I'll work around her schedule. Let me know when and where."

Kade and Holly were sitting at the conference table in Kade's office, going over Holly's deliverables for several meetings on Kade's schedule, when Holly mentioned Jen Spencer.

Having heard Jen's ideas, Kade understood why Charles had invested in Creative Care. Elder care was a multi-billion-dollar industry, and current solutions were poor and pricey. Jen was smart to adopt a marketplace approach to connecting caregivers to those needing care. Building a marketplace took time, and the company didn't have to have one in place at this stage. But it needed enough proof points to interest investors in continuing to finance them.

As Jen had pointed out during her presentation, the caregivers weren't represented or connected in any way. They were siloed individuals, often with limited education, who didn't have anyone to champion them. Additionally, those needing care weren't typically utilizing the Internet in any meaningful way, if at all. So it was a challenge to get these two groups to find each other.

According to Jen, Creative Care could change things. Younger family members were typically the ones on whose shoulders it fell to find care solutions for their older loved ones. The mobile app Creative Care was building would connect caregivers with those who needed to find care for elderly relatives. The app could match them geographically as well as by skill set required/offered. Family members who had used their services could review caregivers. The app could also set up and process electronic payments daily.

But with only four months left until the cash ran out, the challenge would be to make the app work well enough to forge some connections, enable transactions, and create the feedback loop in time to generate investor interest in continuing to bankroll the company. Jen's decision to let two more weeks pass without taking measures to reduce the red ink was exceedingly disappointing. Time was not on Creative Care's side.

Kade scoffed when Holly suggested rearranging an existing dinner engagement to accommodate a working session with Jen. "It's taken her two weeks to decide to act, and now she wants to jump the line? Forget it."

"The line, as you call it, is a meeting with the same software rep you've successfully managed to push off this entire year. He's not going anywhere."

"There is an order to things," Kade said, more testily than she wished. "You, of all people, know this. She can follow the rules like everyone else."

"Why did you accept this job?" Holly excelled at rapid shifts in topic.

"You know why."

Holly closed her laptop lid and crossed her arms. "Apparently I don't. I thought you wanted to help get new technologies into the hands of folks who could benefit from them as quickly as possible."

"I do."

"Which is why you'd rather meet with the software rep of a mature technology you have no interest in than the head of a company building a cutting-edge solution to a large and difficult problem that could help millions of people." Holly swiped her phone off the table, opened the text-messaging app, and moved her thumbs in a rapid dance across the touchscreen's keyboard.

Kade sighed. She never won these battles. "You are an insufferable, impenitent, self-righteous—"

"Truth-telling."

"Manipulative—"

"Creative."

"Bullying—"

"Seven o'clock this Thursday at your place. In and confirmed."

"Wait. What?"

Holly held up her phone's screen to Kade. "She accepted instantly."

"No meetings at my place after hours. It's your own damn rule!"

"And she has your cell-phone number in case anything comes up."

"Fuck."

"You're on your own there. Some things even I can't do for you."

CHAPTER SIX

Jen gave up after the fifth outfit. She went back to the low-rise jeans and dark-blue sweater she had originally tried on. This wasn't a date, and she needed to stop acting as if it were. She could wear a trash bag for all Kade cared, so why did Jen? She didn't. Well, she did, but she was fully aware of how immature she was being.

The time she'd spent with Kade had meant something. During their day on Maui, Kade had maneuvered her way past that of a casual acquaintance and tucked herself into a small corner of Jen's heart. Seeing Kade again was like returning to a beloved old summer home and removing the furniture coverings, revealing a place of comfort, warmth, and fond memories. It hurt to think Kade hadn't felt similarly.

She was being childish. Foolish. She was one of millions of people throughout time who felt more for someone than that person felt in return. There was nothing new or special about it.

And if Kade had felt the same back then, would it change anything now?

Of course not. All it would accomplish to get Kade to admit it would be a little ego boost. A woman like Kadrienne Davenport could have anyone she wanted. She wouldn't settle for the struggling CEO of a tiny company with mixed prospects.

Bringing up their past time together would only add discomfort to an already awkward situation. Either Kade had forgotten, which would leave Jen silently bearing her embarrassment, or she remembered and hadn't wanted to mention it because she wouldn't want Jen to think she was open to rekindling things.

Jen needed to focus only on her mission of getting Kade to contact those in her professional network who could help Creative Care. The company's future was in the balance and needed to command Jen's sole attention.

Kade lived in a luxury condominium in Atherton, one of the wealthiest zip codes in America, only fifteen minutes from her Menlo Park office. A shard of sadness shot across Jen's chest when she imagined Kade inhabiting a utilitarian environment so devoid of warmth that it housed an actual conference room. She scolded herself not to arrive with preconceived notions. Whether Kade surrounded herself with objects, colors, and furnishings Jen would find homey and inviting, or with maddeningly modern starkness, was none of Jen's concern.

Jen exited the elevator on the top floor, which opened to a wide hallway with wood floors and wall sconces, and followed the signs to Kade's unit, which apparently was one of only two on the entire level. A mat that said WELCOME in eight languages rested outside Kade's door. Jen pressed the door bell and smiled when she heard an electronic chime of "Whistle While You Work." At least Kade hadn't entirely lost her sense of humor.

After several seconds, the door opened, and Jen's breath caught at the sight of a barefoot Kade, toweling dry her hair, wearing straight-leg trousers that hugged well-muscled thighs and a sleeveless V-neck blouse that highlighted toned arms.

Jen was immediately swept into the memory of Kade, beverage in hand, walking onto their lanai. Dissatisfied by and keyed up from their chaste good-night kiss, Jen had entered the shared living space in search of the minibar, hoping to find something to take the edge off. The mai tai she'd ordered earlier had failed to deliver any punch, and she wanted something to knock out the thoughts threatening to act out in irrational ways, such as heading straight for Kade's bed.

Then, as now, Kade's hair was damp but not dripping. That night, Jen had caught Kade's outline in the dim outdoor lights and could tell the bounce in her hair was gone due to a recent shower. As Kade had headed outside, the only sounds were the tinkling of the ice in her glass, the sliding of the door, and the ocean waves that became louder as it opened.

Kade hadn't closed the door behind her, and something within Jen had stirred, willfully translating the gesture as an invitation. She hadn't meant to descend on Kade, but she felt a burning need to touch her. And so she'd followed her.

Now, as she stared at Kade's body through the outline of her clothes, Jen recalled every touch her fingers had once trailed across those curves, every glorious hitch in Kade's breath, every lift of her chin and angling of her neck made in encouragement of Jen's advances. The rise and fall of her chest was as scintillating now as then.

"Jen? Jen, you okay?"

Jen's world tilted back on its axis, and the present swung into focus. Kade was frowning, concern etched across her beautiful face.

"Cute color." Kade hadn't followed Jen's gaze, and her concern lingered. Jen pointed to Kade's feet. "Your toenail polish. I like it." *Cute color? Who says that to her boss?* Jen might as well have been wearing a hat with DORK written in all caps.

Kade looked down briefly and shifted one foot behind the other, as if hiding her feet from Jen's view. "Sorry. I wanted to fit in a shower before we got down to business. Please come in."

"Oh, here," Jen said as she entered and held out a bottle of wine. "I don't know if it's proper protocol, and there's no pressure to drink this, but it felt weird to come empty-handed."

Kade accepted the bottle with a smile. "Polite as always."

Okay, that certainly seemed like an acknowledgment of Maui. Were they really going to go there?

"We'll set up over here." Kade led the way to a room that could have been in any office building. She did have an actual conference room here. In her home. Where she lived. Who did that?

Jen set down her purse and laptop bag.

"Would you like a tour?" Kade asked.

"Oh, no, thank you. I'm good." Jen didn't want to see Kade's bedroom or catch sight of photographs of her in the arms of a lover.

She did notice a number of clocks adorning the wall, with placards of major cities in the time zones represented: San Francisco, London, Dubai, Shanghai, Moscow, and Sydney.

Kade's smile vanished. She set the wine on the table, opened a drawer from a wall cabinet, and placed a number of takeout menus in front of Jen. "Take your pick. They're all good."

Jen wasn't hungry but understood this to be part of the evening's agenda, so she fanned through the options. They settled on Mediterranean. While Kade placed the order, Jen pulled up a slide deck on her laptop.

Kade took the seat next to Jen. "You've given our conversation some thought?"

Jen nodded. "I have. You were right. Our burn was too high. We were also taking on too much, so we've restructured and refocused. The developers are cranking on the mobile app, and I'm working to get as many caregivers on the platform as possible ASAP. Which is where you come in."

"When you say 'restructured and refocused,' do you mean you've already taken action?"

Did Kade think she'd done nothing these past two weeks? "Yes. We laid off two people, and most of us are deferring a portion of our salaries until we've secured funding. It extends our runway by at least six weeks."

"I would have appreciated hearing those plans prior to execution."

"You suggested we terminate our VP of sales. We did."

"And had you not abruptly ended our discussion, we might have covered other topics as well. Topics just as critical."

"Noted," Jen said, her ire rising. As CEO, she could hire and fire as she saw fit. She didn't need to run such decisions by the board. Did Kade micromanage all her portfolio companies? If so, no wonder she hadn't had a day off for years leading up to the Women in Tech conference, when she'd had one foisted upon her. She was an unprecedented control freak. A few choice words entered Jen's consciousness, but she let them lap at the shore of her mind, choosing not to cement them as labels for this woman.

Jen watched as Kade stood and began pacing the room. Apparently the dissatisfaction over the conversation was mutual.

"Follow me," Kade said, seemingly having arrived at some decision. She led Jen past a formal dining room and into a den. "Sit," she said, pointing to a couch. Jen did as instructed. As Kade strode to a large wet bar that occupied over two-thirds of the wall and busied herself behind its counter, Jen scanned the room. It seemed devoid of personality or, at least, absent any personal touches. It was functional, serving the purpose of mixing drinks but not being a friendly place in which to consume them.

Kade brought over two shot glasses filled with amber liquid and set one in front of Jen. Without taking a seat, Kade held the other as if to toast and then slammed it. She shook from the effects of what seemed to be a high-proof alcohol. She sat at one of the bar stools, facing Jen. "Your turn."

Jen first eyed the beverage, then Kade. "I'm not much of a…" She stopped mid-grumble. She suspected Kade wasn't much of a hard-alcohol drinker either, and even through the haze of irritation, she recognized the peace offering. Drink in hand, she frowned at Kade, sighed, and then swallowed half of it. Heat burst through her, jolting her as if she'd been electrocuted. She exhaled loudly and made what was certain to be a sourpuss face. "Holy…geez."

Kade smiled. It was an honest-to-God, joyful, relaxed expression Jen hadn't seen since Maui. She wanted to see more of it. She lifted the glass in Kade's direction. "You should do more of that," she said, then swallowed the rest.

"Drink?" Kade asked, the lovely smile still gracing her kissable mouth. Seeing it in person was infinitely more appealing than the vision imprinted in Jen's memory, which was itself enough to arouse Jen upon recall. Perhaps it was the unwelcoming room that contrasted sharply with and brought out this more open side to Kade. The adorable painted toes hadn't hurt. How intimidating could someone be in bare feet?

Jen shook her head. "Smile." She found herself wanting to say, "You're gorgeous," but she thought it might be the alcohol talking. Instead she opted for, "It suits you."

Kade sidestepped the comment. "Do you think we're going to be able to work together?"

Jen returned Kade's smile, though she knew hers wasn't as radiant. "Is 'work together' a euphemism for my having to agree to everything you say?"

"No."

"Then yes."

"Good."

"Kade?"

"Yes?"

"You do know that we've…met before, right?"

Kade smiled in a deliciously mischievous way and cocked her head to the side. "Met?"

Jen wanted to squirm. Was Kade really going to make her elaborate? She nodded.

"Yes, Jen. I remember. Did you really think I could forget?"

"I think…I think you've probably met a lot of people."

"Few as special as you." Kade extended her hand back toward the hallway. "Shall we?"

Jen didn't budge. "Why did you say that?"

Kade had said it in stride but seemed to backpedal when Jen didn't move. "I'm sorry. Shouldn't I have?"

"That's a very disarming thing to say."

Kade took some time with Jen's statement, as if not wanting to scare away their fragile truce. "I thought you asked if I remembered you because you remembered me. Fondly? Or did I misread that?"

"Yes. Fondly."

"And I remember you fondly." Kade said the word hesitantly, as if uncertain Jen would find it acceptable.

"I'm glad."

Kade chewed her bottom lip briefly, seemingly afraid to say the wrong thing. "I remember our time together as special, Jen. I thought that's what you wanted me to acknowledge, and I do. Readily. There's nothing more or less to it."

"Okay."

"Okay?"

Kade seemed so forthcoming, so responsive to what Jen had asked, had needed to know, that Jen wasn't sure why she found it lacking somehow. Kade had been entirely emotionally present during the conversation and obviously concerned about Jen's feelings. So why did Jen feel short-changed?

Jen smiled. "Yes, okay. Thank you for saying that."

"Can I say one other thing?" Kade asked.

Jen nodded uncertainly.

"You look...more tired since I last saw you. Are you getting enough sleep?"

In the same way that Kade's earlier response was oddly unsatisfying, this, too, grated on Jen. Half of her delighted in the fact that Kade was showing concern for her well-being. The other half felt like yelling at Kade, calling her out on her hypocrisy. Kade was one of those "successful" businesswomen who worked more hours than anyone ought, dragging all women along with her impractical, superhuman work ethic. Women unfairly felt like they had to compete with that level of work/life imbalance because of people like Kade. Of course Jen felt like hell—and apparently looked as well as she felt. Women like Kadrienne Davenport, however unconsciously, demanded it of her.

On the heels of the crazy startup hours Jen already put in for Creative Care on a routine basis, she'd just spent two of the worst weeks to date coming up with plans to save her company because *this woman* had scared the living bejesus out of her!

"I'm fine. Thank you." Jen shut down further discussion on the topic by returning to the conference room. With every step she took, she worked to tamp down her anger and flush it into the shadows. It wasn't Kade's fault that women were held to unreasonable standards, having to prove themselves in the workplace time and again while consistently bearing the brunt of family and household responsibilities.

"Water? Wine?" Kade asked before joining Jen at the table.

Jen surprised herself. "Wine, please." There was a saying about drinking something before or after "liquor, never sicker," but she didn't know it offhand, and whatever amber liquid Kade had served wasn't doing enough to take the edge off.

Kade snatched the bottle Jen had brought and tilted her head in silent invitation for Jen to join her. Kade led them into a kitchen, which Jen found wonderfully cozy. White cabinets, pewter fixtures, chopping-block-style wood countertops, a vintage Wedgewood stove, an old-fashioned wood-burning heater topped with an antique kettle, and skylights combined for an open, inviting space completely at odds with the modern conference room and den. Which of the rooms did Kade feel most comfortable in?

"This is nice," Jen said, as Kade worked the bottle opener.

"You didn't want the tour."

"I don't want you to feel obligated to open your home to me merely because we work together."

"You didn't previously strike me as someone in the habit of second-guessing people. Have you changed, or am I one of the lucky few?"

"Second-guessing?"

Kade poured wine into two glasses. "Deciding that my offer was out of obligation."

"I hadn't concluded that it was. I just don't want it to be."

"It isn't." Kade handed a glass to Jen and backed against the counter. "Are we always going to walk on eggshells around each other?"

Jen exhaled, sending strands of hair momentarily skyward. Usually even-keeled and good-natured, she was frustrated by Kade in a way few people in her life could manage. Kade made her feel off-balance, and she wasn't used to it. But they'd squared away their touchy past, and it was time to move firmly into the present. Perhaps she could even benefit from having seen a side of Kade she had acknowledged at the time as being atypical for her to reveal, because Jen wasn't intimidated by Kade as she imagined others would be. And she appreciated that Kade hadn't tried to correct her for using her nickname, which felt natural to her. "No. But can we acknowledge this is a little weird?"

Kade smiled. "Agreed. But manageable." She inclined her head toward the direction of the conference room. "Now let's see what you've got for me, hmm?"

❖

Once Jen got Kade up to speed on the changes she and Jeremy had made over the past couple of weeks, she jotted down notes to take back to Jeremy, refinements that brainstorming with Kade helped solidify. Kade was very much an equal partner in the discussion, asking questions, listening carefully, offering suggestions, talking out ideas. Kade had the perfect segue to the reason for Jen's visit in the first place.

"Where do I come in?"

"I was hoping you might have a contact or two in some of the Bay Area hospitals."

"To what end?"

"To convince them it's in their best interest to partner with Creative Care. If they refer us to family members who need to find caregivers for someone being discharged, then it's not their reputation on the line in recommending a particular individual. Family members themselves are searching for and rating those caregivers on our platform. Plus, the hospital is providing value-added customer service by recommending options for families struggling to find care, which hospitals themselves are rated on. And we're not competing for resources against the hospitals the way we are with assisted-living facilities."

Kade seemed intrigued. "With hospitals providing referrals, the speed with which patients register on the platform could significantly increase. But I don't see how it accelerates getting caregivers to register. You're bringing in only half of the equation needed for an online match between patients and caregivers."

"I know people who work part-time for the University of California who are held to a maximum number of hours per week so the UC isn't forced to cover their benefits. So these people are stuck looking for supplemental work. We can provide that work, with no downside to the university. In fact, they might incur lower employee turnover because we make it easier for their part-timers to find additional work that allows them to stay in the area."

Kade began nodding slowly. "The UC system has a number of hospitals."

"UCSF to start, which is in our backyard and our first test market."

Kade snapped her fingers as if an idea had struck. "If your platform delivers on its promise of improved scheduling and reduced coverage gaps, you could offer it for free to hospitals to incentivize them to partner with you, because it would improve their patient care as well."

"I like how you think, Ms. Davenport."

The food arrived, and as Kade excused herself to retrieve it, she asked, "Do you mind if we eat in the dining room?" Jen didn't, and so she followed Kade.

Far more settled than when she had arrived, Jen was able to absorb her surroundings. The main features of Kade's condo were the many timepieces adorning the walls, which were eerily silent. She also spotted a far more unexpected sight: a tiny steam train with working headlights—and, oh my gosh, smoke—that wound its way throughout the living and dining rooms on a lengthy track along the walls. Along its path were painted scenes of European towns, as well as miniature buildings, trees, and road signs. A number of complicated mechanisms performed tasks during stops along the way, such as filling cars with coal and lumber at one site, and emptying them at another. It was like stepping into a toy store from the past, and all that was missing were children who could appreciate the elaborate display.

Jen stepped over to where Kade had opened the takeout containers and placed serving utensils in each, lending a very casual air to the dining experience. Jen opted for pita bread, hummus, stuffed grape leaves, spanakopita, and cucumber salad, much hungrier now than when she'd arrived.

As they ate, Jen gazed at the clocks. Those with second hands were aligned to the others down to the millisecond. The pieces banded together to create a synchronicity unlike any she'd witnessed. It was the strangest dinner environment. While part of her was enjoying the simple, informal meal with Kade, another part was feeling like she had time-traveled to the rear of a clock-keeper's shop. She didn't have a clue as to what to say, so she ate in silence and studied her surroundings, her eyes straying to the train whenever it passed by.

"Not your typical dining room, I know," Kade said after chewing a bite of bread.

"I don't know whether to be impressed or scared that every single timepiece seems set to the nanosecond."

"My OCD goes into overdrive when one of them lags behind." Kade swept a hand in the direction of the clocks. "I used to have far more, but I couldn't get any work done because I'd obsess about having them all aligned, which is very difficult when different manufacturers and mechanical pieces are involved. I've pared down to these."

"No cuckoo clocks?"

Kade laughed. "Never. They terrified me as a kid. Worse than clowns."

"Have you always been into timepieces?" Jen forked some spanakopita, flakes of which flew across her plate.

"Oddly enough, I wouldn't say I'm into them, exactly. My father was a railway maintenance worker. He was meticulous about keeping a schedule, both at work and home. It was…suffocating, really, his obsession. Mom and I were constantly on pins and needles. In his world, lives were on the line." Kade glanced around the rooms. "It's like half of me has all this because I'm trying to make sense of it, of him, and the other half tries to understand why I failed to get it in the first place."

"Get it?"

"People can get hurt if you say you're going to do something, and you don't."

Jen nodded, though she wasn't really following. "I remember you weren't close, but you talk about him in the past tense. Is he…?"

Kade grimaced. "Very much alive. No, we're not close. Mom kicked him out when I was seventeen. I see him every few years at extended-family gatherings." Kade set her plate aside and pulled two dessert plates closer. She set a piece of baklava on each and started in, closing her eyes as she chewed. "Mmm. So good."

Between the tantalizing moan and the honey that glistened on Kade's lips, Jen instantly forgot about second hands. She wanted to luxuriate in a slow-motion state of glorious anticipation while feeling warm air tingle above her mouth from Kade's breath as she bowed ever nearer. She wanted to lick the sticky sweetness from Kade's lips and linger there as she tasted it. Baklava shot to the top of her go-to desserts.

"Hmm?" Jen said as she came to the realization that Kade had spoken.

Kade smiled, licked the corner of her mouth, and dabbed it with a napkin. "I asked how your grandmother's doing."

Joy surged through Jen that Kade remembered this piece of her life, though she didn't understand why it meant so much. "Thank you for asking. She's…she has good days and bad days. Like we all do." She picked up her piece of dessert and took a bite.

As she ate, Kade touched a fingertip to Jen's bottom lip and slowly traced it along the skin. Jen stopped chewing, fighting not to swoon from the jolt of pleasure that shot through her. Kade took a little swipe and held up a tiny flake of the thin dough as if to show Jen she had a reason for the caress. Jen didn't need any logic at that moment. All she needed was more of Kade's hands on her. She found herself drifting closer, as if pursuing Kade's touch, and forced herself to sit back.

"She's lucky she has you," Kade said, and it took Jen a moment to re-engage in the conversation.

Jen wasn't sure she should eat any more of the baklava, which seemed intent on transforming itself into an aphrodisiac. "I've been lucky to have her. When I was younger, I stayed with her for many weeks every summer whenever my folks drove back East to visit my other grandparents. I love them, too, but I don't know them as well as Nana. She's always had my back."

Jen eyed the half-eaten morsel again and looked up when Kade chuckled.

Kade smiled. "You seem wary of it."

Jen pointed at it. "That's because this baklava has an agenda. This is grade-A, seduction-class baklava." She raised her palms in surrender. "I'm done." She headed to the conference room and packed her things. Kade walked her to the front door.

"You're okay to drive?" Kade asked.

"Yes. Kade…"

Kade arched an eyebrow.

She wanted to ask the question on her mind but decided to shelve it. She hiked her laptop bag higher on her shoulder and stuck out her hand. "Thank you."

Kade didn't shake Jen's hand so much as hold it in hers. This was all Jen needed as incentive.

"Can I ask a non-work-related question?" Jen asked.

Kade nodded.

"Did you ever think about me?"

Kade turned Jen's hand palm down and traced the back of it with her other hand. "If I say no, I'll hurt your feelings. And if I say yes…" She dropped Jen's hand as if suddenly becoming aware of what she was doing.

"I might get the wrong idea?" Jen sighed. "Never mind. I shouldn't have asked. That wasn't fair of me. Good night, Kade. And honestly, thank—"

"Yes."

"You." Though they spoke over each other, Jen heard Kade perfectly. Jen knew she looked the part of a smitten adolescent, but she couldn't help smiling broadly. Damn, Kade could make her feel good. She allowed herself a few more moments to soak up the contentment from not being alone in appreciating their special bond on Maui. Finally, she nodded and took her leave, enjoying the extra bounce in her step.

Chapter Seven

The next morning, Kade sat at the small conference table in her Matlock office, spooning yogurt into her mouth, when a knock at her door was quickly followed by Holly, who let herself in as she always did. Kade folded *The Wall Street Journal* and pushed a bowl of fruit toward Holly, who immediately snatched a piece of cantaloupe with Kade's fork as she sat down.

"Start talking," Holly said, as she popped the bite into her mouth.

Kade focused on scraping yogurt away from the sides of the plastic container. "Productive night overall. Better than expected."

Holly finished chewing and swallowed. "Yes. I got your list. Lists."

"Start with the names I put an—"

"Asterisk by. Yes. I can read. Since when do you bail on Friday spin class?"

"I didn't. I was up, so I went to the five thirty instead of ours."

"Hence the 4:58 email adding another six contacts to the list you sent last night."

"We need to move quickly. If Creative Care doesn't get proof points in short order, they're sunk."

"I get that, but it doesn't explain your level of involvement. Doling out contacts is one thing. Personally attending meetings is another thing entirely."

Kade appropriated her fork and fruit bowl, and dropped several blueberries into her yogurt. She gave Holly a sideways glance before unfolding her paper and pretending to read, hoping Holly would take the hint.

Which, of course, she didn't.

"You like her," Holly said as she commandeered the fruit again and unceremoniously flipped Kade's paper to the table of contents.

Kade sat back to give Holly space. "For a woman who has plenty of work to do, you seem rather inert." Holly ignored her and ran her finger down the index listing. "What are you looking for?" Kade asked.

"Sudoku."

"Not in the *Journal*."

With a look of disgust, Holly shoved the paper away and stood. "What's the point?"

"Work," Kade said. "You should try it."

Holly flipped her off and left.

Kade and Jen's late-Monday-afternoon appointment with UCSF's head of administration, Suzanne Woods, had been a success. Suzanne acknowledged the cost constraints that tied her hands when it came to part-time staff hours and thought it possible that Creative Care could reduce employee turnover. However, she was concerned about losing staffers because caregivers might elect to work full-time as in-home aides registered with Creative Care instead of juggling two part-time jobs. Prepared for this objection, Kade placated her by touting the UCSF brand and reputation, saying caregivers would always want to opt for employment by the UC, other things being equal.

Jen told Suzanne she'd draft a letter of intent between them and create a demo account for the hospital to check out the Creative Care offerings.

They'd driven to the meeting separately, and once they were back in the parking lot, Kade congratulated Jen and wished her a pleasant evening. As she started toward her car, Jen's voice stopped her.

"Do you have dinner plans?"

"Always."

"You eat out every night?"

"That's not what you asked."

Jen shifted her laptop bag to her other hand and furrowed her brow, as if in concentration. Kade found it adorable. "Do your dinner plans involve eating alone, or will one or more people be joining you?"

"I'll be reheating leftovers at seven and checking the Asian markets while I eat. Interested?" Kade only added that last bit because she knew no one would willingly subject themselves to the tasks in her weekly routine.

"No. But how about having dinner with me tonight as a way to thank you for setting up the meeting with Suzanne?"

Kade waved her off. "No need. Providing introductions is part of the job."

"Is joining me for customer meetings also part of the job?"

It wasn't. Kade knew it, and it sounded like Jen knew it, too. She could offer only two plausible explanations for why she'd insisted on joining. Either she didn't trust Jen to do her job, or she wanted to spend time with Jen. The former wasn't true. The more she worked with Jen, the more she appreciated her intellect and spirit. The latter *was* true, but she wasn't comfortable admitting it to herself, much less to Jen.

Kade thumbed in the direction of the building's entrance. "It's been a while since Suzanne and I have gotten a chance to catch up, so I thought I'd take the opportunity and tag along. I'm going to drop back in for a few."

"Which is why you were heading to your car."

Kade popped herself in the head. "My mind was on the meeting. You did great, by the way. See you tomorrow." They were scheduled to meet with another San Francisco hospital administrator Kade knew. She waved and started toward the building.

"You don't trust me, do you?" Jen called after her.

Kade closed her eyes before turning around. She'd been naive to think Jen wouldn't catch on to something, even if it was the wrong thing. She walked up to her and looked at her squarely, willing herself not to soften her gaze when beholding those magnificent blue eyes. "Do you honestly think I'd put my professional reputation on the line by taking meetings with a CEO I didn't trust?"

Jen stared back unflinchingly, refusing to be intimidated, refusing to back down. It was thrilling. "No. Is the only reason you joined me today because you wanted to catch up with Suzanne?"

Kade blinked. "I thought I could help by being here."

"You did. So how can I thank you?"

"Knock 'em dead tomorrow."

"I can do that."

"I have no doubt."

Nana wasn't having a good day. Something she'd eaten had given her diarrhea, and as Doreen recounted to Jen, by the time Doreen realized that Edna had needed an earlier bathroom visit, Edna had soiled the sheets. Doreen had strong-armed Edna into her wheelchair so she could take care of the bed in order to have a clean place to put her. Doreen had wiped Edna's hands and forearms, but her lower quarters were still a mess when Jen arrived. They tag-teamed, Doreen working on the bed and Jen bathing Edna.

Edna was embarrassed when these incidents occurred, which broke Jen's heart. She grew quiet and avoided eye contact. Jen's best defense in these situations was a good offense. She'd tell Nana about her day, from the highlights to the minutiae. Today she included Kade in her update, and even though she'd told Nana everything about Kade shortly after returning from Maui, she started from the beginning, letting Nana stop her if she wished.

When Nana got quiet like this, Jen wasn't sure whether she was indulging Jen by letting her retell a tale or whether, more likely, she hadn't remembered it in the first place. Jen now knew it was the latter, because Nana kept asking versions of the same questions long after her bath.

"You like her. This Kade," Nana said.

"Yes, I do." Jen was rubbing lotion into Nana's feet. Doreen had replaced the plastic mattress cover—ingenious device—changed the sheets, and washed the soiled ones, and now Nana was once again in bed. She was sitting up, propped by several pillows. Jen had covered Nana's left foot with a slipper while she worked on the right.

"Does she know?"

They'd covered this territory. Getting frustrated didn't help either of them, and while Jen occasionally succumbed to a short temper, most of the time she tried to pretend the repetition was a kind of mantra. "I don't think so, no."

"Tell her."

"I should," Jen said, not for the first time. "I'll think about it."

"That means you won't."

Jen smiled. "It means I'll think about it." She covered the foot she'd finished and removed the other slipper.

"When two girls want to date, who asks?"

"There aren't any rules about it."

"But someone must be the boy. To ask."

Jen squirted more lotion onto her hands. "Girls ask boys all the time, Nana. Boys ask girls, boys ask boys, girls ask boys, girls ask girls."

"Do you like a girl?" And they were back. Jen's mind flashed to the train set in Kade's condo, passing through the same territory time and again.

"I do."

"Does she know?"

"I doubt it."

"Girls ask girls. So ask her."

After receiving positive signals from the second hospital administrator they met with, Kade privately delighted in seeing the uncontained joy on Jen's face as they stepped outside. Jen was an attractive woman, whose sharp mind made her all the more so, and when she smiled at Kade, Kade felt its warmth skitter across her skin like a tender caress.

"We make a good team," Jen said at the edge of the parking lot.

"As much as it pleases me to take credit for success when I've done absolutely nothing to deserve it, I respectfully disagree. That was all you."

"He would have never agreed to meet with me, or certainly not so readily, had you not been involved. Without you, I'd be lucky to get onto his schedule by springtime."

Kade tipped an imaginary hat in Jen's direction. "Until next time." She stepped toward her car.

"Wait." Jen stopped Kade's progress with a hand on her arm. "What are your plans for dinner? Please at least let me treat you to something other than leftovers and foreign stock markets."

Kade purposely eyed Jen's hand before meeting her gaze, recognizing the ever-present current between them. It called for boundaries. "On one condition."

"Name it."

"It's not a date."

Jen nodded. "Not a date." She said it so matter-of-factly that Kade doubted she'd gotten through.

Kade tried again. "It's a dinner between colleagues."

Jen offered a sickeningly sweet smile. "What else would it be?"

Kade didn't want to presume Jen was thinking of this as anything other than a shared meal between board members. Maybe it was just she who thought that way about Jen, and it was a one-way street. She dropped it.

"What time were the leftovers being reheated?" Jen asked.

"Seven."

"Pick you up then."

CHAPTER EIGHT

Buoyed by her meeting and thrilled at the prospect of having dinner with Kade, Jen switched into seduction mode—well, as far as she was capable, which wasn't much to speak of. She didn't have an array of suggestive outfits, and she didn't consider herself sexy. Cute, she'd been told over the years. Usually girl-next-door or All-American-girl pretty, compliments she wasn't overly fond of. Also wholesome—a term far worse than anything with the word "girl" in it. One simply did not get their game on with someone wholesome. But she did have certain assets, and she was in the mood to advertise them, despite Kade's not-a-date rule.

Changing out of the classic but drab business skirt, she opted for a periwinkle dress that highlighted her eyes, showed off her legs, hugged her flat stomach, and accentuated her cleavage with its in-sewn C cup. Mid-height heels, earrings, and a silver necklace completed the outfit. She touched on a little makeup and re-curled the ends of her long hair to give it more body. Had Kade not just seen her, she would have put her hair up for added neck exposure, but that seemed a little too desperate.

She placed a call to her grandmother's house and was relieved when Candace, Nana's other primary caregiver, answered, which meant she'd recently begun her shift. Tonight Jen wouldn't be left with a too-familiar last-minute scramble for care coverage.

This was her first night off work in far too long, and Jen planned to enjoy it. Had Kade declined, Jen would have stopped by Nana's before heading home and working until midnight. As she took one last glance in the mirror, she was pleased to see that the crushing blow her Creative Care hours had delivered to her workout schedule hadn't yet resulted in an expansion of her belly, though its previous tautness had long ago given way to its present softness.

When Kade opened her front door to Jen, Jen mentally threw a fist into the air at her reaction. She openly and slowly appraised Jen from head to toe. For a second, she seemed poised to speak. But then she took a breath and slowly exhaled. "Oh boy," she muttered.

Kade had settled for a more casual look, managing to look stunning in simple black slacks and an emerald V-neck sweater, which brought out the green flecks in her eyes.

"You look great," Jen said, and meant it.

"I look like roadkill next to you, but thank you." Kade grabbed her purse from the entryway table and locked the door. "I'm all yours." She said it as she turned and practically ran into Jen, who hadn't moved.

"All mine?" Jen asked, advancing into what little space had remained between them. She cupped Kade's chin and brought their mouths dangerously close together. Her heart rate shot up as she heard a tiny whimper from Kade, who made no effort to step back. "If only this were a date," she whispered, fighting the desire to kiss Kade, whose lips had parted slightly as if in anticipation. She'd only meant to tease, and now she was the one being teased.

She abruptly retreated and dropped her hand, working to regain control of her breathing. "After you," she said, tilting her head toward the elevators.

Kade blinked. And closed her mouth. Then she set her jaw and marched ahead.

During the ride to the cozy Italian restaurant Jen had chosen, they picked apart the meetings they'd had over the past two days in order to refine Jen's message, using their observations of the administrators' reactions to certain ideas. Jen found Kade's experience and input invaluable, once again appreciating that Kade actively sought her take on things versus dictating a to-do list. But Jen didn't want tonight to be about work, and although she mentally filed away recommendations on handling future Creative Care meetings, she wanted to lay some ground rules. Aside from the fact that it wasn't a date.

When she parked on the street in front of the restaurant, she turned to Kade. "Would it be all right with you if we don't talk shop tonight?"

Kade eyed her skeptically. "We can try, but I'm afraid I'm a bit of a one-note wonder."

"I disagree."

"Hugely surprising," Kade said sarcastically.

They sat tucked away in a romantically lit corner of the restaurant, bantering with the waiter over specials and informing him of their selections. He returned with the Prosecco they ordered, poured them each a glass, and set the bottle down before departing.

Jen extended her glass to Kade. "Thank you for everything you're doing for Creative Care, Kade. I've never been more confident of our success."

"May you succeed," Kade said before clinking glasses and sipping the bubbly.

"Tell me about Holly."

"Oh geez. Launch right in, why don't you?"

"I want to know more about you. Tell me how she came to work for you."

"Not much to it. She's the little sister of Cassie, my best friend from junior high and high school. Pretty much a little sister to me, and every bit the pain in my ass that implies." Kade spoke with obvious affection, belying the last words.

"She mentioned she's been your only assistant."

"I didn't want one. She essentially let it be known that as soon as she graduated from college, she'd be working for me."

"Definitely sounds kid-sisterish."

"I think she had a bit of misapplied hero worship back then. I started my first company in order to help her younger brother, Sam, do better in school. He had a terrible time until he was diagnosed with dyslexia. It was ridiculous for such a gifted kid to be left to struggle for so long. Why wasn't this part of every child's health assessment? Why should it be any different than a hearing or eyesight issue?"

Jen knew the basics from her post-Maui research. "So you developed a program that quickly and effectively diagnoses kids early on."

Kade nodded. "Along with some talented software developers, yes. Of course it didn't really help Sam."

"But it's helped a lot of others. Both your companies have, from what I understand." Jen remembered reading that Kade's second venture stemmed from a bad accident involving a man who'd been like a father to her. He'd recovered, and Jen didn't recall his name, but now she'd bet anything that the man was Holly and Sam's dad. The company had developed a hemostatic gel people could carry around as easily as hand sanitizer, which could stop severe bleeding in seconds. Jen had some in her purse.

"I like to think so."

"Then I don't understand why her hero worship was misapplied. Sounds spot-on to me."

Kade frowned and set down her fork. "She should have blamed me for Cassie. I don't know why she never did. None of the Kellers did." Kade slowly twirled the stem of her flute, seemingly studying the bubbles dancing upward to pop at the surface, her thoughts clearly unpleasant ones.

Cassie had been near the top of the list of subjects Jen had wanted to cover this evening, but Kade's reaction changed everything. She didn't want to push Kade, who was obviously pained by her memories. She decided to switch topics, but Kade beat her to it.

"How did you meet Charles?" Kade asked, pushing some salad greens with her fork as if gauging her appetite.

"He was an investor in a friend's company, and she introduced us. Having heard their horror stories of working with VCs, I'm somewhat anxious about taking VC money."

This statement seemed to nudge Kade out of her doldrums. "I'm familiar with Charles's opinion on the subject, but what happened with your friend?"

"Same thing that happens to most women who aim for both a tech career and a family. She was considered a liability almost as soon as she announced her pregnancy, to the extent that she was for all intents and purposes ousted before she hit maternity leave."

"We have laws against that."

Jen scoffed. "We have laws against child pornography and drug trafficking, too. Doesn't prevent it from occurring."

"If that truly happened to your friend simply because she was pregnant, she had a bona fide claim against the board."

Did Kade truly believe her words, or did she expect that all women ought to be able to succeed the way she had, if they just worked hard enough? With all of Kade's years in the Valley, Jen found it difficult to believe she could be so naive.

"The filing of which would have immediately sunk any prospects she might have had to head up another company. Her reputation would have been decimated. You know damn well we're in a white-male-dominated industry. It's hard enough to be taken seriously as a female entrepreneur. A female entrepreneur with children? Nearly impossible." "Impossible" was the word that stilled Jen's tongue, as the next ones that formed in her mind unkindly related to Kade's workaholism, and she didn't want to go there. Yes, she believed women like Kade to be setting an unachievable bar for other women to emulate, especially those with kids. But Kade wasn't to blame. The real issue was that society as a whole regarded the bar a realistic metric in the first place. The scale needed to be revised and leveled out between men and women, and needed to include child and senior care in the equation.

The table fell silent, and Jen wondered if she'd gone too far. She'd never been shy, and standing up for what she believed was, for better or worse, one of the things that gave her the chops to be CEO. Kade took another bite of pasta and chewed it thoroughly. Jen hoped it meant she was giving the matter due consideration. She highly respected Kade's opinions—her real ones, not those she mentioned off the cuff as if from some sound bite.

"I assume this conversation is off the record?" Kade asked.

Given Kade's position at Matlock, it seemed a fair question. "Kade, nothing you and I discuss is for public consumption. I consider you a friend." Another subject Jen wanted to broach.

"It's something I've struggled with. I joined Matlock because of their track record and reputation, and because I'm at ground zero for getting new technologies launched and in the hands of people who need them. But it doesn't come without its own, well, how do I put this delicately? Sexism. I've considered starting my own fund and centering it on women-owned and women-led businesses."

All of Jen's concern about Kade's willingness to be as thoughtful and open in private as she was at work melted away. As Jen considered a Kadrienne Davenport-led fund that supported women, she felt an uptick in her affection for her that she let show.

"What?" Kade asked, repeatedly smoothing the napkin on her lap as if uncomfortable with Jen's reaction.

Almost giddy now, Jen said, "Yes. One hundred percent, yes. Fantastic idea. Oh, Kade, you have to do it."

"I hate to disappoint you, but it's only an idea. Nothing's in the works."

"Nothing about that idea disappoints me, and I would very happily accept an investment from such a firm," she said with a wink.

"Depending on the size of the investment, you'd report to me. Longer term. Still interested?"

"Spoilsport," Jen said, making Kade laugh.

Dinner passed too quickly for Jen's taste. Although they'd covered many subjects, Jen had shelved several important ones so the evening wouldn't turn too serious: Cassie, Kade's father, her obsession with schedules, the no-date rule. On the positive side, Jen had zero interest in adhering to Kade's dating edict and didn't think it fraught with emotionally charged territory, so she decided to start there. She could push the rest out to the coming weeks, a future in which Jen fully envisioned Kade taking part.

Jen surveyed the dessert menu, but the rich pasta was filling, and she wanted to enjoy the comfortable temperature outside. "Do you want dessert, or can we walk? We can grab a decaf next door and stroll downtown."

"Let's do it."

After purchasing their coffees, Jen took Kade's elbow as they walked. She was in a good mood, feeling lighthearted from their discussion and thoughts of Kade potentially advocating for entrepreneurs like her one day. She decided to act like a CEO and take charge. "Can we talk about the no-date policy?"

This conversation starter didn't seem to work initially, as Kade carefully sipped from her cup, eyes forward. "What would be the point?"

"Is it a religious thing?" Jen asked, ignoring her.

Kade laughed. "Hardly."

"You're not attracted to me?"

"What do you think?"

"I think you are. So then tell me. Let's go through your list."

"There is no list."

"One. I don't make enough money."

"I don't care about that."

"Didn't think so. Two, you don't like my career."

"How hypocritical do you think I am?"

"Three. You have a fiduciary duty to the shareholders of Creative Care."

"I do."

"Resign. Charles knows a lot of people who could serve on the board."

"It's not very professional of me to tell him I need to resign because I want to date you."

"It's more professional to remain on the board when you're dating the CEO?"

"We're not dating."

"A fact that should change. Four. You like being alone."

"I'm good at it."

"But you prefer it?"

"I prefer not to hurt people I care about."

"So you care about me." Half statement, half question.

"Not at the moment."

Jen laughed. "We'll come back to four." As they passed a bench, Jen sat and tugged Kade down next to her. She held her coffee in one hand and took Kade's hand with the other. "Five. You're adorable."

Kade frowned. "That's not an objection."

Jen laughed again and lightly bumped her shoulder against Kade's. She set her coffee on the ground and took Kade's hand in both of hers, folding it into her lap. "No. I got distracted."

"You're agitating."

"You think I'm cute."

Kade sighed. "Five?"

Jen wiped the grin off her face and eyed Kade seriously. "I'm not worth it."

"Not funny."

"It's not meant to be. I want to date you, we're attracted to each other, and someone else can take your board seat. So you must think I'm not worth it."

Kade tried to pull away, but Jen held her tight. "Help me understand."

Kade drew an audible breath. "It's the opposite."

"What do you mean?"

"I'm the one who's not worth it. Trust me. Please."

Jen didn't understand. Few people Jen knew were as competent and capable as Kade. How could she hold herself in such low regard? What had happened to give her such a poor opinion of herself? The desperation in Kade's voice to close the subject left no room to doubt Kade's sincerity and prevented Jen from pursuing the matter.

Kade untangled from Jen's loosened grip and stood. She held out her hand.

Jen bent down for her coffee and took the hand that pulled her to her feet.

In a role reversal, Kade took Jen's elbow as they started walking again.

Jen walked silently at Kade's side, arm in arm. Confused. It was like some perverse version of the classic *Just Friends* breakup speech: *It's not you, it's me.*

"Do you know what the two best things about Maui were for me?" Kade asked.

"Your awesome new bikini and the hordes of admirers who hung on your every word?"

Kade laughed. "I did score an awesome bikini actually, but no, not even close. You, first and foremost. And, for a day, forgetting who I am."

They walked on for several more blocks before Kade stopped in front of a shoe-store display. She pointed to a pair of sandals by extending her cup in its direction. "Cute."

But Jen's mind was racing. She could barely comprehend what Kade was talking about because she was back on Maui. Yes, Kade had said she wasn't acting in typical fashion during their day together, but she was funny, warm, gracious, and kind—characteristics that don't suddenly pop up for a day and then disappear. They might be sides to Kade that she didn't express as often as she had that day, but they were hers, and they were genuine, as tonight again confirmed.

She wanted to ask Kade who exactly she was being now, because as with Maui, she liked this person. A lot. She liked that she was motivated by helping others, employed a family friend and instilled within that friend incredible loyalty, and willingly provided support and guidance to Jen on the business front. She warmed at the affection in Kade's voice, the gift of her words just now.

Jen had no desire to play the long-suffering girlfriend to someone emotionally unavailable, damaged. She already played the role of caretaker to her grandmother—she didn't need to replicate that in her love life. But Kade *wasn't* emotionally unavailable. Jen remembered well many of Kade's words.

You've been an absolute gift to me.
Few as special as you.
You, first and foremost.

She had to think through the best way of revisiting this conversation. Kade obviously had put up a wall, but Jen hoped she could find a window. Or a strong rope with a grappling iron.

Aside from an occasional comment one of them would make on something in a shop's display, conversation died down, with Jen sensing that Kade, like her, was lost in her own thoughts.

During the ride back to Kade's, Jen found she was conflicted about how to say good night. She wanted to kiss Kade, but she didn't want to push her over the no-date rule to the point that Kade wouldn't agree to another evening out. And if she were to kiss her, she didn't want a fumbling exercise in the car. She wanted more.

She parked but didn't shut off the engine. "Thanks for tonight, Kade. And thanks again for the meetings. I appreciate it."

Kade reached toward the driver's console and turned off the engine. Then she got out, walked to Jen's side, and opened her door. "Can I have a hug?"

Jen delighted in the innocence of the question. It highlighted for her the sweet side of Kade she'd spent part of the evening remembering. She took the hand Kade extended and swung her legs out of the vehicle.

Kade pulled her into an embrace that they indulgently let linger. Finally, Kade pulled back into the circle of her arms. "Thanks for not pushing."

Jen had been on the brink of doing just that. Holding Kade had felt damn good on Maui, but the Kade she'd known then was merely an outline—a quick sketch of an attractive woman who'd shown flashes of wit and kindness. Lately that framework was being filled in with greater detail, and the portrait emerging was that of a complex, beautiful woman whose intelligence and sense of humor were enticing Jen to want to see the whole picture. Now, having Kade in her arms felt so marvelous, it seemed cruel to have to let go. "Don't think you're getting off so easily next time."

"Next time?" Kade asked with a crooked smile.

"You don't think I've gotten where I am by listening, do you?"

Kade laughed. "Is that the secret?"

Jen reluctantly released Kade and folded into her seat.

"Good night," Kade said, before closing the door.

CHAPTER NINE

Kade had made a lot of mistakes in her life. To this, she could readily admit. Sometimes she wondered if her two startup-company successes had come down to either sheer stubbornness or dumb luck. The number of things she'd done wrong as CEO was one reason she'd decided to move into the VC world, so she could mentor others. Many books, including her own, offered guidance: problems to watch out for, how to hold effective meetings, metrics to follow, recruiting advice, etc. Yet Kade believed the best defense against committing major errors was to listen to the specific issues her companies faced in real time and provide the kind of customized advice that generic articles and blogs simply couldn't replicate.

But one of the biggest mistakes she'd made was having dinner with Jennifer Spencer again, because she couldn't extricate her from her thoughts. By acquiescing to one-on-one time together after work, Kade was muddling messages. Asking Jen for a hug hadn't helped clarify things either. It was unprofessional. Board members did not embrace.

Jen had a way of drawing her in. Jen didn't have to flirt or ask or demand. She just had to be herself, and Kade was rapt. With one glance from those brilliant sky-blue eyes or flash of her captivating smile, Kade's shields dissolved. She hadn't abandoned all her precepts, but it had taken massive willpower to limit their good-bye to the hug she shouldn't have asked for, when she ached to kiss Jen again. While she was in Jen's arms, inhaled her scent, absorbed the warmth of her body, she felt enveloped by Jen's tenderness, and she was lost.

They hadn't communicated since their Tuesday dinner, and this was a big week for Creative Care. The product team was set to deliver version 1.0 of the mobile app today, designed to simplify matching seniors with caregivers. With the platform live, the skeleton referral system she and Jen were putting together with her hospital contacts, and the manual matches the company had been making over the past couple of months to seed the system with its initial transactions, Creative Care would put itself in much better shape to secure funding.

Although hitting the deadline to get the platform live had been Jen's primary objective of the past few weeks, Kade was surprised when Holly told her Jen had requested that she not schedule any hospital-administration meetings this week. Creative Care needed to be moving simultaneously in multiple directions. Surely landing another referral partner was worth a few hours of Jen's time? Jen wasn't one of the staff writing software code.

But why was Kade keyed up? Each of the companies she invested in via Matlock Ventures was undoubtedly feeling the pressure of an important deadline. Startups always had a big customer to try to land, a new software feature to release, an important recruit to close, a marketing campaign to launch, an investor report due. Week in and week out, startup companies could be counted on to demonstrably act on material initiatives that, in the bowels of larger entities, would languish for months. It was one of the most-cited reasons employees gave for joining a startup—they felt they could contribute directly and quickly.

The difference, the reason why her concern over the state of things at Creative Care was a problem: it wasn't one of Matlock's investments. She was paid—and paid handsomely—to invest in, monitor, and advise the companies in her Matlock portfolio. She was a partner in the firm, for God's sake. Yet here she was, colossal idiot that she was, wondering how Jen was faring, wondering how a team in which she didn't have a dime invested was progressing.

Twice today, Holly had had to prompt her to jump on scheduled conference calls. That simply never happened. Both times she'd joined three minutes late, which to Kade might as well have been an hour. Her distractedness was causing her to violate principles she held dear. Arriving late to meetings was disrespectful and wasteful, two things she loathed. And today she'd disrespected colleagues and wasted their time because she couldn't get Jen out of her thoughts.

Right before six p.m., Kade messaged Holly to come into her office. She needed to take action with respect to Jen, though she was fuzzy on what that meant exactly, with "action" and "Jen" being the only consistent themes floating through her brain. She thought Holly could help her flesh out details of some sort, even though asking Holly for assistance on this particular subject was sure to entail unending harassment.

Kade fidgeted with her pen. "I need your help. And I'm not really sure where to start."

Holly handed her a piece of paper. Before Kade could ask what it was, Holly said, "Jen's address. Also in your calendar. No, she's not expecting you. Bring food." She turned to leave but stopped at the sound of Kade's voice.

"Wait," Kade said, not quite following.

"You've been thinking about her all week."

Flustered, Kade couldn't disagree. "I wanted to check on how things at the—"

"You want to see her."

"*Company* are progressing." Kade wasn't sure who she was trying to fool.

"I checked in with Jeremy Corbin. They're running behind, but with all hands on deck, he thinks they'll launch on Sunday instead of today. He sent Jen home."

"I really should do some work tonight," Kade offered weakly, knowing she was seeking an excuse from doing any.

"If you don't go see her, do you think you'll be any more productive tonight than you've been the past few days?"

"And if I do go see her, I've learned nothing."

"You're afraid you'll hurt her."

Kade nodded.

"That means you care."

"That means I'm selfish because I want to see her anyway, fully knowing the consequences."

Holly took a seat in one of Kade's visitors' chairs. "What's the name of the man I'm going to marry?"

"Wait. What? Who?" Kade's head was spinning. Holly was getting married?

"I don't know. That's why I'm asking. Since you can predict the future, I figured I'd cut to the chase." Holly wiped her hands in the air. "No more bad dates."

"Be serious."

"No. Serious is exactly what neither of us should be right now. You like her. You're checking in with her, not committing to share a sarcophagus throughout eternity."

"Wow. Romantic."

"So lighten up." Holly stood. "I'm rejiggering a few things on your schedule this weekend, so be sure to check. Bring wine."

Jen lived in a small ranch-style house on a quiet street. Kade used the old-fashioned knocker to signal her arrival. When no noise was forthcoming, she tried the doorbell. This tactic brought footsteps, which grew louder as someone approached. Kade saw Jen peer through the beveled glass at the top of the door, then her eyes widen. The door opened.

Jen didn't look anything like her usual sunny self. She looked tired. Defeated. Her eyes were red in the way of an all-nighter versus an illness or good cry. Her hair was sticking out of its loose ponytail and probably hadn't been brushed today. She was in gray sweatpants and a well-worn yellow T-shirt with several holes in the stitching near the collar. Kade couldn't help but notice she was bra-less, but it was a fact, not a turn-on. Her feet were in boot-type slippers. Even disheveled and glum, Jen was the most appealing woman Kade had ever seen.

Kade held up the bag of Thai food and a bottle of wine. "I come bearing gifts."

Jen didn't release her grip on the door. "We don't have a meeting," she said tentatively, squinting at Kade as if trying to visualize her calendar to confirm the veracity of her statement.

"No, we don't. May I come in?"

"How do you know where I live?"

"Resourceful assistant with too much time on her hands, apparently."

Jen didn't move, and Kade questioned for the hundredth time why she had thought to come here.

"I know it's your personal space, Jen, and I'm not here to invade it. I brought these whether you want me to stay or not. Please. Take them." She held out both items to Jen.

"I'm a mess. My house is a mess. My company's a mess."

Kade returned the objects to her side and smiled. "One of the things I advocate to entrepreneurs I work with is to try to break problems down into small, actionable pieces. Everything you mentioned is fixable, though I'm not sure I agree with your assessment. Can I help?"

Jen frowned. "Probably," she said dejectedly.

Kade wasn't sure why her help would be a bad thing and tried to shake off the mild sting Jen's tone evoked. "I'd like to, if you'll let me."

Jen moved aside and let Kade in. She took the lead down the hallway, past a dining room and into a kitchen. Jen was apparently using the kitchen table as an office. Handwritten notes, bullet points, arrows, and asterisks were strewn across printouts of PowerPoint slides. Her laptop was nearby, next to which a glass of water sat on a coaster. Jen started picking up and arranging the papers into some sort of order.

"Hungry?" Kade asked as she set the bag and bottle on the counter.

"Very."

"How about I dish out dinner while you do whatever it is you think will make you feel better about…" She waved a palm in Jen's direction. "You. Though you look perfectly fine to me."

Jen scoffed. "I look like roadkill. Real roadkill. Not your kind."
She retreated down another hallway.

As Kade prepared dinner and uncorked the wine, she took in
her surroundings. The kitchen was small but bright and comfy, with
buttery-yellow cabinets, white tile, pale-yellow walls, and lots of
windows. It seemed the kind of place suited for a young family,
where kids could do homework and parents could fix meals. Warm
and open, like Jen.

Kade was setting out napkins as Jen returned, looking more
refreshed. She'd brushed her hair, retied her ponytail, swapped jeans
for the sweatpants, and tossed a fleece pullover over her T-shirt. The
slippers remained. "Better?" Kade asked.

Jen's nod was unconvincing.

Kade sat and indicated the wineglass at Jen's place setting. "I
wasn't sure if you wanted any, so no worries if you don't."

Jen half-smiled and took a seat. For someone who claimed to
be hungry, she picked at her food disinterestedly.

Without knowing what to say, Kade ate in silence, reluctant to
pressure Jen for information. Jen seemed to have a lot on her mind,
and Kade figured she'd come around to speaking it. This might be
the first uncomfortable silence to ever pass between them.

"Kade," Jen said, her eyes on her plate and her voice barely
above a whisper. "I need you to do something for me."

Kade stilled her hands and fought the urge to drag her chair
beside Jen and take her into her arms. "Name it."

"You once asked if what you said was off the record. I need that
now. I need you here as my friend, not my board member. If you
can't do that..." Jen swallowed with difficulty, as if she were on the
verge of crying. "I need you to please leave."

Kade was out of her chair in an instant, squatting next to Jen
and taking her hands in hers. "Of course I'm here as your friend. I
promise."

A dam broke. Jen tugged her hands free and covered her
eyes, and she started to cry. Kade did drag her chair over then and,
ignoring the awkward position, pulled Jen to her. She whispered
soothing words, rubbed her back with one hand, and held her head

with the other. She would leave it to Jen to decide what, if anything, she wished to share, and when.

Jen apologized for getting Kade's shirt wet, though Kade didn't care. She poured Jen a glass of water and took it to her. After several sips, Jen stood and said, "Living room." Kade followed.

Jen sat on the couch and patted the cushion next to her, taking Kade's hand as she joined her. "We're behind schedule. The payment gateway isn't integrated, the social-media platform is taking up five times more CPU than anticipated, and the dashboard is slow to load. Oh, and a five-year-old with a coloring book would be more helpful than our current design contractor."

Kade eyed Jen with amusement.

"I've spent countless hours on the fund-raising deck, and it's shit. *I* wouldn't invest. How can I convince someone else to?"

Kade sensed the question was rhetorical, so she continued to let Jen say her piece. She had a number of thoughts on how to tackle the issues Jen was bringing up, but she'd promised to be a friend, and right now that meant listening.

Jen sank lower into the cushion and smiled mirthlessly. "I have no idea what I'm doing, except failing spectacularly." She took a deep breath. "That about covers it."

"May I make a suggestion?"

"Please."

"Let's finish eating. Then why don't you walk me through the deck as it stands, no caveats by you or interruptions by me. I'll jot down some notes along the way and then put together some thoughts while you get some sleep. We'll tackle next steps afterward."

Jen shook her head. "You're sweet to offer, but I don't want to take advantage of you. I'm just unloading. I'll be fine. I'll figure it out." She covered Kade's hand. "But thank you."

"How about this then? Lie here." Kade tugged Jen and arranged her until her head rested on a pillow in Kade's lap.

Jen stared up at Kade skeptically.

Kade slid the elastic band from Jen's hair and began a gentle scalp massage. "Come up with an alternative suggestion and tell me about it in twenty minutes."

Jen sighed. "I already know my plan. Read more guidance. Consult my advisors. Rework the deck."

"Great. Then you shouldn't have any trouble repeating it in twenty minutes, assuming you haven't come up with something better."

"It's a waste of time," Jen murmured as her eyes fluttered.

"Planning is never wasted."

"Mmm."

Jen woke languidly, emerging from a restful sleep she hadn't remembered settling down to. As her eyes adjusted, she started at the realization she was on the couch in the living room. She quickly rose onto her elbows, working backward in her mind until landing on the recollection of resting her head in Kade's lap. Kade wasn't next to her, so Jen listened. Nothing. She swung her legs down and headed to the brightly lit kitchen. Kade was seated at what had been Jen's makeshift workstation, Jen's laptop displaying various text, and Kade studying a PowerPoint slide that seemed about midway through one of Jen's printouts. The food and dishes had been put away, counter cleaned, wine corked.

"Hi," Jen said, blinking to adjust to the light and glancing at the clock above the sink. 1:28 a.m. "What are you doing here?" Jen was curious, not accusatory.

Kade met Jen's eyes and broke into a lovely smile that Jen was sure she'd never get her fill of. It was the kind of smile that somehow captured and projected one of life's sweetest moments, like the instant a bride-to-be says "I do" or a father playfully tosses his giggling toddler into the air. She fleetingly wondered whether she was the impetus behind it, and in the seconds before she was awake enough to properly discard that thought, she reveled in the simple beauty of Kade's delight.

"How are you feeling?" Kade asked.

"Not sure yet."

"There's coffee if you're interested. Half caff."

Needing extra time to make sense of the scene in her kitchen, Jen poured herself a cup before settling at the table across from Kade. She nodded to Kade's pile to signal she awaited an answer to her first question.

"I hope you don't mind. I took a look through your slides to see if anything jumped out at me as something you might build on or take in a different direction." She flipped the deck closed and pushed it aside. The wattage of her smile dimmed considerably. "Up to you whether you want to go over it." She raised her hands as if in surrender to what she seemed to think was an impending upbraiding. "No pressure. I was here, that's all."

Here, yes. Kade had certainly been here for her tonight. Jen needed Kade to understand. She stretched across the table for her hand, which was hesitantly supplied. "I don't want you to think I don't value your feedback, Kade. I do. Tremendously. I just don't want you to get the idea that your experience and startup knowledge are all I value you for. I'd rather fumble around in the dark, trying to figure things out on my own, than have you believe that. Does that make sense?"

Kade squinted slightly, as if trying on Jen's words to see if they fit. "It's all I know."

It saddened Jen to hear Kade boil herself down to such a small thing when Jen knew there was so much more to her. The very fact that Kade was here, that she'd come over to check on Jen in the first place, proved it. But Jen had no illusions of breaking through Kade's well-cemented self-assessments tonight. She wanted Kade to see exactly how much she did appreciate her feedback. "Then let's see whatcha got for me," she said with a wink.

Kade made Jen take her through her slide deck before giving any guidance, insisting the unprinted material and anecdotes Jen supplied with each page were equally as important, because they showed a potential investor how well-versed Jen was with the information. Investors wanted to see confidence in leaders and be confident those leaders had a solid handle as to what was going on in their company and industry. She made several more notes, crossed out some text, and typed a few things into the word-processor program on Jen's laptop.

Then she went through each slide, starting by asking Jen what her own thoughts were as to the strengths and weaknesses of the material, and ending by counseling her as to what she covered well and what could use a bit more work. They powwowed for over an hour before Kade slid Jen's laptop toward her and covered several additional topics she thought would further strengthen Jen's message.

For Jen, it was a treasure trove. Kade didn't bulldoze or condescend. She nudged directionally but required Jen to do the heavy lifting—the hard work that would bring it all together with the objective of landing additional funding for Creative Care.

"Feeling better?" Kade asked after they were done.

"Infinitely."

Kade sipped her coffee and held the mug in her lap. "You're there, Jen. A few tweaks maybe, but you've got this."

"That means a lot, coming from you."

Kade nodded, too automatically, like she'd heard it all before.

Jen needed to explain, though she hadn't put her finger on exactly what she was trying to get across. This wasn't just business to her. "I want to make you proud of me."

Kade yawned, no other reaction to what Jen said. "You're doing everything you need to."

"I mean *you*, Kade. Not because you're my colleague."

Surprise alighted in Kade's eyes. "Why?"

"I don't know," Jen said, skirting the truth. Kade was important to her. But Jen sensed Kade wasn't ready to hear it and would flee as soon as she did.

Kade smiled distantly before setting her beverage on the table. She patted Jen's leg, the way a relative would. "I should get going," she said as she stood.

"Wait," Jen said, grabbing Kade's hand and entwining their fingers as she got up. "Stay."

Kade looked down to their joined hands and then up to Jen's face. Confused. Searching.

"It's nearly three. Your shoes are already off. Come." Jen tugged her reluctant guest down the hall to her bedroom and parked her in front of her dresser. She opened a drawer and removed an oversized T-shirt.

"Jen, I—"

Jen thrust the shirt against Kade's chest and guided her into the bathroom, which barely held the two of them. She opened the cabinet behind the door and sorted through a few shelves before setting an unopened toothbrush, hand towel, and washcloth on the counter. She grabbed toothpaste from the medicine cabinet, spread it on her toothbrush, and shoved it into her mouth. It was the antithesis of sexy, but she wanted to signal that she wasn't making a play for Kade. At least not in this particular moment. As she started brushing, she backed out and closed the door behind her.

From within the guest bathroom, Jen knew she was pressing her luck. She gave forty-to-sixty odds that Kade would take her up on her offer. Maybe thirty-seventy. She moved quickly in order to try to limit the amount of time Kade had to cycle through her objections.

Having changed into a T-shirt, Jen was first to re-enter the bedroom—a good sign, as Kade hadn't yet bolted. She left a bedside lamp on and crawled between the sheets on the side of the king-size bed farthest from the bathroom. Straddling the fence between turning her back to Kade and watching Kade enter her bedroom potentially wearing nothing but a T-shirt and underwear, Jen kept her eyes on the door. This was an opportunity she refused to miss. She pulled the top sheet and blanket on the empty side lower in invitation.

Kade exited the bathroom hesitantly, wearing the T-shirt Jen had provided and carrying her folded clothes. She used the pile to point down the hallway. "Good night, Jen." She swiftly headed out the door.

Jen threw back the sheets and followed Kade, who had already set her clothes on the coffee table and was grabbing a throw from the back of the couch when Jen arrived.

"I don't want you to sleep on the couch," Jen said.

"Guest bedroom?"

Jen snagged Kade's hand and marched her back to her bedroom. "Not happening. My bed's so big you could send up flares and I wouldn't find you." Pulling her to the edge of the bed, Jen gave Kade a gentle shove, landing her on her butt. Then she rounded the mattress and slipped under the covers facing Kade, giving her the final say as to whether to join her.

Kade remained still for several moments and seemed to arrive at a decision. She crawled into bed and lay on her back as close to the edge as possible.

Amused, Jen said, "I won't bite."

Kade moved in roughly one inch.

Jen laughed. She got onto her knees, stretched across Kade's torso, scooped her outer hip, and tugged. She knew Kade wouldn't budge unless she acquiesced to the action, which she surprised Jen by doing. Now she was actually in a normal sleeping position.

"Do you usually sleep on your back?" Jen asked as she switched off the lamp.

"Yes."

"Good, because I usually sleep on my side or stomach." And with that, Jen snuggled against Kade and laid her arm across her waist. She figured Kade would have said "no" had she asked permission, and this way Kade would have to request that she move, if that's what she truly wanted. Jen would do so, of course, but she left it up to Kade. Jen was exactly where she wanted to be. She nestled closer. "Thank you for tonight."

Jen felt a tiny bit of movement that she took to be a nod.

"Thinking about your schedule tomorrow?" Jen asked.

"Maybe."

Jen chuckled. So predictable. "What's on tap?"

"Eight o'clock breakfast, nine o'clock spin class, ten thirty shower and change, Stanford recruiting event at noon."

"Ha ha."

Silence.

Jen lifted her head to look at Kade even though it was too dark to see. "You're not serious."

Jen felt Kade's chest rise and fall and heard her exhale in short bursts. Laughing. "If you plan on leaving that early, be a dear and let yourself out."

"No breakfast in bed?"

"I can set out a granola bar right now for you to enjoy first thing."

"Nah." Kade put her free arm around Jen. "I'm thinking I might not want to get up in four hours." She kissed Jen's hair. "Or ever."

Once again, Kade surprised her with her sweetness.

CHAPTER TEN

Slightly disoriented, Kade woke to unfamiliar surroundings. But unlike waking up in a hotel, words that came to mind were homey and warm, not functional and efficient. She'd slept well, though it had taken a while to fall asleep, her body warring with her brain over what it considered reasonable proximity to Jen. Her body wanted to be in close contact; her mind preferred the couch.

Since Jen wasn't in the room, Kade humored her body's desire to soak up Jen's scent while she had the opportunity, so she rolled onto her stomach and rested her face on Jen's pillow. She recognized the hint of apricot from Jen's shampoo. For another indulgent moment, she wondered what it would be like to wake up each day, enveloped in Jen's fragrance, surrounded by Jen's body, cared for by Jen's heart. It would be pretty damn wonderful. But there was a pesky thing called reality, and she needed to get back to it.

After using the bathroom and brushing her teeth, Kade unhooked and donned the terry-cloth robe from the back of the bathroom door, swapping it for last night's T-shirt. She padded down the hallway and into the kitchen. Jen was seated at the table, dressed in jeans and a Henley, sipping from a mug and reading *The Wall Street Journal.* Kade could happily wake up to this scene every day. Then again, if she was going to continue fantasizing about the perfect morning welcome, she'd scale back on the amount of clothing Jen wore and, for as much as she loved the *Journal,* opt for a greeting that didn't involve leaving the bedroom.

Good thing she stacked her weekends to avoid the kind of temptation Jen represented.

"You get the *Journal*?" Kade asked.

Jen sat back, gave Kade her full attention, and unleashed such a beautiful smile that Kade felt her own face light up unexpectedly.

"Good morning. Not usually, but I know you read it, or at least you used to, so I went out and foraged. There's OJ, milk, and cream cheese in the fridge."

On the counter, Kade spied a bowl of fresh fruit, a bag of bagels, slices of tomato on a cutting board, and an empty mug. "How are you not married?" she said as she poured coffee.

"I could ask you the same thing."

Kade chuckled and grabbed the milk. Before adding a splash, she ticked off reasons, extending her thumb and fingers as she listed each. "Easy. Workaholic. Can't cook. OCD about being on time. Intimidating. Inflexible. For starters."

Jen took up the task and started counting. "How about helpful, sharp, insightful, sweet, and funny?"

Kade eyed her skeptically as she returned the carton to the fridge. "Sure, if we've moved on to you."

"You're very frustrating."

"See? Another one. Add it to the list. Stubborn, too, while you're at it." She sat across from Jen and changed her tone. "How are you feeling today? Seriously."

"Yesterday morning, Jeremy was ready to kill me because I was fluttering about the office like a moth on steroids, moving from person to person as if they were porch lights, checking their progress every two minutes. He sent me home. So seriously? I feel renewed, energized, and confident. All thanks to you. Seriously."

Kade cupped her mug in her hands and smiled. She knew she shouldn't put too much weight behind Jen's words because Jen had most of the topics she needed to cover already in her deck, which merely required some rearranging, amplification, or subtlety, depending on the subject. Yet they filled Kade with genuine pleasure, like the first shafts of sunlight after a long snowstorm. "I'm glad."

"You have a beautiful smile."

Kade cocked an eyebrow in response.

Jen laughed. "Please add 'great at accepting compliments' to your list. Hey, I have a proposal."

"Uh-oh." Kade indicated the newspaper and the food. "Was all this to butter me up?"

"No, not especially," Jen said, and then seemed to reconsider. "Is it working?"

Kade gave her a mock glare.

"Remember our two ground rules from Maui? A single day, no work talk."

Kade nodded.

"Will you take today off and spend it with me?"

Kade shifted in her chair, and Jen seemed poised to deflect potential objections.

"Hear me out. You could easily get one of your ambitious, anxious-to-prove-themselves underlings to cover for you at the recruiting event. Why don't we go to San Francisco, walk along Crissy Field, have lunch in the Marina—"

"Wait," Kade said with a raised palm. "Let me get my phone." Kade dashed to the living room and shuffled through her clothes pile. Besides the Stanford shindig, something else was slated for that evening, something she couldn't remember offhand but would leverage to politely decline. Jen's offer was far more appealing than anything she had lined up, but she needed to be able to defend against it. All it would require was a quick reminder of her schedule to fend off Jen, say her good-byes, and get back on track. While she consulted her device, Jen continued.

"I don't want to see everything on your plate. It's Saturday. My presentation's in much better shape than it was before you got here, I've got a clear path forward, and I...what's wrong?"

Kade couldn't believe what she was seeing. Then again, considering her assistant, she could. All obligations had been adroitly removed from her calendar, and in her inbox was an email from Holly detailing extremely plausible yet incredibly convenient reasons why she was suddenly completely free this weekend. She didn't even have time to concoct a viable story, since Jen was standing next to her.

Jen took the phone Kade was handing her. "What?"

"What does it say?" Kade asked, waiting for Jen to read the screen.

Jen shifted her gaze to the calendar on display. The entire day was blocked off. Jen appeared confused. "It says, 'Day with Jen' question mark."

"Right."

"Wait. This is your schedule today?"

Kade nodded and slid into her chair. "Apparently. Holly rearranged things."

"You're not working?"

Kade shook her head and thought she could tell the exact moment the coin dropped for Jen. Jen tilted her head and graced Kade with a slow smile that took hold of her whole face. Then she squealed like a schoolgirl and practically jumped into Kade's lap, throwing her arms around her neck and hugging her. When she pulled back to look at Kade, she was grinning.

"You know what this means, don't you?" Jen asked.

Kade shook her head, all thoughts of excuses becoming jumbled and incoherent with Jen this close, the unbounded joy in her eyes intoxicating.

"It means I must kiss you." And she did.

At first, it was only a firm press of her lips on Kade's, barely longer than sisters or friends might exchange if they hadn't seen each other in years. Then Jen bussed Kade's lips a few more times in quick succession. And then it all changed.

Jen quickly shifted from having both legs to one side of Kade to straddling her instead. She ran a hand into Kade's hair, starting at the base of her neck. Then she caressed Kade's cheek before sliding to her chin, which she gently cupped. She dipped her head until her lips hovered against Kade's upper lip, which she softly teased with her tongue. By the time she followed suit against Kade's bottom lip, Kade longed for more contact.

Kade slid her hands down Jen's back and lower, between denim and cotton, cupping her ass and pulling her close. Impatiently, Kade surged forward, her mouth and tongue demanding more from Jen—more contact, more pressure, more everything.

Jen's hands moved to her neck and then snuck inside the open collar of the robe. She smoothed her fingers beneath the swell of one breast, then glided her thumb over the nipple, teasing it to attention.

It felt so good, almost as if Kade had never been touched before. She seemed ready to justify anything in order to have this day with Jen, this intimacy. They were talking about only one day. What could go wrong? But something niggled at the back of Kade's mind. Kade desperately did not want to hurt Jen. They couldn't continue down this path.

With effort, Kade broke their kiss. She gazed at Jen, blown away by how attractive she was with swollen lips and flushed skin, and unsure as to why she was on the receiving end of her attention. With the pad of her thumb, she brushed Jen's bottom lip. "You're beautiful," she said, hearing the conviction in her own voice, knowing the inadequacy of her words.

She reached for Jen's hands, then kissed each one before holding them in the small space between them. "As much as I want this, I don't think we sh—"

Jen shushed Kade with an index finger to her lips. "No thinking. A single day, no work talk," Jen said again. She ran her fingers through Kade's silky strands and shifted her gaze to follow her hands. "That's the deal." She found Kade's eyes once more, as if to convey unhesitant and complete acceptance of the terms. Then Jen climbed off Kade and held her hand out, the invitation clear.

Kade took it and followed her to the bedroom.

Jen found it difficult to take the short path to her room. Her legs seemed rubbery, the journey long, the path fuzzy, as her brain struggled to impart instructions to her lust-filled body. Kade was behind her, their destination and its implications unambiguous. They were going to have sex—finally, Jen thought—and she couldn't be more eager or willing. Yes, it came with caveats, but Jen wasn't the planner Kade was. She would rather take what she could today than push it off to an unknowable tomorrow.

She stopped them at the edge of the bed—Kade's side, Jen thought happily. She had a moment of inaction, feeling nearly overwhelmed by all the choices they could make over the next few hours. But as she looked at Kade and saw her unmistakable need, her unflinching eyes, Jen felt grounded, sure. She took Kade's face in her hands, lingering several moments to simply enjoy and absorb the affectionate gaze being leveled at her by the woman who had captured her heart. Jen didn't need to dissect that last thought, to overanalyze the conclusion. It was there, nothing frightening or worrying about it.

She kissed Kade with every ounce of devotion she was feeling. She wanted to show Kade that while she was more than ready for this, it was uniquely Kade with whom she wanted to share it. And then she purposely shifted into a different gear, one she hoped would encourage the hunger between them and not stifle it with too much emotion. Jen knew what was in her heart, but she suspected Kade wasn't yet there. Moreover, Kade might never be. So Jen decided to do all she could, which was to give of herself in this moment.

Jen broke the kiss and led Kade's hands to the edge of her shirt, folding her fingers over the hemline, a clear signal of what she wanted. Kade didn't disappoint, inching the material upward, exposing first the top of Jen's jeans, then her stomach, then her bra, before tugging the shirt over her head and tossing it onto the corner of the bed. The thought flicked across her mind that Kade probably had a thing against throwing clothes on the floor. She'd find out soon enough.

Grabbing the lapels of her own robe, which she concluded looked far better on Kade than her, Jen tugged Kade forward for a bruising kiss. She wanted to claim, to possess. Their tongues danced and dueled, jockeying between dominance and submission. Jen felt behind her for Kade's hands, which were on her back, and again positioned them where she wanted, this time at the clasp of her jeans.

Kade broke the kiss and focused on Jen's face as she unbuttoned and unzipped. "Take them off," Kade said once she lowered the zipper. The command sent a jolt of arousal to Jen's center, and she inhaled sharply. She wriggled them down and stepped out of them, holding them up to Kade by a finger through a belt loop, interested to see what Kade would do. Kade threw them on top of the shirt, and Jen wondered what it was costing her not to fold them first.

Kade advanced on her then, caressing the exposed skin, running her hands along Jen's back and waist, arms and neck, sides and stomach. Then she squatted, moving them from Jen's calves to the backs of her knees to her thighs, first one leg and then the other. As she rose, she nudged her nose in a line over Jen's bikinis, starting at the lowest part of the front-facing fabric and tightening her grip on the backs of Jen's thighs as she seemed to sense the sudden weakness in Jen's legs. Jen gasped at the contact, steadying herself with her hands on Kade's shoulders, wild with desire as Kade stood to face her.

Jen again took Kade's hands and brought them around her body, setting Kade's fingers at the clasp of her bra to complete the command.

But Kade shook her head. Instead, she took Jen's hands and led them to the knot in her belt. "Take it off," she said as she slid an arm around Jen's neck, while the other caressed the curve of Jen's breast beneath the sheer fabric. Jen didn't think Kade was playing fair, and she liked it. How was she to concentrate on disrobing Kade, with Kade touching her this way?

Jen kept her eyes on Kade's as she worked the simple tie, enjoying the concentration on Kade's face to try to control her breathing. Once the robe was unfastened, it fell open, revealing the lacy bikinis she'd only glimpsed beneath the T-shirt last night. Her eyes never leaving Kade's, she bent her knees, sliding the underwear down long legs as she went. The dark curls at the juncture of Kade's legs signaled a playground Jen wanted to explore, and she could hardly contain her desire to tug Kade forward and stroke her with her tongue until she cried out her pleasure. Instead she stood, laid her palms on the skin above Kade's sternum, and slipped them beneath the thick fabric. She glided them up and over Kade's shoulders, the movement further parting the robe to completely reveal her breasts. With one more upward motion, the robe fell to the floor, and Kade stood naked before her.

Jen stopped and stared. Kade's body was near perfection, exceeding Jen's greatest fantasies about it, fantasies that had begun as soon as she'd seen Kade wearing a jade bikini over a year ago, images that had only grown in number since meeting Kade again. She licked her suddenly dry lips, almost unsure of where to start with the things she wanted to do. The only thought that materialized was that they were too far apart, so Jen crushed her body to Kade's and kissed her, surrendering to the feel of skin against skin.

But barriers still separated them, small yet unacceptable ones, which needed tending to. Body still flush with Kade's, Jen fumbled for her bra clasp. But Kade's hands were suddenly there, and she whispered against Jen's mouth, "Let me." Kade undid the clasp, slid her fingers up Jen's back to the straps, and gently pushed them off her shoulders. She moved just enough that the space she created between them allowed the bra to fall, and it dangled from one end by Kade's fingers. With the swing of her arm, Kade added it to the growing clothes pile.

Kade's mouth traveled along Jen's neck in a sensual exploration. Her hands went to Jen's waist, and she dipped her fingers in between bikinis and skin, tracing along the edge of the fabric. She brought them around to the front, her knuckles grazing the hair between Jen's legs. Then she slipped back around and worked her fingers lower, barely dipping into Jen's wetness from behind.

Jen whimpered, her breath coming shallowly. If Kade stroked lower, she'd be well on her way to orgasm. But Kade went back to the waistband and slid the bikinis down until they fell. Jen stepped out of them, and Kade bent to pick them up—at least that's what Jen thought initially. Once Kade's hands and nose started reacquainting themselves with Jen's lower body, Jen quickly discovered Kade wasn't too concerned about leaving clothes on the floor.

This time, after Kade's nose nudged at Jen's center, her mouth followed. She traced her tongue into the shallowest of Jen's folds, enough to tease and extract another whimper. And then she shifted gears. With her mouth still against Jen, she prodded her backward until Jen's legs hit the mattress, and then she gave her a light shove, sending her prone on her back. On the floor on her knees, Kade spread Jen's thighs and plunged her tongue into her, using her upper lip to keep pressure where Jen needed it. Jen felt stirrings of her orgasm, and Kade seemed to sense it, too, shifting to take Jen fully into her mouth while delving into her with her fingers. She pulled out to the very edge before pushing deeply into her, repeating her motions, maintaining pressure with her mouth.

Making mostly unintelligible sounds, interspersed with an occasional "oh" or "God" or "yes," Jen climbed until she shattered, left to a blissful state of satisfaction, muscles spent and weak.

Kade crawled next to her on the bed, delivering soft kisses to her temple, shoulder, underneath her chin, along her throat.

Jen tenderly brushed some hair out of Kade's face and acknowledged to herself the wonder she was feeling. "What did you just do to me?"

"I think the more appropriate question is: shall I do it again?"

Jen smiled and held Kade's chin in her palm. "Not until I've had a chance to memorize every inch of your body with my mouth." Jen kissed her leisurely at first, taking time to savor their connection and let her body recover. But tasting herself on Kade's lips was a powerful restorative, and as she began to feel reinvigorated, she kissed her more passionately and scooched them until they were lengthwise on the bed. She rose onto her elbows, hovering over Kade, and locked eyes with her. "Let me." She hadn't sensed any odd power dynamic between them, any indication that Kade needed to be constantly in charge, but she wanted unrestricted access to her and decided to err on the side of clarity.

Kade didn't specifically acknowledge the comment, and she never stopped touching Jen. She simply went along with everything Jen said and did, every silent suggestion and plea Jen made, somehow making it clear without words that she was completely present in the moment and fully expected Jen to be as well.

Jen worked her way down Kade's neck and clavicle, using lips, tongue, and teeth to express her unadulterated enjoyment of every aspect of Kade's body. Her breasts in particular, weighty handfuls of smooth, creamy flesh, deserved careful perusal. She swirled her tongue around the puckered skin of Kade's areola before sucking the nipple into her mouth. Kade was on the quiet side as lovers went, and Jen appreciated slightly more verbal feedback, so she decided to say something. Kade had expressed no hesitation in meeting her lover's needs, so why not incentivize her?

Jen grazed Kade's nipple with her teeth. "Do you like that?" Jen asked, substituting her fingers for her mouth while she spoke. With her dazed, unfocused eyes, Kade managed to find Jen's and nod. "Tell me," Jen said. "Tell me how I'm making you feel." Jen took Kade's breast into her mouth.

"I can't…mmm…concentrate. When you…oh…"

"Should I stop?"

Kade raised her head. "God, no."

Jen smiled and continued lavishing Kade's ample chest with attention, but she let her hand drift lower, and then lower still. As she teased Kade's sex, Jen felt Kade tighten, and she heard a more ragged edge to her breathing. She slid a finger along Kade's wetness and heard her breath catch. "Tell me."

"Feels…good…so good. Please." Kade gripped Jen's head, and Jen could tell she was fighting an internal battle between trying not to clutch too tightly and being absolutely unwilling to let go.

Jen pushed inside, deep and slow, and Kade moaned. Jen kept up outside pressure with her thumb, set a steady rhythm between Kade's legs, and laved her breasts with her tongue.

"Yes…there…that's…" Kade's muscles clenched, and her breath held for a moment before she cried out in release.

Jen shifted higher and rested along Kade's side, half on Kade, half on the bed. With her fingertip, she drew a languid line down her nose, lips, chin, and throat. Propped on her elbow, resting her head on her hand, she kept her eyes on the movement of her finger, watching as it traced haphazard patterns across Kade's face. "You're beautiful."

Kade grabbed Jen's hand and kissed the traveling digit. She leaned forward and kissed Jen on the mouth.

"What are you thinking?" Jen asked.

Kade took Jen's hand and interlaced their fingers. "Let's stay local. Skip the drive. Picnic in the park. Maybe rent a couple of beach cruisers and bicycle around the lake. Dinner here or at a place you like." Kade caressed Jen's cheek. "More…vocalization lessons." Light danced in Kade's eyes, and Jen blushed, hot.

"Best idea ever," Jen said, lifting their combined hands and kissing Kade's. "Let's start now."

Chapter Eleven

In the late afternoon, Jen lent Kade a T-shirt, athletic shorts, and a baseball cap. She packed a blanket and an insulated lunch bag into a backpack, and they stopped by a deli to grab food for their outdoor picnic. They rented bicycles and meandered along a path through the woods before settling down on a flat, grassy area close to the lake.

As Jen unpacked their food, she removed a bottle of sunscreen, even though the hottest sun of the day had passed. She held it up with a salacious grin. "Need me to do you?"

Kade snatched it out of her hands and kissed her, laughing the entire time. "You're terrible. And yes, I do." With a wink, she added, "But not here."

"You're very easygoing about your sexuality in public. Is that because no one recognizes you in a baseball cap and ponytail?"

"I wouldn't care if they did."

"I don't remember reading about the fact that you're a lesbian."

"Need more proof?" Kade held a grape between her teeth and shared it, stealing an awkward kiss as Jen took half with her mouth. She chewed and swallowed. "Exactly what kind of reading were you doing?"

Jen flushed. "I kinda Googled you after Maui."

"Stalker," Kade said before sampling the salad.

"Seriously. You're a big fish in a small pond. I would think your sexuality would have hit the blogosphere, with jealous misogynist homophobes spewing all kinds of vitriol about a woman's place being in the kitchen and what not. The fact that you're succeeding as a woman, and as a gay woman, is enough to prompt Internet chatter in Silicon Valley, at the very least."

"I think I'd actually have to *be* with a woman to start said rumor mill."

Jen swallowed a bite of chow mein. "When was your last relationship?"

Kade kept her eyes on Jen but didn't respond.

"What, there are so many, you can't keep track?"

Kade shook her head. "I've never been in one."

Stilling her fork mid-air, Jen stared at her as if Kade's nose had grown several inches. "I'm not talking long or even healthy. When's the last one that lasted even a month?"

Kade shook her head again.

Jen half-smiled, definitely feeling the sting of Kade not trusting her with this information, which she didn't consider particularly revealing. Dropping her utensil into the plastic container, she covered Kade's hand with her own. "Kade, if something's too personal or private, just tell me. I will totally respect that. But please don't lie to me."

Kade withdrew her hand, and there was no mistaking the hurt in her eyes. "I'm not." She set her fork down and grabbed her half-full water bottle. She stood and wiped off her shorts. And then very quietly, she said, "I wouldn't." She walked toward the water fountain, ostensibly to fill her bottle, which didn't need it.

Jen watched her distractedly, not really seeing. Shocked. If Kade had said she could get an elephant to walk a tightrope or Congress to balance the budget, Jen might have believed her. But this was beyond comprehension. Kade was thirty-three, successful on any scale, smart, sweet, and sexy as hell. And good God, great in bed. It defied logic that she'd never been in a relationship.

Yes, she worked too much, which would be challenging for a lover. And yes, she was quirky when it came to time management. But even her obsessiveness on that front seemed very manageable. Jen herself had seen Kade make last-minute calendar adjustments that were no different from what others would do. And when she took the day off, which Jen was experiencing for the second time,

Kade barely checked her phone. It's like she simply needed to mentally prepare for what came next, and then she was fine with it.

Jen owed Kade an apology. She desperately wanted to understand why Kade prevented herself from getting close to anyone, but right now she needed to set things right. Quickly lidding their food, she followed the path Kade had traversed and found her propped against a tree, looking out at the water. Jen walked over to her and grasped for her free hand, but Kade moved it and held the bottle in both hands. "I'm sorry I assumed you were lying."

Kade didn't react, although her jaw muscles clenched.

"I'm sorry I hurt your feelings," Jen said, hoping to get through.

Kade said nothing.

"I see so much in you, it's hard for me to understand why you haven't been with anyone."

"Let's finish lunch and head back," Kade said, pushing off the tree and walking back to the blanket, effectively cutting off conversation.

They sat quietly, Kade pushing some noodles around her paper plate, Jen eating while watching Kade not take another bite.

"Are you not going to talk to me any more today?" Jen asked, frustrated with herself and with Kade. "I said I'm sorry and I meant it. Will you please forgive me?"

Kade looked skyward, as if it might contain whatever guidance or strength she felt she needed right now. She set down her plate and took a sip of water. Then she shifted her eyes to Jen. "Apology accepted. If anything, I should consider it a compliment that you think I could ever be in a relationship. But here's the truth, and once I say this, I don't want to revisit it, and I hope you'll respect that.

"The people I've cared about most in this world are the ones I've hurt the deepest. My father lost his job because of me, my mother lost my father because of me, we both lost the man he once was because of me, and my best friend…" Kade's voice had grown softer and softer until it broke with emotion. Her eyes glistened. "My best friend lost her life because of me. I won't let myself hurt anyone else." Kade tucked her knees against her chest, her arms wrapped around them protectively.

Jen's heart broke. The pain Kade lived with and her guilt were massive weights crushing her ability to see herself in a different light, to see herself as Jen did. She could no longer stay away, no matter how stiff and unapproachable Kade made herself. She positioned Kade between her knees so Kade's back rested against her chest. Jen put her arms around her and held her. She would hold her for as long as Kade allowed.

❖

The rest of the afternoon passed in near silence. Their late lunch and return bike ride meant it was pushing five o'clock by the time they arrived at Jen's. Kade was subdued, and Jen didn't know what to say or do to bring back the lightheartedness and playfulness that had been present earlier in the day. She feared Kade would call an early end to their time together. And she was right.

"I should go," Kade said almost as soon as they entered Jen's house.

Jen walked up to Kade and put her arms around her. "That wasn't our deal. I have you until tomorrow morning." She felt faint stirrings of hope when Kade slid an arm around Jen's waist and rested her chin on her shoulder.

"I'm not very good company," Kade said.

"The good news is, I am." Jen kissed Kade's nose. "I have ways of taking your mind off whatever's got you in a funk."

Kade smiled halfheartedly. "Yes, you do."

"Shall I use them? I don't want to pressure you if you really want to leave. But I'd love it if you'd stay."

Kade sighed and took both Jen's hands in hers. "I want to stick to our deal. If I say I'll do something, I want to do it."

Jen fought hard to maintain a neutral expression and not pull away, though Kade's words stung. She wanted Kade to stay because of her, not out of some sense of duty.

Kade lightly tucked some strands of hair behind Jen's ear. "Mostly, though, if I'm being honest, I want to stay because of you."

Jen felt the rejuvenating effect of those words immediately, as if she were taking her first drink of water after days in the desert. Had Kade read her mind? How much could Kade see?

Kade tenderly ran two fingers from Jen's cheekbone to her jawline, then slid them across Jen's lips. She softly kissed the mouth she'd just touched. "So, Miss Funk-eraser, what do you have in mind?"

How did Kade keep finding ways to nestle into Jen's heart even more fully than she already had? Kade managed to approach the very crux of her from new angles and sneak into tucked-away places during the light of day.

Jen tugged Kade behind her and indicated that she sit at the kitchen table. "Time for my secret weapon." She left the room briefly and returned with her prize, which she set on the table.

"Boggle?" Kade asked. "Boggle is your secret weapon?"

Jen really didn't care what they did, as long as it got Kade's mind off her somber thoughts. Well, she did care, and she had very specific ideas of how she could get Kade's mind onto other, more intimate things, but they needed a bit of a segue before jumping back into bed. As Jen grabbed two pens and memo pads from the junk drawer, she said, "My grandma loves this game. She taught me when I was young and always beat me until my vocabulary improved, sometime around high school." She set the items on the table and went about pouring each of them a glass of white wine from the fridge. "Then at least I had a chance. We'll see how I fare against the likes of Kadrienne Davenport."

"Do you two still play?"

Jen shook her head. "Her mind's not as sharp as it used to be, and she has trouble concentrating. Books, games, puzzles—they're tough for her. So you'll have to be her stand-in." Jen served the wine and sat across from Kade.

"I get the feeling no one could do her justice."

"She's definitely special. But so are you."

"Special as in 'unique' or 'different,' like my horrific perm in eighth grade?"

Jen laughed. "Unique and different, for sure. But more like a unicorn or fairy."

"How often do you see her?"

"I try to see her several times a week, at least. She doesn't always recognize me, which can be hard. But I know who she is."

"Part of her probably perceives you're there."

"I'll never find out, and I don't need to. I'm in her heart, and she'd do the same for me. I wish you could meet her."

"Why can't I?"

"A single day, remember?" Jen had been purposely brushing the idea aside, much preferring to think of their time together as a beginning, not an end. She wasn't deluding herself that Kade would change her mind. But Kade made her happy, and she wanted to give herself over to those feelings instead of concern herself with something outside her control.

Kade nodded. "I'm sorry it can't be longer."

"It can if you want it to be." It was the extent to which Jen would push.

"It's not about what I want."

Jen covered Kade's hand with hers. Kade seemed so earnest, like she wanted to give them a chance. This was bittersweet for Jen, the idea that Kade wanted more from their relationship yet seemed resigned to a different outcome. "I know. And while I disagree with where you stand on the subject, I understand it. At least I'm trying to. And since I have you for a little while longer, I intend to make the most of it." Jen handed the plastic cube to Kade for her to randomly mix up the letters so they could play. "Shake. You know the rules?"

"I think so," Kade said as she shook the pieces. "We get until the sand timer runs out to write down all the words we find using letters from adjacent cubes. Three letters long or more, the longer the better in terms of points." Kade shimmied the letters until they fell into place and set the cube down. She gave Jen a try-to-beat-me look. "Good luck."

Turning the sand counter upside down to start the game, Jen said, "I won't need it."

Two games later, Jen's prescient words left Kade arguing for a different result. "Deedy is not a word," she said.

"It is too a word. It means industrious or earnest."

"If that's a word, then so is deev."

"You do not get credit for folklore. It's not in our chosen dictionary."

"I think your dictionary and rules leave a bit to be desired. Best three out of five?"

"No. We said two out of three. I win."

"What's the prize?"

"I've already won it," Jen said as she stood and extended her hand to Kade.

Kade took it. "Bragging rights?"

Jen pulled her up. "Oh, I've won much more than that," Jen said as she led Kade toward her bedroom. "Exploration rights."

"If this is what I get for losing, why would I ever want to win?"

"I thought you liked to come out on top."

"You realize there's no dignified response to that," Kade said as Jen stopped her at the foot of the bed.

"Yes. I'm counting on a raunchy one," Jen said, tugging Kade's shirt off over her head. "Don't disappoint me."

Kade pushed Jen onto the bed, swiftly following and covering her with her body. She grinned lasciviously before dropping out of view. Before Jen could question where she was going, fingers curled into Jen's waistband and stripped her. A wet, hot mouth was between her legs, a talented tongue working her center. Taking. Delivering.

Neither Kade's response nor Jen's position was refined, and the indecency of the entire scene quickly stoked Jen's arousal higher and higher. Board games as foreplay. Who knew?

Since they'd eaten lunch so late, they weren't too hungry for dinner, but with their recent workout, they both wanted a snack. Jen sliced the baguette and cheese they'd purchased at the deli, while Kade rinsed some blueberries, opened a bag of marcona almonds, and refilled their wineglasses. Jen placed the food on a tray and carried it into the living room. Kade followed, beverages in hand. Although it was too warm for a fire, Jen went all Girl Scout on Kade and decided to start one anyway. She pressed a button on the wall, and the gas fireplace alighted. "Ambiance," she said as she joined Kade on the floor, giving her a quick kiss on the mouth.

"Impressive. Did you learn that during a wilderness expedition?" Kade asked as she settled on the throw she'd laid out on the carpet.

"I did. I know how to trap rodents and snakes for food using only rope and a knife. And I can identify all thirty-two plant varietals best known for retaining fresh water, to help me survive in a pinch. How are you going to help?"

"Survive in the wilderness?"

"Yes."

"Hmm. Strong cell-phone signal?"

"Try again."

"Um. Stick with you?"

"And do everything I say? Please. Like that would happen."

Kade flicked her head in the direction of the bedroom. "Hey, I'm highly trainable, with the right motivation." She winked.

Jen blushed. "You cede control temporarily. Then you take it back. If we're trying to survive in the wilderness, you'd have to do what I say."

"Note to self: no backwoods trips with Jen. Although at least I wouldn't get bored."

"Watching me try to MacGyver our way to safety?"

"No. Listening to the creative stories your overly active imagination comes up with trying to make me believe one word of what you're saying."

"You doubt my survival prowess?"

"In Silicon Valley? No. In the Outback? Yes. Had you been able to name a single one of your houseplants, I might have been more inclined to believe you. 'Greenus plantitus' was an admirable try though."

Jen nuzzled Kade's neck. "I can light a fire in other ways."

"Show me."

As they lay in bed that night, Jen said, "Will you tell me about Cassie?" Touching two fingers to Kade's lips, she stopped what she knew would be an immediate protest. "Not what happened to her.

But what you remember about her. What you did together, how you met, what she was like. The good things."

Kade idly toyed with Jen's fingers. She seemed to be studying them as she touched each knuckle, vein, scar, bone, and freckle, but Jen suspected she wasn't really seeing anything. "After my dad lost his job, he couldn't find work in our town, so we moved. Cassie's family, the Kellers, lived two doors down from the place my parents rented. Mrs. Keller brought over some cookies to welcome us, and Cassie came with her. We were both eleven. Most of the kids in our neighborhood were either much older or much younger, so we naturally gravitated toward each other.

"We did everything together. We were both tomboys, so we mutilated dolls, shot baskets, played foursquare and capture the flag with other kids, flew wooden airplanes and boomerangs, batted balls, played catch, climbed trees, poked tadpoles, everything. For birthdays and holidays, we'd ask our parents for the same things so we could play together. Tennis rackets, skis, skateboards.

"She had three siblings, so there was always a kind of barely controlled chaos at her house. Whereas at mine, after he lost his job, my dad became militant about sticking to routines and schedules. He became more and more strict, whereas Mr. and Mrs. Keller were go-with-the-flow kind of people. I think I just felt freer around them since my house was full of rules.

"I was very much a rule-follower, whereas Cassie was a rules-are-meant-to-be-broken kind of girl. Adventurous. Friendly and outgoing. Very inclusive. Similar to you, I think. If she was with a group and saw a kid off to the side, alone, she'd be the first to invite the kid to join them.

"She could have been best friends with anyone, but for some reason, she chose me. And while she was alive, the world shone a little brighter."

Jen could hear the affection and wonder in Kade's voice. For all the heartbreak Kade had experienced, Jen felt profoundly glad for the many years of close friendship Kade had found with Cassie.

"Were you in love with her?"

Kade gave a short laugh. "I've asked myself that. Probably, but I certainly didn't know it at the time, and even now I'm not convinced. She was so boy-crazy in high school, she was never on my radar in that way. I definitely loved her, but I'm not sure I was in love with her."

Jen planted a kiss beneath Kade's chin. "Thank you for telling me about her."

Kade adjusted their positions until Jen was on her back with Kade's head on her lap. "What about you? Who have you been in love with?"

"Nancy Drew."

Kade nodded. "Granted."

"Elizabeth Bennett."

"I was thinking nonfictional."

"Oh, ruin it. Hmm. Let's see. Robert Downey, Jr."

"Nonfictional people you actually know."

"Well, there was Jody Green from my softball team."

"Softball. Really? And did you drive to the games in a Subaru?"

Jen smacked Kade's shoulder.

"Ow. Sorry. Okay, Jody Green. High school? College? City recreation?"

"My coach in high school. I had a huge crush on her."

"Four out of five lesbians crush on their softball coaches. I'm talking love here. Doe-eyed, 'til-death-do-us-part, Juliet-and-Juliet kind of love."

"Jody Green."

"You and Jody had a thing?"

"No. She was married to Mr. Green, my science teacher." Jen deflected the pillow that was tossed at her face and laughed. "I'm still waiting for my Juliet." Jen tried to tug Kade higher, so Kade readjusted until her arm rested across Jen's torso and her chin lay against Jen's shoulder.

Kade closed her eyes and lightly caressed the skin above Jen's sternum. "Juliet's too young for you."

CHAPTER TWELVE

When Jen woke, she immediately knew from the slight chill she felt beneath the sheet that Kade wasn't in bed. Jen had needed to throw back her usual covers and stick with only the top sheet in order to sleep, since Kade emanated tremendous heat when snuggled against her. Alarmed at the thought Kade might have left without saying good-bye, Jen didn't even bother to hit the bathroom before grabbing the closest shirt and throwing it on as she sped down the hallway to the kitchen.

Even before she entered, Jen could smell maple syrup and coffee. She rounded the wall and found a spatula-wielding Kade minding Jen's griddle, in which two pancakes were cooking. She surmised they were the first to be poured, because a nearby bowl contained a generous amount of batter. On a rear burner was a small pot of what appeared to be a strawberry compote, because although she wasn't close enough to view the bottom, she could see strawberry smears along the inside. On the counter sat a can of whipped cream, a bottle of champagne, a carton of orange juice, two champagne flutes, and the butter dish.

When Kade saw her out of the corner of her eye, her expression of concentration morphed into a captivating smile that took over her face, giving her a youthful, happy glow. Stunning, Jen thought. Kade walked up to Jen and kissed her firmly but quickly. "Good morning. Perfect timing. I planned to get you up in a minute. Mimosa?" Kade peered at the pancakes again and flipped them before working to pop the champagne cork.

"How did you know that one of my all-time favorite breakfasts is strawberry pancakes with whipped cream? And that I'd take a mimosa over a Bloody Mary any day?"

Before pouring the champagne, Kade took another peek at the griddle. Apparently deciding the pancakes weren't ready, she continued with the beverages. "I asked Holly to find out from Jeremy what you like for breakfast." Then Kade looked anxious for a moment and added, "She would have done it in a very roundabout way and, knowing her, probably asked him what everyone on the team likes, putting it in some sort of business context. She wouldn't have made it sound like I wanted to know."

Jen advanced on Kade and took her face in her hands. "I wouldn't care. Thank you for your thoughtfulness." She kissed Kade sweetly and stepped back to look into her sparkling hazel eyes, which shimmered more gold than green this morning. She reached for some of the dark strands of hair that rested below Kade's collarbone and sifted its soft silkiness through her fingers. "You're beautiful." She took her time with another kiss.

Kade broke it off, flicking her head toward the stove and looking truly apologetic. "Sorry, I've got to—"

"Go, Julia Child. I'll be back in two seconds." Jen escaped for a bathroom and tooth-brushing break, and to throw on some shorts. By the time she returned, mimosas were poured, new pools of batter were cooking, and two pancakes were on a plate next to the compote.

"I wasn't sure how much whipped cream or maple syrup or butter you like, so you'll have to apply your own," Kade said, keeping an eye on her cooking.

"The only way I'm eating both of these is if you promise to sit and eat with me when those are ready. The rest can wait. Otherwise, you're taking one of these."

"Deal."

Jen proceeded to pour copious amounts of maple syrup and strawberries both in between and on top of the stack, and she shook the can of whipped cream gleefully. "This looks so good." She sprayed it into a big happy face, starting with an outside circle for the head and ending with the smile. She was no artist, but she thought it was a pretty good self-portrait at the moment. Then she took a seat and waited, resting her chin in her hand. Watching Kade at work, whether in the kitchen—self-professed non-cook that she was—or otherwise, was a pursuit Jen didn't think she could ever tire of.

Once Kade had prepped her own stack, which housed only a small dollop of whipped cream, she joined Jen at the table. She held out her mimosa to Jen. "Thank you for the best Saturday I can remember having in…" She appeared to work backward to the solution. Then she winked. "How about, thank you for a lovely day?"

Jen smiled and extended her beverage. "It's been delightful. Unanticipated. And speaking of lovely, thank you for this breakfast." They clinked glasses and began eating, though Jen's progress rapidly slowed.

She was fighting an internal dilemma that had begun as soon as their weekend together had started: work to convince Kade not to bind them to an arbitrary period or stick to the agreed-upon terms. Kade had been clear from the get-go as to what she could and couldn't give. Had they not bound their twenty-four hours and instead left it open-ended, Kade would almost surely have never agreed, and they wouldn't have shared their wonderful day together.

But now that it was coming to a close, Jen wasn't satisfied with the agreement. Or at least she wanted to strike a new one. She could get on board with sticking to "one day" if they could set up another one, and another after that.

The more she thought about each forward tick of the universal second hand counting down their time together, the poorer her appetite became. This made her feel worse, given everything Kade had done to make this morning special for her. Try as she might to keep the tears at bay, she was losing the battle.

"Jen, what's—"

Jen cut her off by setting down her fork with a clang. She clasped her hands, unable to make eye contact. "Kade. Listen. You've been amazing in every way this weekend, and I don't regret any of it. You've been forthcoming about what you're capable of offering, and I've gone ahead and spent time with you under your conditions, fully aware of our agreement. And now that it's coming to an end, I'm sad. I'm sad and I'm frustrated and I'm…wanting more."

She looked at Kade then, because it was too important not to. "I want more. I don't say it to make you feel guilty. You're carrying plenty of that. But I…" She searched for the right words. Say them and be done. Lay it out there. "I really like you. And I want you to know that."

Jen needed closure, and she needed it now. Drawn-out good-byes wouldn't help either of them. She stood next to Kade's chair and offered her palms to Kade. Kade slid her hands into Jen's and stood with her, their eyes seeming to search the other's for a sign telling them what to do next. "Take your time, finish breakfast, don't clean up, leave it for me. I'm going to shower and get to work to try to take my mind off you, which I know will be an utter failure."

Jen touched the pad of her thumb to Kade's lips and gently caressed them, tracking the movement with her eyes. She released a sigh, involuntarily conveying the disappointment of not being able to get through to Kade how much could be between them, if only Kade would consent. "You're an extraordinary woman, Kadrienne Davenport. Never forget that." Jen kissed Kade sweetly, softly. Not a kiss of passion but of farewell.

Then she left the room.

❖

Noon spin class was a spectacular fiasco. The instructor was the guy who loved house music—strong beats and no words. It was a storm of electronic tones that sounded like noise to Kade. She couldn't get lost in it. And what she really wanted above all else was to get lost, to move her mind onto any other subject than the one it was currently fastened to like the jaws of a pit bull.

Normally she could push through his class by requiring more and more from her body, leaving no room for any thoughts other than begging for the current hill climb to end or quenching her thirst. Today, every beat of the bass pounding through the speakers sounded like "Jen, Jen, Jen," and every crank of her hand to increase the level of pedaling difficulty came with illogical thoughts of whether Jen would be waiting for her on the down slope.

Showering afterward was a dismal experience as well, since it brought back the one they'd shared last night after another round of making love. Having sex, she amended in her mind, attempting to distance the weightier characterization. They'd lathered, rinsed, teased, and tasted each other until the water ran cold and they had to warm each other back up in bed. Kade recalled all too well Jen's demanding mouth at her breasts, each thrust of her fingers, each spoken request that Kade tell her what she wanted and where she wanted it, her gasp as she came, Jen's hands and body keeping her upright, supporting her, holding her.

Kade had no one to blame but herself. She should have left well enough alone after Maui. Seeing Jen again, working with her, talking with her, laughing with her—Kade enjoyed it all too much. She was like a kid in winter, skating on a lake's thin ice after a storm, knowing better but thrilling at the freedom and sensation, the twirling and propelling, the joy.

She hadn't sufficiently gauged how deeply Jen had taken root in her soul over a year ago, hadn't accounted for it when agreeing to spend this weekend with her. She'd simply glided on the frozen water with Jen because she wanted to. It was as close as Kade had ever come to being in a relationship. But Kade knew it would come—the din, like thunder, signaling the impending crack below their skates. If they continued seeing each other, the only certainty in Jen's future would be a break in the ice that Kade would somehow cause. She didn't know how or when, but she felt its inevitability.

The only answer was to rid herself of thoughts of Jen, and the first and most obvious step was to contact Charles and resign from Creative Care's board.

Kade didn't care that it was Sunday. Having known Charles for over a decade, she could call any time. Her attempt went straight to voice mail, and she left a message asking him to call her back. She followed up with a text as well, asking to talk. The sooner she could get off the board, the faster she could put Creative Care and its CEO behind her and return her attention to Matlock Ventures.

❖

Jen was struggling. Nana's life was now built solidly around routine, because people with dementia tended to feel less stress when they knew what to expect. But with Jen's demanding schedule, it was often difficult to adhere to routine. When she visited after work, she usually did so after Nana had eaten dinner. Tonight, Jen wanted to eat with Nana, to share in some sort of breaking of bread with a family member as a kind of healing measure against her schism with Kade, and it was turning out to be a mistake.

Nana didn't recognize her and didn't trust the food she was trying to feed her. Nana loved mashed potatoes, but she wouldn't accept them from Jen. Often when Nana was this out of sorts, it meant a poor night's sleep or physical discomfort, such as a bladder infection. Jen was close to having to call Candace, the caregiver on duty, in from the other room to see if she'd prove more successful in getting Nana to eat.

"I want to go home," Edna said.

"You are home, Nana."

"Take me home."

"Grandma, you've lived here for forty years. I'm not sure where you want to go."

"Why won't you take me home?"

The conversation repeated on a seemingly endless loop before Jen tried a different tack, knowing that arguing with a person suffering from dementia wasn't necessarily the best course. Instead of slumping and showing such an obvious sign of frustration, Jen remembered to try to think from Edna's point of view. She sat up straight and smiled, presenting herself as interested and helpful. "What's at home that you need to do?"

"Joseph's home alone with no one to take care of him."

Jen surmised that Edna was thinking about Jen's father as a boy. "He's been growing into such a great person, Edna. He's so happy to have you as his mom." Jen was trying to move Edna's focus away from what seemed like concern over her parenting skills.

"He needs to be fed."

"You know what? He's not home right now. Tonight he's at your sister's, remember? And she's already fed him."

"She doesn't cook like I do."

"You're right. She doesn't. That's another reason he's so lucky to have you." She held the fork to Nana's lips again. "These are definitely not as good as yours, are they?" Edna finally took a bite.

"No," she said after swallowing.

As Jen continued to feed Nana, she began to feel better. Every time she visited, she ran into a different challenge, at times minor, at other times massive. Whatever her expectations might be for a particular visit, they would almost surely be upended somehow. And while she definitely hadn't planned to become a caretaker in her twenties, it came with its own rich set of rewards. Jen had always been an empathetic, compassionate girl, and being able to help her beloved grandmother during this stage in her life made Jen genuinely happy.

Thoughts of Kade wormed their way through Jen's mind and into the conversation. She asked, "How did you know Grandpa was the one?"

Nana swallowed another bite of potato and smiled. "Such a handsome lad. I hope he remembers we're out of milk."

Jen often wasn't sure what Nana remembered. Her long-term memory was excellent, short-term terrible, and mid-term, such as when her husband died ten years ago, hit-or-miss. While Nana actually was out of milk, her use of present tense suggested she could be thinking of an incident from thirty years ago. Since Nana was likely to forget Jen's question before another minute passed, she decided to let it drop.

"Agains and tomorrows," Nana said.

"Agains, Nana?" She was about to tell Nana it wasn't a word but swallowed the correction. It meant something to Nana, and she'd hear her out.

"I knew Ben was the one for me because he was the only person I wanted to see again and again, tomorrow and the next day." She grinned and lightly touched Jen's nose. "That's how he got his nickname."

"Bennigan?"

"It's actually Ben Again. I'd tell my friends, 'I get to see Ben again.' That's how it started." Then she grabbed the fork from Jen's hand and scooped a bite of potato. "Ben Again. I can't wait." She smiled and closed her eyes while she chewed.

Peacefulness settled over Nana's features, in sharp contrast to her agitation from earlier. Whether Nana was looking forward to Ben returning from the store shortly or their reunion in an afterlife, Jen hoped that one day, somehow, the universe would grant Nana her wish.

As much as Jen wanted to experience the kind of love her grandparents shared and had a particular individual in mind for the journey, in this moment, the serenity evident in Nana's expression filled Jen's heart. How lucky was she to have grown up in a loving, supportive family, surrounded by people who weren't afraid to let their feelings show?

She'd told Kade the truth: she had no regrets. Tomorrows weren't in their future, and the time they'd shared hadn't been nearly enough. But she and Kade had experienced something raw and real, powerful and intimate. Breathtaking. Maybe she should be feeling bereft and heartbroken, but right now, having experienced at least a little of what Edna and Ben had, she felt grateful.

CHAPTER THIRTEEN

Monday afternoon, in the Creative Care conference room, Jen awaited Jeremy's assessment.

"It's really solid, Jen. Light-years from only days ago." Jen had finished taking him through the revised fund-raising presentation, into which she'd incorporated Kade's feedback. "I should be able to add the changes to the roadmap and product slides by end of day tomorrow, no problem."

"That would be great."

"How did you pull all this together so quickly? You look pretty good for someone who can't be getting a lot of sleep."

Jen blushed. "I got some help."

"Jen-ni-fer Spen-cer," Jeremy said in a sing-song tone. "Look at you. Exactly what kind of help did you get and from whom?"

She raised her hand defensively. "Before you say anything, it was a one-off deal off the record."

Jeremy eyed Jen thoughtfully. "Tell me this doesn't have anything to do with breakfast in bed with our illustrious board member. Strawberry pancakes perhaps?"

She could deny it, because it technically wasn't breakfast in bed, but she knew what he was getting at. "Kind of."

"She's straddling a fine line when it comes to objectivity, isn't she? That is, when she isn't straddling you?"

Jen felt her eyes widen and her flush deepen. She grabbed a stack of sticky notes and tossed it at him in protest. "I can't believe you said that," she said, keeping her voice down.

He laughed. "It's only us."

"She came over to check on me Friday, after *someone* sent me home. You saw the state I was in. She swooped in and offered really helpful advice—as my friend, mind you. Not my boss."

"And she left on…?"

"Sunday morning. But in terms of her objectivity, keep in mind that there aren't any matters pending before the board, so it's not like she's in danger of bias. And second, she was very clear that we wouldn't repeat this weekend."

"How do you feel about that?"

"It's the right thing for the company. Startups come with enough drama of their own."

"What about for you?"

She toyed with a dry-erase marker, spinning it on the table top. "That's harder, Jer. I really like her."

"Then what's the problem? Can't she resign from our board so there's no conflict of interest?"

"She could, but that would require interest on her part."

"Then she's not half as smart as her reputation gives her credit for."

Jen smiled, appreciating Jeremy's default reaction to err on her side. "In her defense, she has her reasons. Look, you and I are going into fund-raising mode, which means our already crazy hours get worse. It's hard enough getting to Nana's. I can't take on relationship drama, too. Let's focus on closing our funding round. I've started compiling a list of the VCs we want to try to talk to, those familiar with our industry who do a lot of early stage investments. I'll ask Charles and Kade to add to it. We need to move quickly on setting up meetings."

"Sounds good."

"I also want to do that team event we talked about. Unfortunately, I won't be able to join, but check with your guys and see if we can do it this week. They've been working around the clock and hit it out of the park this weekend. Giving them a play day is the least we can do."

"Roger that."

❖

Thank God for Holly. The two startup co-founders Kade was meeting with showed no signs of understanding that their allotted time was one hour. Promptly on the hour, Holly interrupted their droning-on by knocking and entering, then standing in the doorway as a silent prod to Kade's guests.

After walking them out, Holly closed the door and took a seat.

"Wow. What did you think of her?"

"The meeting was interminable, and once again I owe you for saving me."

"I mean Penelope, the CTO. So rare to see a woman in that role. And what a stunning one."

Kade glanced at the doorway as if she could conjure the departed visitors. "Penelope?" Had one of them been a Penelope?

"Did you not notice the shapely legs, sculpted eyebrows, perfect olive skin, and flowing black hair?"

Kade reflected on the meeting. She couldn't recall anything except for how bored she was and the growing number of seconds that seemed to be packed into each slowly passing minute, as if the minutes had eaten too many carbohydrates. "No."

"Well, since you're not dead yet, that can only mean you're thinking about another woman."

"Was she really that pretty?"

"Good God. Do you need to be hospitalized?"

"What I need is for people to stick to the schedule."

"Why bother? If you're not going to pay attention in your meetings, why don't I just cancel the rest of your appointments today? Then you can focus on agonizing over Jen instead of pretending you're not thinking about her."

"I'm paying attention."

"Uh-huh. Name one takeaway from that meeting."

Kade gazed at Holly, ransacking her mind for a tiny foothold to whatever Penelope and her colleague had gone on incessantly about.

Holly inclined her head as if to say, "I rest my case."

"It's your own fault for encouraging me and rearranging my schedule," Kade groused.

Holly laughed. "So you'd spend time with a smart, hard-working, attractive woman who seems genuinely nice. How horrible of me."

Kade slumped in her chair and rubbed her temples. "She wants more."

"Okay, scratching 'smart' from the list."

When Kade refused to acknowledge the jab, Holly became more serious. "Kade, women always want more from you. How is this different?"

"This isn't a hookup at a conference in some random city."

"Then what is it?"

"Important."

"Exactly. So do something about it."

"The problem is I want to."

"The problem is you think there's a problem. But you wouldn't be you if you didn't. Where's your phone?"

Kade swiped it off the credenza behind her and held it up.

"Dry run," Holly said. "Pretend I'm Jen. Ask me out."

Kade gently set the device on her desk. "I already told her we couldn't see each other again."

"Which is likely preventing her from thinking about you as well as it's stopping you from thinking about her. Now get your game on."

"There's no point."

"You don't have enough time between now and your next appointment to work out, and you're worthless sitting here with your head between her—I'm sorry, head in the clouds. So channel your energy like you're asking her out so you can purge your thoughts of her for a few hours. She'll never know."

"Pretending to ask her out isn't going to help."

"Then ask her for real."

"Not an option."

"Then what do you have to lose by indulging me?"

"This is a waste of time."

"Okay. Tell me about Penelope's company, and I'll go."

"Holly." Saying Holly's name in a threatening tone was as useful as telling an excited puppy not to wiggle. Holly was unfazed. Kade sighed and grabbed her phone. "Fine."

What *would* she say to Jen if she were to actually pursue such a fantasy? She stared at the screen, but it didn't provide any clues. Annoying. With all the technology she was exposed to, shouldn't there be an app that lit up the screen with civilized suggestions? She sent Holly a text.

Holly studied her phone as if waiting for more.

"That's pretty much all I've got," Kade said.

"'Hi?' Hi is the sum total of what you say to a woman you can't stop thinking about?"

"What's wrong with a greeting?"

"You're asking her out. Get to the point."

"Don't pressure me."

"You do realize I can access every one of your accounts and jump into any conversation or start one as if I'm you, right?"

"You wouldn't."

Holly arched an eyebrow.

"This is you not pressuring me?" Kade went back to typing and was done nearly instantaneously.

"'How's your day going?' You can't be serious," Holly said.

Kade tossed her phone down. "I'm terrible at this." Holly started typing into her own messaging app. When her phone chimed, Kade read the message aloud. "You're so fucking sexy, you make me cream my pants." Kade laughed. "This is going in my personnel files in case I need to use it against you."

Holly bent down and kissed Kade on the cheek. "I'll call you Hot Stuff. Call me whatever strikes your fancy."

Moments after Holly left her office, Kade's phone chimed again.

Hey, Hot Stuff, want to come over for cake and I scream your name?

Kade replied,

You're fired.

Jen had had a good run of late. The caregivers she'd found for Nana had been reliable and competent. It took more of Jen's time to search for, contract with, pay, and schedule them, but the cost savings versus an agency or assisted-living facility was worth it. Nana didn't have a significant nest egg, and every dollar counted. But every once in a while, things like today happened. One of Nana's regular caregivers called in sick. Jen tried a couple of backup providers and left messages. Thus it fell to Jen because Nana couldn't be left alone.

Similar struggles Jen had faced early on were the impetus for Creative Care. Jen was convinced there was a better solution out there than the DIY strategy she was employing or the home-care-agency option.

Since a gap in coverage for Nana was relatively infrequent, Jen could often take it herself. She'd installed high-speed Internet at Nana's house for that reason. She wasn't even half as productive on such days as when she was in the office or worked from home because she largely had to keep to Nana's routine. But Nana did have a number of hours in her day when she could rest, watch TV, garden, or otherwise occupy herself with proper direction. Jen did call an agency when she had outside commitments on her calendar, such as her meeting with Kade today. Unfortunately, since Jen wasn't a regularly paying client, she was low on their priority list for fulfilling last-minute needs. And so she waited.

Many times during the past year, as Nana's dementia had become more pronounced and Jen was slammed at Creative Care, Jen weighed the additional cost of using a home-care agency. But she'd already performed that spreadsheet exercise a number of times and always returned to the same conclusion, which didn't require any math. Nana came before Creative Care. And Jen felt obligated to help Nana "extend her runway," as Kade would say—lengthen the amount of time before she ran out of cash.

As she prepared Nana's breakfast, Jen hoped at least one of her backup options would come through before her meeting. She knew Kade was going out of her way for her not only by connecting her with people in her network, but by attending herself as well as allowing Holly to take time away from Matlock business to do the scheduling. She also knew punctuality was one of Kade's hot-button issues, and she wasn't eager to press it.

❖

"She's still not here," Kade said to Holly after excusing herself to make the call. Jen was late to their meeting with Brian Marshall, one of the hospital executives who had agreed to discuss Creative Care. Kade was stressed enough about whether she could play it off in front of Brian as if she were completely indifferent about her colleague. But she had poor coping skills when it came to being late. When things ran off schedule, things went wrong.

All of that festered within Kade as worry. Was Jen all right? Had she been in an accident? No. It was too premature and apocalyptic to start thinking that way. Nothing good came from doing so.

"I understand, but she doesn't work for me," Holly said. "I don't have her schedule and don't know where she is. I've sent an email, a text, and left a voice mail."

"So have I. Have you tried Jeremy Corbin?"

"Yes, and to the best of his knowledge, Jen was planning to meet with you and Brian."

Kade's phone buzzed. "Hold on. Let me see if this text is from her." Kade switched applications and clicked on the most recent message.

Kade—something's come up. I'm so sorry I can't make the meeting with Brian. Will reschedule posthaste. Please apologize for me. –J

Instant relief at knowing Jen was alive and apparently well flooded her, then vanished as quickly. Jen didn't seem any worse for wear, which Kade was grateful for, but the poor—rather, complete lack of excuse—chafed. Several seconds passed, yet oddly enough, Kade's continuous scowl failed to change the contents of the message. She swiped it off the screen and returned to her call in progress. "Something's come up. She's cancelling." Kade took a deep breath, and it, too, failed to change the fact that they were late, a situation she loathed.

"At least she's okay," Holly said.

Kade ended the call. Yes, she was thankful Jen seemed to be in one piece, but Kade had put her reputation on the line for her. A big deal. Kade's word was her bond. Her word meant far more to her than any object she could own. She wasn't about to let someone who obviously didn't share her priorities negatively affect her standing in the industry.

No, it was wrong to jump to conclusions. Jen cared deeply about Creative Care and wouldn't jeopardize its future for something trivial.

Kade returned to Brian's office with a choice to make. Having gotten up to speed on Creative Care, she could take the meeting herself with the same goals of getting his hospital to refer patients to the company and spreading the word that his part-timers could likely find supplemental work by registering on the platform. Or she could do what she should have done in the first place: get off Creative Care's board and focus on the job she was paid to do at Matlock.

It was like having a little cartoon angel on one shoulder to Kade's devil on the other. The angel's argument was aided by Kade's loyalty to Charles, since his unresponsiveness to her messages likely meant he wasn't bouncing back as well as he'd hoped. And so even though part of her wanted to remove all traces of having ever been associated with this meeting, she listened to the part that fundamentally believed in what Creative Care was building. "Brian, unfortunately Jen has to deal with an emergency and won't be able to make it. She apologizes profusely and would be here if she could. If you'll indulge me, I still think it's well worth your time to learn about the Creative Care platform, even though I'm a poor substitute for her."

The satisfaction that usually accompanied a successful meeting eluded Kade that evening. Picking disinterestedly at lukewarm leftovers, her mind refused to give her reprieve from thoughts of Jen.

CHAPTER FOURTEEN

K ade deserved an explanation. Two, now. Jen's failure to show up for the second of their scheduled meetings this week infuriated her.

One of the most important things in a VC's arsenal was her network. Success in the industry was predicated on knowing the right people to connect at the right time. Kade made introductions between company executives when she saw a match between the technology one of her portfolio companies was building and a more mature company looking for ways to drive revenue or innovate on a number of fronts.

Startup executives routinely asked for those connections, always wanting the name of someone high up in the food chain in order to reach a key decision-maker more quickly, thus expediting a sale. But Kade and her colleagues never played these cards lightly or often. Doing so would only frustrate a previously friendly contact, who wouldn't hesitate to stop returning calls or emails if they doled out his or her name indiscriminately. Kade insisted that there be a strong fit between demand and supply. She hadn't gotten where she was by burning bridges.

The fact that Jen was MIA on meetings with two contacts in Kade's network made her bristle. This kind of thing simply didn't happen in her industry. A CEO would have to be on his or her deathbed to skip a meeting stemming from a VC introduction. Short of Jen's hospitalization, which she was not hoping for whatsoever, Kade wasn't ready to accept many excuses, certainly not the woefully inadequate "something's come up," which she'd received twice now.

After the earlier meeting with Brian Marshall, Kade had called Jen, in part to let her know that Brian had agreed to be a referral partner. But she mostly wanted to confirm that Jen was fine and able to attend their second meeting. Jen hadn't picked up, so Kade had left a voice mail and followed up via email. Jen finally responded that she was well and confirmed she'd be there. To have Jen now bail a second time with the same anemic excuse was insulting and disrespectful.

Unannounced arrivals weren't part of her usual MO, but today Kade found herself practically stomping up the cement steps to the Creative Care office after she'd once again been forced to handle a Creative Care meeting alone. The entrance was made of glass, so she could see several cubicles, monitors, plants, and other office paraphernalia, but no people. A pull of the handle failed to gain her entry. She rapped on the glass door. No one answered. To the far right of the door, she spied a handmade sign saying DELIVERIES, with an arrow pointing to a black button beneath, which she pressed. After still no answer, she turned to leave but saw something move in her peripheral vision. A shaggy, sandy-haired, twenty-something man with an unkempt beard pushed the door open.

"Can I help you?"

"I'm looking for Jen Spencer."

"Everyone's at Disneyland."

"I'm sorry?"

"Yeah. My brother's in town so I had to bail. Bummer. Feel free to stop by tomorrow if you want."

"Thanks." Disneyland? Kade surprised herself by calmly descending the stairs instead of yelling profanities. She no longer required an explanation from Jen. All she needed was to cancel any remaining meetings they had and extricate herself from further Creative Care commitments. She would not allow anyone to sully her reputation.

Back in her Matlock office, Kade plunged into work. She'd recently met with a virtual-office-assistant company, and she needed to decide whether to recommend to her partners that they make an offer to invest by sending a term sheet and, if so, what the terms of the offer should be.

Kade spent the rest of the day researching the startup and contemplating other areas in which the technology could be useful. One of the most satisfying aspects of her job was future-tripping like this. The business term for people like her was "visionary." For Kade, being a visionary was like having a pair of virtual-reality glasses she could put on, allowing her to view things from different perspectives. She was always able to ask herself, "What if?" Searching for answers to that question propelled her forward and helped her land on ideas that took shape in the form of finding new ways to apply existing technology.

Kade lost herself in the world of artificial intelligence. When her calendar popped up a reminder about dinner, she decided to continue working at the office instead of going home to do the same thing. She phoned in an order for delivery, closed multiple browser windows related to her research, and tried to scan the daily stock-market news until her food came.

But the words on the digital pages failed to take root in her brain because it kept reverting to Jen. Her mind warred between wanting to check in on her and wanting to yell at her. Jen's own messages contained no hint she was in anguish but didn't placate Kade in the way they usually would. She wanted visual proof that Jen was healthy and in one piece.

On the other extreme, Kade couldn't get over the slight of Jen's failure to stick to their well-defined plan. Jen hadn't provided any suitable account of her absences, and perhaps worst of all, this hurt Kade's feelings. Why wouldn't Jen tell her the truth about her reasons for cancelling? Did Jen feel she wasn't trustworthy? It wasn't as though Jen was withholding information about nuclear codes. This was about nonattendance at a business meeting, and Jen couldn't trust her with the reasons behind it?

If this was how Jen planned to handle future meetings, the only thing Jen could be sure of was that Kade wouldn't be involved.

Although Jen's absenteeism was a disaster professionally, it left no question for them personally. Closing the door on their relationship had done little to prevent Kade from staring at the virtual handle, and the impulse to ignore her own edict remained strong. Now, however, that door was sealed, and it was for the best. Kade had been wading into deep water with her, which would only end up causing Jen pain. As much as Kade struggled against Jen's powerful draw, she cared too much for Jen to disregard the probability of hurting her.

The death knell to their relationship rang, and the sharp stab of disappointment it brought was as familiar as the sound of a clock striking the hour. Heartache was nothing new to Kade.

During dinner, while she finished reading this morning's *Wall Street Journal*, which in reality meant rereading the same paragraph over and over and absorbing nothing, Kade glanced up to see Roger Daniels in her doorway. One of the firm's senior partners, Roger had been instrumental in recruiting Kade. He was one of those average-looking, bland-featured men you couldn't describe even if you'd been stuck in an elevator with him for hours, but in the intellect department, he had few peers. She'd taken the job in part because she wanted to learn from him.

She invited him in and offered some of the takeout. He declined as she knew he would, but given that his seniority should mean she'd never expect to see him at the office so late and the number of times she did, she suspected his ongoing divorce had something to do with his office hours, and she felt a little sorry for him. As he sat, he pointed to the full-page article open on her desk and asked a question about it.

Caught, Kade gave him a bemused smile. "I'm pleased you asked. My key takeaways? It's written in English, it's in today's *Journal*, and it contains information."

Roger laughed. "Happens to the best of us, Kadrienne. Have we put too much on your plate?"

She waved him off. "Not at all. A little research overload, I think."

"Is this the virtual-assistant company?"

Kade nodded. "What's the best excuse you've ever gotten for someone cancelling an important meeting on you?"

Roger didn't seem to mind the pivot. "Hmm. Probably a toss-up between a spouse's water breaking and acute appendicitis. How about you?"

"East Coast blizzard that shut down Newark Liberty, JFK, and LaGuardia for two days."

"Seems reasonable."

"Worst excuse?"

"I'm not sure. When one isn't given, I suppose."

Kade nodded.

"Emergencies aside, it's my experience that people cancel when they've determined something else has come up that's more important. If I'm not among their priorities, fine with me. Why do you ask?"

Kade was reluctant to admit to Roger that she'd scheduled multiple meetings to help Creative Care's prospects. With the number of hours she logged in a day, she didn't necessarily feel she was short-changing her own portfolio or research, but his take might be different. So she approached the subject less directly. "I provided some introductions to relevant industry execs for one of Charles Jameson's companies, Creative Care, to help them gain traction ahead of their next financing round. Meetings were scheduled, but I heard from a couple of contacts that the CEO cancelled on them without explanation."

Roger nodded and steepled his fingers as if in thought. "What do you think of Creative Care?"

"You mean like, 'Other than that, Mrs. Lincoln, how was the play?'"

Roger smiled. "Yes."

"Huge market opportunity. I like what they're building, and eBay and Amazon have proved that the marketplace angle can work. Certainly replicable with the right pricing model and distribution strategy."

"Should we be taking a look?" Roger asked seriously.

"You know I can't act on this one, Roger. I'm not impartial."

"I realize that, but our bylaws allow a different partner to advance an investment when another has to recuse him or herself."

"True. It hadn't occurred to me."

"What about the leadership team?"

Kade's head started to spin. A Matlock investment in Creative Care? She forced herself to focus on Roger's question. "I'm on the fence at the moment. The CEO is capable, bright, affable...well-versed on the technology...and until recently I would have said driven. Both she and the CTO seem to have fantastic rapport with their team and have been able to recruit remarkably well as a result. The head of product is solid, too."

"But you have reservations about the CEO."

Kade cocked her head, thinking through her issues with Jen on a professional level, trying for objectivity. "Our styles are very different, so it's hard for me to judge."

"Try."

"I don't have any evidence to support this, but I wonder if she's popular among her team because she doesn't force them to work as hard as they should. They're months behind on getting their minimum viable product out the door, and I wonder about the causes. They're taking steps—the right ones, too, I think—to address the delays, and it seems they're on track again, so I'm not even sure there's an issue."

"There's an issue if she's not showing up for meetings."

"I agree. It bothers me. Plus, this behind-schedule team that's rapidly running out of money recently flew down to Disneyland for a day. A weekday." She didn't mention what she thought of Jen's desire to provide severance to a VP of sales who hadn't sold anything, let alone hiring him in the first place.

Roger nodded slowly. "I don't have to tell you this, Kadrienne, but if you don't think she's the right person for the job, you'll need to disclose your concerns to potential investors."

"I know." As a board member, Kade knew prospective investors would solicit her feedback, as they tended to call existing backers and customers to vet a company's team and technology before investing millions of dollars.

She hoped Charles's recovery was proceeding apace so he could retake his board seat in short order. Under no circumstance did Kade wish to have to share her thoughts on Jen's leadership skills.

CHAPTER FIFTEEN

The first sign of something amiss was the quiet rap on the door before Holly entered Kade's office. The second was the gentle shutting of the door behind her. The third was the tentative way Holly stood just inside before slowly walking toward Kade's desk, wearing a concerned expression Kade hadn't seen in years and having lost all color in her face.

Immediately anxious, Kade sat up straight on the edge of her chair. "Your parents?"

Holly shook her head.

"Are your brother and sister okay?" She arose and took Holly's hands in hers, then sat them both down in the visitor chairs. "Tell me what's wrong."

"Your mom called. It's your father. He's had a stroke. A pretty severe one, apparently."

Kade was up and rounding her desk. "Why didn't she call my cell phone? What line is she on?" None of the light indicators signaled a call on hold.

"She's working the phones. She didn't want to talk to you until she had more information and had spoken directly to his doctor."

Kade threw up her hands and felt the internal shift as she moved from worried to angry. "Well, what am I supposed to do with *that* information? And why is *she* involved?" She sat abruptly. "Thank God it's no one in your family." Completely rattled, she stood just as quickly and threw up her hands again. "Did anybody look at his calendar? Maybe he scheduled the damn thing and it's all going according to plan." She began pacing between the door and where Holly sat. "Notice it wasn't a heart attack. You actually have to have a heart in order for that to happen."

She made the mistake of looking at Holly, whose mouth was quivering and whose eyes were misting. And she started to lose it. She crossed one arm over her chest and held her head in her other hand as she cried. She didn't say anything as Holly took her into her arms, her staggered breathing the only sound in the room.

Jen believed the chances Kade would answer her door were slim and that they would plummet farther once she realized Jen was on the other side. She owed Kade an explanation for her no-show to two important meetings, and she hadn't yet figured out what to say. The truth was simplest but carried weighty consequences. Jen wasn't much for lying, but she didn't want to admit the reason behind her absences.

To Jen's mind, last-minute issues with Nana's care should rightfully be considered family emergencies. Nana needed care, and Jen needed to provide it, one way or another. But the treatment her CEO friend had received after announcing her pregnancy—a situation that Charles confirmed was all too common in venture-backed startups—was eye-opening. Her friend immediately became damaged goods because she dared to have a family while being a C-level executive, signaling that her job was not the sole thing she lived for.

Female entrepreneurs in Silicon Valley were already on precarious footing, and Jen didn't want to give any indication she couldn't handle what was on her plate. She believed if she used "family emergency" as an excuse more than once, she would earn a reputation for being unable to solve that emergency. If she was seen as unable to live up to her basic responsibilities as a woman—the family-caretaker role unequally imposed on women—how could she be trusted to run a company? Moreover, using the same excuse twice or more could suggest she wasn't a problem-solver—a skill required of chief executives—because she should have found a solution after the first occurrence.

Jen believed if she signaled that her family was her top priority, her tenure as a CEO in the Valley would be short-lived. "Something came up" was a terribly weak excuse, but its repeated use didn't automatically signal that the same issue kept arising or that she couldn't adequately address it.

Given all this anxiety, she still might not have had the courage to show up at Kade's door unannounced. But her concern had skyrocketed when she'd received a puzzling email from Holly in response to a request to get on Kade's schedule.

Time out.

That was the message.

What did that mean? Was Holly taking time off? Even if she was, it seemed likely that, of her own choosing, she was at Kade's disposal 24/7. Was Kade taking time off? Or was Holly suggesting some sort of truce between Kade and her in a fight she hadn't realized she was in?

Jen rang the doorbell, its humorous tones failing to entertain her this time. The song snippet ended and silence greeted her. She tried again. No muffled footsteps. Nothing. Fully expecting the door to be locked, she tried the handle, and it opened. She poked her head inside and didn't see or hear anyone. "Kade?" she called. Why was the door unlocked?

She entered and felt around for the light switch. Kade was normally tidy, but something was off tonight. First a shoe, then a purse, then another shoe, then keys littered the floor in a line toward the dining room. Following these was an earring and a second earring. The condo was dark.

A tryst, with clothes being shed in a lust-filled frenzy, was the first thought that came to Jen's mind and made her hesitate. On top of the stress she'd been feeling about Nana's situation and Creative Care's funding status, Jen didn't think she could handle seeing Kade with another woman, regardless of the fact she had no claim on her. But the objects appeared to be Kade's, and the place was quiet. "Kade?" She didn't follow the path, which led toward Kade's bedroom. She would leave that for last, if necessary, preferring to find Kade in a less intimate setting if possible. Instead, she followed her instinct, which took her to the den with the wet bar.

The lights lining the bar mirror reflected from it and dimly lit the room. Kade was curled into a seated position sideways with her feet on the couch, hugging her knees, a fairly full bottle of expensive-looking liquor and a three-fingers-full glass on the coffee table in front of her. She wore a thick cotton robe Jen couldn't tell the color of but guessed pale blue. Briefly raising her chin, she looked at Jen blankly before resuming her position. What appeared to be a wooden boxcar from the train that normally traveled around the dining and living rooms sat in her lap, and she rotated its wheels absently with one hand, holding tissues in the other.

Jen had never seen Kade so undone, so lifeless. Usually bursting with bustle, this Kade seemed small, like a child in time-out. Mascara lines formed small smudges beneath puffy, red eyes, and her hair was unkempt, as if she'd run her hands through it for hours. Jen was at a loss for what to say or do. She rounded the table and sat on the couch by Kade's feet, tenderly stroking the back of Kade's calf after settling in.

Kade shifted, curled next to Jen, and rested her head on Jen's thigh. She sobbed quietly, her short, staggered intakes of breath tearing at Jen's heart. Jen sat back and stroked Kade's hair, letting her release some of the pain.

Jen didn't know how much time had passed before Kade shifted again, sitting upright, blowing her nose and wiping her eyes. "Sorry," she whispered, swallowing with difficulty. Instead of telling her not to apologize, or saying things would be all right since she didn't know what Kade was dealing with, Jen asked, "What can I do?"

"My father…" Kade struggled to take in air as she spoke while she cried. "Stroke."

"Oh, Kade. I'm so sorry."

"No." Kade picked up the boxcar and smacked it against her knee. Over and over, she cried, "No." With each repeated word, she hit it, which must have hurt tremendously given its solid wood structure. But it began to give way, and soon it smashed into pieces.

The few remaining in her hand were thrown to the ground. Kade jumped to her feet and grabbed a pillow from the couch. She strode to the other side of the room and sat against the wall, strangling the pillow, shaking her head. "I hate him. I hate him. I hate him. I. Hate. Him. Jen, I hate that man, and I'm not like you. I'm not good like you. I'm not…I don't…No. Why should I see him? Why should *I* go? I don't care. I don't care. I don't care if he dies. I don't care what happens to him. I. Don't. Care…I can't go. I can't. I can't." And then she kept shaking her head, still clinging to the pillow like a lifejacket.

Jen rose and sat cross-legged before Kade, their knees touching. She rested her hands on Kade's legs above the knee. "Hey."

Kade wouldn't look at her.

Jen tugged on the pillow until it rested between them. She laid her forearms on it and opened her palms faceup in invitation.

Kade slid her hands into Jen's, and Jen clasped them.

"No one can make you do anything you don't want to do. You need time to work out what's right for you. Take it."

"Jen?"

"Hmm?"

"Will you stay a little while?"

Kade wasn't hungry, but Jen accepted her offer of leftover ravioli and spinach salad. While Jen reheated the pasta and added tomato and feta to the salad, Kade washed her face and changed into faded jeans and a fleece pullover. She downgraded to wine, which Jen partook of, and set them up on the small deck off the kitchen. Although it was warm for late fall, she turned on the outdoor overhead heater to keep them both comfortable.

"Glad you stopped by?" Kade asked with a crooked smile, cupping her wineglass.

"I am, actually. You needed a friend."

Kade sighed. "I don't have a great relationship with my father."

Jen arched a brow as if to sarcastically say, "Really?"

"I know. Hard to tell, right?"

"Want to talk about it?" Jen asked.

"Not really."

"Are you going to visit him?"

Kade shifted her gaze to her wineglass. "That's the sixty-four-thousand-dollar question. He's only ninety minutes from here." She lost herself for several moments as she gently swirled the liquid around, watching it slosh. "My mother thinks I should."

"And what do you think?"

"She probably feels leftover guilt from kicking him out and divorcing him. Now that Gordon's alone in a hospital room, she probably feels bad for him."

"And how do you feel?"

"Is this your psych degree talking?"

"I think you have some unresolved feelings about him. I think he hurt you."

Kade nodded. "Enough that Mom left him because of his emotional abuse. Of both of us."

"Were you ever close?"

"Until I was ten, very. Then the first incident happened."

"Did he harm you?"

Kade shook her head. "Not physically, no. I think I mentioned that Gordon performed crucial railroad maintenance work, things like measuring deviations of critical distances and lighting the heaters and dousing the frozen switches to keep them running after a winter storm. He took me with him in the afternoons after school. He was always a disciplinarian, but not Draconian until later."

"I imagine he's the source behind your strict adherence to punctuality?"

Kade nodded. "After one storm, when he was working through his maintenance checklist, I spied Hecker's Hill in the distance. Best sledding runs for miles. I *begged* him to take us on a few runs, since he always carried a sled in his truck during winter. And he did. We had so much fun. But we lost track of time and it got dark, so he planned to get an early start to finish checking the switches from that day.

"The next morning, along one of the routes he didn't get to because of me, a train derailed. Only two minor injuries, thankfully, but extensive property damage. The investigation concluded that improper maintenance caused it, and he was fired. He never forgave me."

Kade took a long pull from her wine and leveled her gaze on Jen. "And after the second incident, I never forgave him. And here we are."

Jen dragged her chair behind Kade's. She gathered Kade's hair and laid it over the front of one shoulder. She began to massage Kade's neck, sliding her fingers beneath the fleece to contact skin. "What's your current thinking?"

"Mmm. More of that."

Jen chuckled. "About your dad." She kneaded an especially tight spot above Kade's right shoulder blade.

"Why should his stroke change anything? He and I barely speak. What would be the point?"

Jen continued massaging Kade in silence. Was Jen judging her, or was she only considering the possibility because she was judging herself through Jen's eyes? Kade knew she was being immature but didn't want to discount her feelings. Her father had hurt her deeply and never apologized. Wasn't it the natural order of things that the child should look to the parent for direction? For understanding and forgiveness?

"I know you'd visit. In my shoes." Kade twisted in her chair to look at Jen. "But you're a better person than I am."

"What makes you say that?"

Kade resumed her position. "You see the good in people, even where there isn't any."

"I don't know anyone who doesn't have some decency in them."

"You haven't met enough venture capitalists."

Jen laughed. "If you were ill, would you want your only human interaction to come from nurses and doctors and others paid to see you? Or would you want someone who cares about you and genuinely wants to see you to visit?"

"That's the thing. I wouldn't be going because I care or because I want to. I'd be doing it out of a sense of obligation."

"But doesn't that obligation stem from a sense of human decency? From treating others as you'd wish to be treated?"

"No. It stems from a mother's guilt trip."

"You say potato." Jen continued her massage, and several minutes passed in silence except for an occasional appreciative moan from Kade. "Let me ask you this. If he died today, would you feel bad you never visited?"

Kade gave this question some thought. "Emotionally abandoned children hold onto hope, however illogical in light of all facts to the contrary, that their parents might stop disappointing them by simply accepting and loving them for who they are. So, yes, I think part of me would regret it, because I'm too stupid and naive to accept the truth even when it's been staring me in the face all my adult life. I'd beat myself up over it because my heart would wonder if we ever could have reconciled, when my head knows very well it could never happen."

"Isn't that one answer? To visit because you don't want to always wonder if things could have been different between you?"

"He hasn't exactly been busting down my door."

"So he needed to make the first move? And now that he can't, he's SOL?"

Kade sat forward in her chair, out of Jen's reach, and turned around to face her. "You have no idea how he treated me."

"You're right. I don't. But you have a chance to show him how it's done. Be the bigger person."

Kade was rapidly losing her temper. What right did Jen have to tell her what to do? "*Reward* him?"

"Reward yourself. Let go of the pain and disappointment."

Kade stood, her anger flaring. "I find *nothing* rewarding about seeing that man. Been there, thank you. And now *I'm* the bad guy because I'm not rushing to his bedside with open arms? His health setback does not suddenly earn him a get-out-of-jail-free card from having to actually act like a parent or never having to answer for what he did."

By this time, Jen was standing as well. She raised her hands in supplication. "I'm sorry, Kade. I didn't mean to upset you. You need to do whatever's right for you."

"Yes, and I don't need your permission to do it."

Jen returned her chair to its original position and picked up her dishes. "Why don't I rinse these and head out? You've had an unsettling day, and I didn't intend to add to it. Thank you for dinner."

Before Jen could take a step, Kade said, "I want to talk about you cancelling on me. Twice."

"I don't want to talk about work right now."

"I do. Jen, what gives? You don't blow off meetings like these. I put my name on the line for you, and you—"

"I didn't blow them off, Kade. I told you. Things came up. I wouldn't have cancelled if they weren't important."

"What things?"

"You wouldn't understand."

"Try me."

"Another time. When you're not already upset."

"I was upset with you way before I found out about my father. I'd appreciate an explanation. A real one."

"And I'll give you one." Jen took a deep breath. She hadn't been sure whether to tell Kade the truth about her absences. In the best of circumstances, Kade still might not have understood. In her present state of mind, the chances seemed remote. "I'll make it right with these people. I will. I'll reschedule. You don't have to come. I can handle it on my own."

"Not with my contacts, you don't. I've had Holly cancel our meetings."

"I saw them get removed from my calendar. I hoped it was a mistake."

"It was a mistake. Mine. For offering in the first place."

"You said you believe in what we're building."

"I do."

"But not anymore?"

"Tell me about Disneyland."

"Oh, for God's sake."

"That's why you cancelled our second meeting?"

"You think I'd blow you off for Disneyland?"

"You didn't?"

"That doesn't deserve an answer."

"You seem to be good at not answering lately. Do you have any desire for Creative Care to succeed?"

"What is that supposed to mean?"

"I question your leadership."

"Because I rewarded my team with a day trip? My team that's been working around the clock and every weekend to deliver version 1.0 on an accelerated schedule? My team that's taken a pay cut to get us through funding? That team?"

"Reward results. Not attempts."

"Wow."

"Have you forgotten they're nearly three months behind, by your own estimation?"

"That's on the management team. Not staff."

"Again with the leadership question then."

Jen stared at Kade, incredulous. How dare she question Jen's reward system of her team or presume to know anything about the results they had achieved? Whether a project was completed on time was only one measure of performance and said nothing about quality.

She'd heard enough. Without another word, she opened the sliding screen door and set her dishes in the sink. Belongings in hand, she was about to shut the front door behind her when she stopped.

Itching for a fight, Kade had baited her, and Jen had bitten. She smirked at the irony of having suggested, moments ago, being the bigger person. While Kade had every right to an explanation for Jen cancelling on her and every right, given her board seat, to critique Jen's management skills, Kade was hurting. Constructive criticism and open dialogue weren't possible this evening, but acting with compassion was never off the table.

With a sigh, Jen went back inside and returned to the deck. She squatted next to Kade and rested a hand on her thigh. "If you decide to visit your father and want someone with you, I'll go." She stood and kissed the top of Kade's head before heading out for real.

Chapter Sixteen

Before Kade could grasp the antique knocker on Jen's front door, it swung open. By way of greeting, Jen handed Kade a travel mug full of hot coffee, a gift bag, and a card. "The card's for you, and the bag's for your father," she said as she grabbed her own mug and locked her door.

Kade was confused. Jen was the one doing her a favor, yet she was the person receiving presents? "What are these?"

Jen shrugged. "They're from the team. I don't know what's in the card, but your father's present is an MP3 player for audiobooks and includes a gift card for six books. The device is small, which may be tough for him, but the setup is easy, so anyone can help."

Kade stowed the present inside the trunk. "Wow. How incredibly thoughtful."

Jen took the coffee out of Kade's hand and indicated the card. "Open it."

Kade did. The greeting card showed a group of cartoon bunnies holding a heart balloon out toward a separate bunny, captioned We're Here for You. Enclosed was a certificate for a massage by a professional in-home service. "Holy cow," Kade said, looking to Jen for an explanation. "Aside from Jeremy, they've never even met me."

"True, but they know you're part of Creative Care and that you've been instrumental in helping us. When they learned about your father's stroke, they decided they wanted to do something for both of you. I had nothing to do with it. I'm merely the messenger." Jen slid into the passenger seat and closed the car door.

Kade followed her lead and started the engine, though her thoughts were on the gifts. Contrary to Jen's assertion, Jen had a lot to do with how the Creative Care team comported themselves. Jen set a tone at the top that forged a cohesive, principled team. Aside from the layoff, staff turnover was nil, and the employees' collective decision to forgo a portion of their salaries was a testament to their belief in and loyalty to Jen.

Kade had recognized early in her career that a company's greatest asset was its people, though nurturing them wasn't her forte. As such, she strove to hire managers who put their staff's concerns above their own and weren't afraid to tell her when she was wrong. Managers like Jen, she realized.

Kade had had this sense of Jen's skills early on, yet it had gotten lost beneath her indignation. Now that most of her anger had dissipated, she could see more clearly. When she measured Jen's strengths and weaknesses against other startup CEOs, Jen earned high marks. All startups endured growing pains; Kade had every confidence that Jen could course-correct whenever the business warranted swift, decisive action, and these gifts reminded her that Jen's team would likely remain by her side through it all.

As Jen set her coffee in the cup holder, she said, "Apologies in advance if I have to hop on some calls this morning."

"Not a problem. Thank you again for doing this," Kade said. "Especially on a weekday."

Jen pushed the seat back into a more comfortable sleeping position and curled up, shifting onto her right side. She closed her eyes, settling in for the long drive.

"We won't stay long," Kade said.

"However long you need."

And wasn't that the main difference between them? Jen was a nurturer, a caretaker. Even in the face of Kade's badgering about her leadership style, Jen had offered to join Kade for this visit. Kade hadn't been too proud to accept, confident Jen's presence would give her courage.

"I don't want to take any more advantage of you than I already am."

"I offered. How is that taking advantage of me?"

"I was selfish to accept."

Jen shifted until she rested on her left side. Kade sensed that blue eyes were studying her.

"Because you don't think you deserve it?" Jen asked.

Tension began to build between Kade's shoulder blades, and she tried to relax her grip on the steering wheel. She didn't want to talk about herself. That wasn't the point of starting this conversation. She took a deep breath and kept her voice low and even. "I just wanted to thank you. You being here. It means something to me. That's all."

When she flicked her eyes to the rear and right-side mirrors, Kade could see Jen's eyes on her in her peripheral vision. She somehow felt more exposed now and wished Jen would shift back toward the window, even though she knew the protection offered by remaining beyond Jen's direct gaze was imaginary.

"You don't get it, do you?" Jen asked.

Kade bit back the sarcastic "safe to say" reply on her lips.

"People care about you. And when people care about you, it means they want to help you. It makes them feel good, knowing they're helping, or at least trying to." Jen peeled the fingers of Kade's right hand from the steering wheel. She held it for a minute before speaking again. "That's one of the hardest things for you to hear, isn't it? That I care about you."

Kade didn't answer. She didn't have to. Jen seemed content to let the discussion peter out. Kade expected Jen to ask about the minefield that lay between her and her father, but she never did. She simply closed her eyes and held Kade's hand.

The nursing home where Kade's father had been transferred accepted Medi-Cal, a combined federal and California program designed to help low-income individuals pay for medical care. As Kade pulled into the lot, it took only one glance to see that the building was decades old and poorly maintained. An elderly man in a wheelchair was parked on the curb outside, his head tilted unnaturally far to one side, his mouth hanging open, his eyes closed. No one else was around.

Inside, the reception desk was empty. A wheelchair-bound woman sat against the wall, working her mouth in such a way as to indicate she had few to no teeth remaining. Another elderly man slowly pushed himself along in his wheelchair backward, his slippered feet taking tiny steps and making little progress. In the distance, Kade could hear someone mournfully wail over and over, a cross between the sound of a cat in heat and a perverse version of a Buddhist monk's "om." Also in the background, someone's call button sounded repeatedly, as if this facility used such devices for something other than garnering immediate attention.

Kade scanned the desk for signs that someone still utilized it and that perhaps the employee stationed there had merely taken a break. Based on the desk calendar and Styrofoam coffee cup, it seemed recently occupied, but she had no way to tell when the person would be returning. As she and Jen looked around for signs to indicate where they might find someone with information, a nurse walked by.

"Excuse me," Kade said.

The nurse stopped and nodded.

"I'm here to visit my father, who was recently transferred here, but I don't know his room number."

"Someone should be with you shortly," he said, and continued his journey.

Kade and Jen looked at each other skeptically. Another few minutes passed with the painful mantra/wail in the background and the insistent call-button signal, and Kade's patience lapsed. She stormed down the hall to wide double doors and pushed a side panel to open them. A sign indicated that this precaution prevented ambulatory patients with dementia from escaping. Kade approached a nurses' station where a nurse consulted something on a computer screen. Although her "be right with you" translated into several more minutes of waiting, the nurse finally assisted them, providing Gordon Davenport's room number and indicating the correct hallway.

Kade hesitated outside of Gordon's door.

"You can do this," Jen said, squeezing Kade's hand for encouragement. "Are you sure you don't want me to stay in the lobby? I can, you know."

They'd already covered this ground. Kade appreciated Jen's offer, but she felt somehow stronger with Jen by her side, like she could better handle whatever happened once she went through the doorway. She shook her head and took a deep breath.

Kade entered her father's room. At first glance, which was all she devoted to it, it seemed designed for function versus comfort, more like a hospital room than a living space. She set her eyes on a man she hadn't seen in nearly four years. His bed was to the right, perpendicular to the door, head against the wall. Opposite Kade, attached to an adjustable wall-mount stand, was a TV, the sound muted.

Gordon didn't move his head or otherwise acknowledge her. A feeding tube disappeared into his right nostril. His gray hair had lost the rest of the black strands that had remained the last time she'd seen him. A day's white stubble dotted his chin and cheeks in a patchwork that seemed unlikely to grow in everywhere it used to, as if he'd lost swaths of hair follicles with the passing years. His brown eyes were open, looking at but not focused on the television. His cheekbones were more pronounced than she remembered.

But even combined, none of these differences were more shocking than the drooping left side of his face. The asymmetry seemed to start somewhere above his eyebrows, because the left one sat lower than the right. It looked as though he'd firmly pressed the left side of his face up against a window and it froze in that position, like someone had pushed his face down and held it while setting it in acrylic.

Kade had seen enough. She backed out of the room, pushing against Jen until they were in the hallway. She couldn't start seeing him as fragile, as a victim of an attack on his brain that had deprived it of oxygen. Any chance of Kade ever seeing him as a man who needed her for any reason had died when Cassie did. His treatment of Kade had been hard enough for her to cope with after the incident that caused him to lose his job, but it was unforgivable after Cassie's accident.

She strode quickly down the hall and out to the parking lot. She opened the passenger side of her car and got in, tossing her key fob onto the driver's seat and shutting her door. Shortly thereafter, Jen opened the driver's side door, scooped up the keys, and sat. Kade crossed her arms in an effort to discourage any attempt by Jen to touch her for comfort or out of compassion. She deserved neither but knew Jen well enough that her instinct would be to reach out to her.

Jen sat for several moments without speaking. Finally, she asked, "Would you like to go home?"

"Please."

Jen started Kade's car, adjusted the mirrors, and got on the road. They were well into the return trip before either spoke. "What do you think of that facility?" Jen asked eventually.

"Seems functional."

"No other thoughts?" Jen was pushing.

Kade had nothing to say.

"Would you want your mom living there?" Jen asked.

"We're not talking about my mom."

"It's dingy, dark, and depressing."

Kade didn't speak.

"It smells like urine."

Again silence.

"Kade."

"I don't know what you want from me."

"I want what I've always wanted. You to be you."

Kade snorted. "What, are you some oracle now? I have to search for the answer to your riddle?"

Jen smiled. "I like the idea of being a kind of guide to you, however opaque."

"You just like telling me what to do," Kade grumbled halfheartedly.

Jen flicked her eyes to Kade and gave her a salacious smile and waggle of her eyebrows. "Sometimes."

Kade stared at her and burst into laughter. She reached over and briefly covered Jen's thigh. "Thank you. For today."

"Anytime."

They sat in comfortable quiet, with only the hum of road noise and the occasional burst of wind from a passing vehicle.

Some time later, Kade started to talk, unsure what was propelling her. Did she owe Jen an explanation? Was she trying to assuage the guilt she was feeling for visualizing her father as a monster who didn't deserve to receive human kindness? Could she be any more unfeeling?

"Our parents, Cassie's and mine, used to switch off taking all the kids to the mountains for skiing and snowboarding. On our last trip, Dad drove. We took the Kellers' SUV, since it had the most room, and rented a cabin, like we always did. Cassie and I were both seventeen and pretty good skiers by then."

Kade was tired. They'd been on the mountain since nine, and she could feel it. She was also exhilarated. She and Cassie had graduated to black-diamond runs, and this was their first full day playing with the big boys, as they liked to call it. Holly, who was five years younger, had stayed on the intermediate runs. The eldest of the Keller children, Jackie, remained on the bunny slopes and flirted with the male ski instructors. Sam, who was even younger than Holly and didn't like snow, stayed inside with Kade's father, playing board games.

They'd promised Kade's dad to meet him and Sam at the car at five p.m. Holly was already out of her skis and heading to the lodge. Kade and Cassie didn't have to worry about finding Jackie, who would already be in the lodge, fawning over some stud. It was four thirty p.m., and the lift lines remained long. If they went up for one more run, they'd be about fifteen minutes late.

Kade's father was a gruff man who became angry when his timetables went unheeded. Kade bent down to unlatch her boots but felt Cassie's ski pole poke her shoulder.

"You seriously want to wait around for a half hour? We can get one more run in."

"*No way. We'll be late. My dad will probably leave us stranded. And if he doesn't, we're toast. I probably wouldn't see the light of day for a month. Nope. Not worth it.*" Kade flipped open a couple of latches.

"*He's not going to leave us stranded. My parents would kill him. His bark is worse than his bite. Fifteen minutes is no biggie. We can offer to do extra chores or something around your house. Come on. Time's a wastin'.*" She pushed forward several feet and looked back at Kade. "*You know you want to.*"

"*Cassie,*" Kade implored. "*No.*"

"*You seriously don't want to?*"

"*Of course I want to, but—*"

"*Let's go!*" Cassie pushed off with her poles and headed for the chairlift without turning around. Kade wanted to get one more run in, but she didn't want to upset her father. She looked down at her boots and back up to Cassie, and repeated the fruitless gesture. Cassie was getting farther and farther ahead. Kade resecured her boots and followed.

There were two different runs off this hill, and by the time Kade pushed off the lift, she didn't know which slope Cassie had taken. She hoped she'd chosen the one they'd been using all day and not the one reported to be a level of difficulty higher. But either one would have them down the mountain within a minute or two of the other.

The run had been electrifying, and Kade was glad for Cassie's encouragement. But as she waited at the bottom of the hill, one minute turned into two, two to five, five to ten. Fear of her father's wrath rapidly changed to fear that something had happened to Cassie. And as soon as she heard the commotion coming from the ski-patrol snowmobiles, she knew in her gut that Cassie had been hurt.

The end, at least, had come quickly. Cassie's inexperience had led her slightly off course, where first responders said she hit a patch of ice. It occurred near a copse of trees, and she sped into one without slowing. The best of helmets couldn't have withstood the impact. Cassie had died instantly.

It turned into the longest, most painful day of Kade's life.

Kade wasn't sure when Jen had taken hold of her hand, but she was glad for the comfort while she finished her tale. She stared down at the joined hands in her lap. Tears were inevitable, and she let them come.

"It wasn't enough that I'd just lost the person who meant everything in the world to me. It wasn't enough that I saw the absolute devastation on the faces of Jackie, of Holly, of Sam, and soon, Mr. and Mrs. Keller. It wasn't enough that I was already blaming myself for her death, and still do." Kade swiped at her tears. "No. My father had to say, 'You killed her.' You see, had I been where and when I said I would, Cassie would still be alive."

Quietly, almost too quietly for Jen to hear, Kade said, "He was right, but he never should have said that." Kade shifted away and stared out the passenger window.

Jen had no idea what to say. She didn't want to offer platitudes that Kade had no doubt heard numerous times about not blaming herself and it having been an accident. But it *had* been an accident, and Kade *shouldn't* blame herself.

Kade's hang-ups suddenly made sense in a way Jen couldn't have anticipated. Kade was so young when Cassie died. The playfulness Jen found beneath Kade's surface had been shoved down, pushed out of sight by a woman—at first a young woman—who felt the need to punish herself. The inability of Kade to calmly deal with her father's stroke was grounded in a childhood of pain and regret. Jen instantly comprehended Kade's eccentric need to adhere to schedules, especially when coupled with the train derailment from her youth. And most importantly, Jen now understood Kade's insistence that she'd only hurt Jen. Her reluctance to pursue a relationship was driven by a history of causing pain to people she loved, an honest albeit irrational belief that she was behind it.

Indignation flared within her at Kade's father, for how could he say such a thing? But right now, the most important matter was caring for Kade. Jen squeezed Kade's hand. "No, he shouldn't have, and thank you for telling me."

"I don't want you to think I'm an unfeeling jerk when it comes to him. I mean I am, but I have my reasons."

"I don't think you're an unfeeling jerk. I can't imagine why your father said that to you or how hard it must have been to hear that on top of losing Cassie. I can understand why it's been difficult to forgive him."

Kade shifted in her seat to face Jen. "You would have."

Jen shook her head. She didn't want Kade comparing herself to her, especially if Kade felt she came up short. They were different people who dealt with things in different ways. One wasn't necessarily better than the other. Jen didn't mind if Kade looked to her for advice on how to cope with something, but she did mind if Kade felt *lesser* for it. Kade had told her she didn't feel worth being part of a relationship, something Jen disagreed with and didn't want to contribute to. "We don't know that. I don't know what it's like to lose my best friend in a horrible accident, let alone be blamed for it on top of blaming myself."

Chapter Seventeen

They continued the journey in silence for some time.

"I could have him moved to a better facility," Kade said after a while.

"You could."

"I don't have to visit."

"Kade?" Jen glanced over several times, waiting for Kade to look at her. When she did, Jen said, "You don't need to decide anything today."

"I'm going to disappoint you."

"It's not me you need to worry about."

"It matters to me. What you think."

"Why?" Jen knew she was pushing, but Kade was letting her in, and Jen wanted to know how far Kade had come on the subject of their relationship.

"Because you're important to me."

And there it was, offered without hesitation or doubt. Kade was admitting what Jen had hoped for but not expected. Right now, work disagreements didn't matter. Fostering what was between them did. Jen was caught between responding earnestly and poking fun at the venue Kade had chosen to reveal this tidbit. The car? Seriously? At least it was a long stretch of highway requiring minimal driving skill. She caressed Kade's hand with her thumb. "You're important to me, too."

Kade seemed talked out, and the ride continued in relative quiet. About a half hour from Jen's, where Kade had picked her up, Kade asked, "Doesn't your grandmother live off this stretch of highway?"

"Good memory. Yeah. About ten minutes from here."

"Will you be seeing her today?"

"Not sure yet."

Kade looked at her watch. "Do you want to stop by now? Since we're already out this way and unexpectedly free? I don't need to be anywhere until two."

Jen brightened. "Are you sure? I'd love for you to meet her, if you're interested."

"Absolutely."

Glancing at the dashboard clock, Jen did some quick mental math. "It's close to noon, and she does better at receiving visitors during meals, so it's probably as good a time as any."

"Is there anything I should know? What to say or not to say?"

"We'll get our cue early. If she recognizes me, it should be fine. Some days she thinks I'm only a caretaker, and those can be more difficult. I'd say if she starts asking the same question over and over, instead of continuing to answer, which can get frustrating, try to move to a different topic. And if she says something completely wrong, don't try to correct her. Go with it. What else? Smile."

"Sounds like you've learned a lot."

Jen laughed. "I'm adept at making mistakes, but I'm also good at learning how not to repeat them. It's been trying. But I don't know. I love that woman. Even when she forgets who I am, I like to think she knows me and simply can't indicate it. The sound of my voice, the touch of my hand, something's getting through. If she perceives more than she can convey, I'd never want to be responsible for depriving her of love, comfort, or human interaction."

"Does she know she was the catalyst for you to start Creative Care?"

"Not often. It's a relatively recent addition to her life's timeline, and her newer memories are the first to fail. But it doesn't matter. I know she's proud of me."

"She should be."

Jen tamped down the response that immediately came to mind: *Even if my leadership is questionable?* The wound was still raw, and because of that, revisiting their argument now wasn't likely to prove helpful. What mattered was that she was about to share some time, however brief, with two people she cared for. But before Jen gave voice to whatever version of "thank you" was on her lips, Kade spoke again.

"I mean it, Jen. You should be proud of what you've accomplished and what you're building. But none of that's as important as the person you are. I'm sure everyone in your family is proud of the woman you've become."

Jen kept her gaze fixed on the road, working to prevent her tears from spilling over so Kade couldn't see the impact of her words. She'd been hurt that Kade had challenged her effectiveness as CEO, especially as she believed Kade didn't have all the facts and had jumped to conclusions. She felt Kade failed to recognize that their differences in leadership styles didn't mean one was better than the other. But more disheartening had been Jen's sense that Kade didn't appreciate how important it was to her to take care of her team. It was core to who Jen was. Now it seemed Kade did value the ways in which Jen was different.

Having collected herself enough to keep her voice steady, Jen said, "You're doing it again."

"What am I doing?"

"Saying something disarming. Twice in a row, in fact. First telling me I'm important to you and then that I'm not such a bad person. A girl could get a big head."

Kade tucked her hands between her legs and shifted her focus to the passenger-window view. "I'm not good at telling people how I feel about them."

Jen silently chided herself for teasing. True, Kade didn't often speak about her feelings, but Jen thought it akin to people who didn't swear much. When they finally cursed, it was all the more effective. Kade tended toward actions instead of words. In Jen's ideal world, she'd prefer both, but given a choice, having someone like Kade follow through time and again meant far more than idle talk.

She pulled Kade's hand onto her lap. "You do one better, Kade. You show us." Kade's suggestion to visit Edna was a perfect example of little ways in which Kade did exactly that. Hell, the woman started companies to help people she cared about.

When they arrived at Edna's, Jen introduced Kade to Doreen, who was in the kitchen. Nana was sitting in her lounger, watching TV. Jen approached from an angle, seemingly so as not to startle her. "Hi, Nana," Jen said as she took her hand.

Nana turned her attention to Jen, and her features softened. She smiled warmly. "Hello, sweetheart." Kade wasn't sure what to expect, but visions of Jen's grandmother wearing a pink polyester robe and slippers flew out the window. This woman was dressed in tan slacks and a black-and-brown argyle sweater, her short gray hair was stiff from hair spray, she wore several bracelets and a necklace, and she had a modest amount of makeup on. Stylish wasn't a word Kade would have normally associated with a person with dementia, but she was learning. The thought struck Kade that the simple act of readying herself for the day was probably important for Edna in maintaining a sense of normalcy and independence, much the same as trying to extend the amount of time she could live in her own house.

Jen bent down and kissed her cheek. "Nana, may I introduce you to someone?"

Nana sat forward and started to push herself up, using the armrests for leverage. She moved with difficulty, and her arms shook as she rose from the chair. Kade was surprised Jen didn't try to dissuade her from getting up, but she realized Edna would likely be most comfortable greeting strangers from a standing position. Jen positioned herself behind her, ready to help if needed.

Once Edna stood, Jen moved between them and extended her hand to indicate that Kade draw nearer. "Nana, I'd like you to meet a friend of mine, Kade Davenport. Kade, this is my grandmother, Edna Spencer."

Edna offered her hand to Kade and smiled. "Nice to meet you, Kade."

They shook hands. "Nice to meet you, too, Mrs. Spencer."

Edna shooed away the greeting with a wave of her hand. "Nonsense. Mrs. Spencer sounds like an old lady. Please call me Edna."

Kade immediately liked her. "Edna," she said with a nod.

Turning to her granddaughter, Edna said, "Are you staying for lunch?"

With a questioning brow, Jen eyed Kade. Kade gave her a "whatever you want to do" shrug. "Sure, Nana. We'd love to, if it's not too much trouble."

Edna waved her hand again. "Don't be silly. Doreen and I will whip up something."

Edna took Jen's arm and headed into the kitchen. As Kade followed, Jen said, "Whatever you two are making smells terrific."

Edna furrowed her brow. "We're not making anything."

Doreen was stirring something in a Crock-Pot and glanced up with a smile. "The sesame chicken is ready, and there's plenty. We've also got rice and broccoli."

Edna kept her eyes on the pot as if trying to process this information.

"We decided to use the slow-cooker today, which we usually don't do." Though Doreen said this to Jen and Kade, Kade thought it likely that Doreen added this comment to help jog Edna's memory. "Edna, why don't you attend to your guests while I serve?"

Seemingly confused, Edna stared at the counter.

Jen jumped in by opening the refrigerator and peering in. "Nana, it looks like you've got iced tea. I wouldn't mind a glass." She pulled out the pitcher. "Would you like some? We can drink it in the family room until lunch is ready."

Edna nodded slowly at first, then seemed to put on a cheerful expression that conflicted with her physicality. "Yes, sweetie, thank you." She turned to Kade and extended her hand. "Hi. Edna Spencer. And you are?"

Dismissing the immediate thought that Edna was joking, Kade flicked her eyes to Jen for some sign of what to do. Jen's expression was apologetic. Taking the cue from Edna's term of endearment for

Jen, Kade leveraged their relationship so that she was something of a known entity instead of a complete stranger. She didn't want Edna to feel that her personal space was being violated. "Hi, Mrs. Spencer. I'm Kade Davenport, a friend of Jen's," she said as she shook hands.

"Nice to meet you, dear. Please call me Edna."

Jen shoved the iced-tea pitcher into Kade's hands and grabbed a stack of glasses from a cupboard. She cradled them in one arm and offered the other to her grandmother, who walked with Jen into the family room. Jen turned and mouthed something to Doreen as they left the kitchen, and Kade noticed she carried four glasses. Jen indicated for Kade to take them while she helped Nana sit in her armchair. She didn't allow much time to lapse before picking up the conversation again, and Kade wondered not only whether she was attempting to keep Edna on track, but if such a try was typically successful.

"Kade and I work together occasionally, Nana," Jen said as she poured.

"Is that what they call it now?" Edna asked.

"Call what?"

"Hanky-panky."

"Nana!" Jen blushed.

"I wondered if it's a euphemism." To Kade she said, "My Jennifer likes women, you see."

"Nana, stop." Jen's expression was one of embarrassment and amusement, as if she were pleased for her grandmother's teasing even if she wished for a different subject.

"It's no wonder a pretty woman like you caught her attention."

Jen looked at Kade with laughter in her eyes as she handed her a glass. "I am so sorry." To Nana, she said, "No euphemism. We really do work together. She's my boss, actually."

Edna made a face of distaste and motioned with her hand as if shooing away something unappealing. "Eh. Computers." She turned to Kade. "You're not here to talk computers, are you?"

Kade felt the edges of her mouth swing upward. "No, ma'am."

"Took some getting used to, Jen with girls. But she's known since she was five." Nana gave Kade a thorough once-over. "What are your intentions with my granddaughter?"

"Nana! We're not…" Jen made a little whimper and gave Kade a beseeching look as she sat next to her on the couch.

"I intend to learn from her." Kade flicked her eyes to Jen. "She's a 'go with it' kind of gal, whereas I tend to be more uptight." Nana settled her gaze on Jen, full of affection. "We can all learn from this one. Wears her heart on her sleeve, like her father. Life is too short to hold ourselves back from those we care about."

Jen must get her openness from her grandmother, Kade thought. Assuming Edna was a typical Spencer, she envied this side of Jen's family. They reminded her of the Kellers, people who seemed thankful for each day they were given with loved ones and weren't afraid to say so.

Jen returned her grandmother's smile. "I have you to thank for a father who's in touch with his emotional side. How is Dad? I haven't talked to him in a while."

Moments passed in silence while Nana's expression turned contemplative, as if she seemed unsure of the answer. "I don't know," Nana said vaguely.

Kade caught the quick flash of Jen's eyes in her direction. Whether it was an acknowledgment that Nana wasn't clear on details or that Kade should speak, she didn't know, but it might be both. Kade wasn't sure if Edna was having a bad day or if her memory loss was routine, but she remembered the few pointers Jen had given her and decided to try shifting the conversation to an earlier time period, hoping it would cause Edna less confusion. She pointed over her shoulder to a photograph on the wall. "Do you mind if I take a closer look at that picture? What a gorgeous steam locomotive."

Edna followed the direction of Kade's attention. "Not at all. Please. That was taken during the first real vacation Ben and I took together after we had Joseph. Ben was a circus fanatic as well as a train buff, so we left Joseph with my parents and went to Milwaukee for the Great Circus Parade. That was us posing in front of the train that hauled the circus-parade wagons."

Standing in front of the photo, Kade said, "That's engine number 4960. Built in 1923." She turned to Edna. "Did you know the 4960 is still being used today?"

Edna's face lit up. "Oh, Ben would be so happy. Are you an antique-train devotee as well?"

"No, but my father is. He had a number of favorites he taught me about when I was little, and this beauty was one of them." She returned to her seat. "Would you mind telling me about the parade and your vacation?"

Edna waved her hand as if slighting the events. "I don't want to bore you with an old woman's memories."

Jen perked up. "Nana, please," she said enthusiastically. "We'd love to hear about it. I don't remember this story."

Contentment saturated Nana's features as she settled in to tell them some of her history.

Following lunch and multiple stories from Edna involving circuses and steam trains, they returned to the car. Jen handed Kade the keys and slipped into the passenger seat. After Kade started the engine and pulled onto the street, Jen said, "Thanks for turning our visit into one of the best I've had lately, and please don't take offense that she obviously couldn't keep track of who you are and how we know each other. She loved you. She simply glowed today because of you."

"She's a pistol. I'm not at all offended. It's not as though she's doing it on purpose."

"True, but you'd be surprised how easy it can be to forget it's the disease and not the person. She can get angry and frustrated and lash out, and I have to do my best to keep calm and root out the cause, which is often pain. Thankfully not only is she generally mild-mannered, but also I'm getting better at recognizing when something's wrong. When she falls, for example, believe it or not, a UTI is usually behind it." Jen paused and glanced at Kade. "Sorry. TMI."

"I'm sure it's been difficult to find ways to keep her in her home. I don't know how you do it, with such a demanding job."

Something occurred to Kade she hadn't considered before meeting Edna. "Can I ask a question and have you not get mad at me?"

"Normally not, but you get a free pass because of today. Shoot."

"When you've said 'something's come up,' is Edna, or caring for Edna, the something?"

Out of the corner of her eye, Kade could see Jen's jaw clench, the hesitation itself answering the question. With the level of involvement Jen was clearly providing her grandmother, Kade could think of no competing alternative. Kade heard Jen release a heavy sigh.

"Off the record?" Jen asked.

"Your silence has already answered. Jen, why didn't you just tell me?"

"I..." Jen didn't say any more.

"Did you think I wouldn't understand?"

"Kade." Again nothing followed. Silence stretched between them.

"Does your team know?" Kade finally asked.

"Yes. Jeremy's known all along. It's been helpful in recruiting. We find that sharing my experience helps us close our top candidates since most employees join because of our mission. Plus, on the odd times I have to leave, I'm pretty up-front with my whereabouts because I don't want them thinking I'm running out to play golf or something while they're pulling sixty-hour weeks. They know I'll be back online as soon as I can. You have to understand these people see me every day. They know how hard I work. They're not going to question my loyalty to the company or my priorities."

Unlike you.

Jen hadn't said it, but the implication was clear.

More miles passed without a word.

Kade felt stomach-punched. Was she so hard-nosed and inflexible she couldn't understand that caring for a family member took precedence over everything? She swallowed. Maybe Jen wasn't throwing punches. Maybe the ache in her gut was from the voice inside her head that said Jen hadn't told her because she might not have accepted the excuse and possibly even retorted that better planning would have obviated the need for Jen to bow out.

With Kade having practically run from her father's room after mere moments, the way the morning had played out was stark commentary on exactly how receptive Jen would think Kade would likely be when it came to caring for her grandmother. As deeply as Jen's judgment cut, Kade couldn't deny it was born of experience. It was hard to admit Jen had viable reasons for her vagueness about her no-shows.

Kade pulled into Jen's driveway and set the car in Park.

Jen spoke first. "Please don't take my not telling you personally. I would have said the same thing to Charles or anyone else on the board."

Great. She was interchangeable with everyone else in Jen's estimation. She took a deep breath and shifted in her seat to face Jen. "I'm sorry I let you down."

"You haven't. I didn't give you a chance."

Kade shook her head. Nothing she could say would change why Jen made the decision to be opaque with her excuses.

Jen took her hand. "Don't blame yourself. Please. You need to worry about you. Dealing with Nana's care hasn't been easy, but I'm an old hand at it, and she and I are close. This stuff with your father? While I do think you should consider spending time with him, it can't be at your emotional expense. Promise you'll focus on you and what you need."

My MO, Kade barely refrained from saying. She put the car in reverse, needing to leave before she heard more requests from Jen to look after herself. Jen was always thinking of others. Gordon would be in good hands if Jen were his daughter. "Thanks again for today." She briefly touched Jen's thigh. "You being there made a difference." As she watched Jen head inside, she had the feeling Jen could make a difference to her in all the ways that mattered. She amended the thought. Jen *will* make the difference to someone. Some incredibly lucky woman.

❖

Before Kade could sit at her desk, Holly was already rapping on her doorframe and shutting the door behind her.

"How is he? How are you?" Holly asked as she took a seat in front of Kade's desk. "Are you okay?"

"I don't know." Kade took a deep breath and looked at her. "I didn't stick around long enough to talk to him."

"It couldn't have been easy."

"I couldn't reconcile the man I've been so angry with all these years with the fragile one staring at the wall. I didn't want to feel sorry for him. I don't want to admit that to you, but it's the truth."

"You know I could never blame you for having conflicting feelings about him after how he treated you."

"Well, it's bound to get more conflicting. I need you to research skilled-nursing facilities around here." She shook her head and raised a palm to ward off any misguided praise. "Don't. It's a reflection on how bad his current place is and on Jen for pointing it out, not on me as some do-gooder. Also, I need you to bring your PI skills to bear on Jen's grandmother, Edna Spencer. I'll send you her address. Late husband Ben, son Joseph, goes by Joe. Find out her closest lifelong friends and where they live. Start with Joe for his buy-in and consent, telling him it's part of a Creative Care board initiative or something, and ask for names of Edna's friends. See if we can get one or more of them to visit, on my dime. Find out what kinds of outings they'd enjoy. If transportation's an issue, book a car and driver. All on the down-low, please. I don't want Jen to have to lift a finger or worry, or know I'm involved."

Holly looked up from the notes she was jotting into her tablet. "I was hoping she's why I didn't hear from you, versus you having a bitter fight with your dad and being booked for homicide."

"You'd have been my one phone call."

"What's the scoop? First, you write her off for bailing on you, and next she's going with you to visit your dad. Now this kindness toward her grandmother."

"If I was kind, I'd have assumed that, when she canceled on me, something major was in play, which was her grandmother's care."

"She could have told you the reason."

Kade didn't bother to respond. "Edna's a kick. I'd like to do something for her, and I can't think of anything more beneficial and therapeutic than spending time with a friend."

"I've read about programs where volunteers take therapy dogs to visit seniors and hospice patients to improve their quality of life."

"Excellent idea. If Joe's on board, ask if Edna's fond of dogs."

Holly uncharacteristically bit her bottom lip, as if she were slightly trepidatious. "What?" Kade asked.

"What about something like that for your father?"

Jarring memories roared to life for Kade, and she looked away. Their four-year old black Labrador retriever mix, Mittens, a tiny puppy when then seven-year-old Kade named him because of his white paws, had become a bone of contention in the Davenport household after the derailment fiasco. Gordon grew more and more disdainful of the animal, which he had originally brought into their home as a playmate for Kade. When they moved cross-country to settle into the neighborhood where Kade would soon meet Cassie, Gordon had refused to take the dog along. An anguished Kade put up flyers in the neighborhood, and her mom posted a photo and description of Mittens as free to a good home. A young couple responded, wanting a companion for their dog.

Kade never spoke of Mittens to anyone. Losing him was one in a string of heartbreaks during her youth. Cassie was a balm to her soul throughout that time, never more so than when she so easily and joyfully befriended a despairing little girl who'd recently lost her best friend.

Her poker face was never firmly in place in Holly's presence, and the concern she saw in Holly's eyes signaled she was doing a poor job of concealing the sting of those childhood memories. Knowing her voice would sound like she was chewing gravel, she shook her head. Perhaps refusing to allow a companion animal to visit a patient would be forever negatively etched on Kade's karma, but at the memory of Mittens's scared eyes, folded ears, and tucked tail resulting from Gordon's vitriol, she couldn't send any defenseless creature his way. In his current state, Gordon was as dangerous as a kitten, but for how long?

Holly deftly sidestepped. "Since you're asking about local facilities, are you planning to visit him again?"

"Jen thinks I should."

Holly crossed her arms and huffed. "So much for my estimation of her. She probably thinks children should play ball in the street, too."

Kade smiled at Holly's fierce protectiveness. "In her defense, I believe she thinks it would be at least as much for my benefit as for his."

"Well, you are into self-punishment."

"You are my assistant, after all," Kade teased her.

Chapter Eighteen

Jen's day was crawling by like a slug through molasses. She'd sent a personalized email to numerous VCs, containing a teaser and overview of Creative Care that mentioned they were starting their fund-raising cycle, and she'd heard crickets. Each day she updated the metrics in her PowerPoint deck so the story she and Jeremy would tell prospective investors included the latest information, nearly all of which was good news. Signups were growing on both the senior and caregiver sides, positive user reviews were coming in daily, and Jen had gotten several more local hospitals into the referral program. So why wasn't she getting meetings?

When she had initially raised her seed capital, Charles had been immediately interested and quick to invest. Instead of involving his lawyers and having them draft a formal term sheet listing the key elements of his offer, he'd sent Jen an email with several short bullet points, and they had a deal. This time around, it seemed she was contacting far more people yet garnering much less interest.

Jen was usually inundated with the volume of emails she received, but now when she wanted to see new unread messages, it seemed her inbox contained only items she'd already responded to or could ignore. She even caught herself clicking the Refresh button more than once, a pointless exercise since messages were delivered in real time. Her marketing intern stopped by her desk, and Jen was happy for the distraction.

"What's up?" Jen asked.

"An ice cream guy out front says he needs to talk to you."

"He's barking up the wrong tree."

"That's what I told him, but he insists he's not trying to sell us anything. He won't leave."

Being CEO sometimes felt to Jen like she was the only adult in a roomful of toddlers. Yet aware that her position demanded she not give in to her occasional desire to whine, she strode to the front entrance. A young blond man with a Van Dyke beard and spiky hair, sporting a backpack and, bizarrely, a pink balloon in the shape of a monkey, waited inside their suite door.

"Can I help you?"

"Jen Spencer?"

"Yes."

"This is for you." He handed her the balloon and consulted a folded paper in his hand. "From a…Kadreen Davenport."

"Kadrienne?"

He snapped his fingers. "Right. Please lead your team downstairs and over to the empty parking lot behind the closed department store."

"Why?"

He grinned. "You'll see. It won't take long, and she says to tell you to trust her."

Jen eyed the man suspiciously. "My whole team?"

He nodded. "See you in the parking lot." He hiked his backpack higher on his shoulder and left.

Jen was standing in her company's reception area holding an animal balloon. From Kade. The whole thing was so unbelievable that she gathered her troops as requested, knowing whatever Kade had up her sleeve would be worth their time.

Once outside, Jen noticed the afternoon sun glinting off a rolling ice cream cart the young man stood by. As he pushed it forward, he waved for everyone to follow him, which they did, chitchatting and openly wondering why they had been called outdoors. Once they arrived at the lot of the shuttered "for lease" building, the young man went to work.

And that's how Jen found herself finishing an ice cream bar and watching her team simultaneously eat frozen treats while assembling and flying old-fashioned airplane glider toys. Several of her software engineers had unfolded a large vinyl mat "target" the man had provided, competing against each other to land their flyers on it. Her marketing intern and head of product were taking turns making massive bubbles with large bubble wands. Although there was an animal balloon kit with instructions, everyone on her small team drifted to the airplanes and bubbles. The man informed Jen the ice cream and toys were paid for and her team's sole responsibility was to take a short break to enjoy them.

Content to soak up the sun and the camaraderie of her team now that the short indulgence of the ice cream bar was over, Jen let her thoughts turn to Kade. This outing was incredibly thoughtful and exactly what her team needed. She'd never considered Kade particularly mindful of the wellbeing of staff and had often sensed substantial differences in their leadership styles. But Kade was batting a thousand in leading high-growth companies to lucrative outcomes, which meant she'd recruited, retained, and managed talent well. And the instructions Kade had given to the young man definitively included all Creative Care workers. Jen couldn't be more pleased with the result.

She sat on the pavement, her back against the sun to provide a little shade, and texted Kade.

Your thoughtfulness is very much appreciated. The Creative Care team thanks you.

Knowing Kade, she probably had only certain segments during the workday in which she allotted herself time out for text messaging, so Jen didn't expect to hear from her any time soon. But her phone buzzed almost immediately.

np.

Why was Jen surprised Kade knew texting shorthand for "no problem"? The woman had been at the forefront of technological advances for over a decade. As she waited for more of a response, she returned to her musings.

Kade was a dichotomy. Professionally, she was a shark, gliding through rough business waters with power and grace. Personally, she was more like a child learning how to swim, needing guidance and reassurance, afraid to let go of the pool's edge. It was maddening, knowing how adept Kade was in certain aspects of her life and how untried and cautious in other areas. And as with a young swimmer, Jen couldn't be upset or angry with her. Kade was the only one who could set her own pace.

Jen frowned. No additional response seemed forthcoming. Did Kade even know what Jen was thanking her for? Was Holly the one behind the afternoon break? Another text came through.

How's the list coming?

Kade was referring to the list of venture capitalists in Creative Care's industry that Jen and Jeremy were putting together, as she'd volunteered to provide introductions to VCs she knew. They'd come up with the list, but Jen hadn't sent it to her, hesitant to keep relying on Kade's help and confident she could find another investor like she had the first time around with Charles. But now Jen's hope was fading, and Kade's question immediately left her feeling deflated. She deflected.

Getting there.

More than a minute ticked by without a response, so Jen stood and pocketed her phone, assuming Kade had moved on to other things. As she considered corralling the team, her phone buzzed. Kade.

"Hi," Jen said.

"Not for one minute do I believe you haven't finished it. What's up?"

Jen took a deep breath. She struggled with accepting help when she believed herself capable of handling a matter. "I don't want to keep imposing on you."

"Jen. I'm your ally and resource. Use me."

Grateful they weren't meeting face-to-face, Jen didn't bother to stifle the heat in her cheeks at the adult video clip her mind suddenly played of how she could best use Kade: hazel eyes growing darker with need, breath catching, body arching, muscles clenching. Circumventing those thoughts, she reconsidered her own hesitancy to take Kade up on her offer.

Entrepreneurial spirit pumped through Kade's blood, and she genuinely relished working with company leaders to improve and innovate. She was experienced and pleased to share her knowledge. So why was Jen dragging her feet?

Because the idea of being a substitutable executive in Kade's stable of suits was demotivating. She wanted to be of unique interest to Kade. She wanted things between them to be personal, intensely so. She didn't want to be just another CEO in Kade's portfolio.

Yet as she looked around at the fierce competition taking place over glider landings, something dawned on her.

Kade didn't think of her solely as a colleague. The likelihood that this special outing was being replicated across all of Kade's portfolio companies was as probable as Kade purposely playing mind games with her. Yes, Kade was interested in Creative Care's success, but the notion that she might be *specifically* interested because of her feelings for Jen, even if Kade wasn't conscious of them, kindled within Jen excitement for things to come that had nothing to do with work.

While she understood the rationale behind Kade's fear of things developing between them, Jen didn't require special handling. People who were important to each other occasionally hurt each other, but the joy of being together easily outweighed the inevitable rough patches.

They could go slow. Jen could be patient. She'd happily remain at Kade's side, coaxing her, guiding her to dip her toe in the relationship waters, reassuring her while slowly increasing her exposure.

Jen didn't know how to convince Kade to give them a shot, but Kade was worth the effort of trying.

"Kade?"

"Hmm?"

"What was the motivation behind my team's treat today?"

The line remained quiet as Kade seemed to contemplate the question. "You."

Jen considered her reply far longer than she normally would, surprised by the confession but not by the warmth infusing her. Kade had been thinking of her exactly as she'd hoped.

Before she could respond, Kade said, "You've been on my mind and I…I shouldn't have…" Jen heard her sigh. "I've set ground rules and then undermined them, which is completely unfair to you. I'm sorry, Jen."

Wait. That wasn't the point of Jen's question whatsoever. She wanted to return to the part about being on Kade's mind. "Kade, that's not why I—"

"But when it comes to work, I haven't let you down, have I?"

Everything shifted with those words. The surge of pleasure from Kade's admission vanished. Jen was the one who had let Kade down by not trusting her enough to tell her the truth about her absences, yet Kade was responding by heaping more blame on herself, the last thing she needed. And as much as Kade's reluctance to give their relationship a try had frustrated Jen, Kade had been entirely forthcoming about what she could and couldn't offer, and why. "You haven't let me down in anything. Work or otherwise."

"Then send me your wish list. You can include your template, but let's start with folks you want to work with that I can introduce you to. Creative Care has a great story, solid numbers, and a strong team. What it doesn't have is a lot of cash. So let's move."

Though it was an important task, it was also one of the few critical work-related messages Jen could ever remember not giving a damn about. Clearly regretting her gesture of support for Jen and her team, Kade was keeping the conversation on work, which was not at all what Jen wanted. "Kade, did you hear what I said? You haven't let me down. Please acknowledge what I'm telling you."

"I heard you. I've got to hop on another call. Send me the list."

The call ended, taking with it Jen's good mood. The shrieks and laughter of her team grated on her in a way they never had. All she wanted from them was to trot back inside and stay until they delivered results that would make Kade proud. She chuckled at the irony before calling everyone in.

Chapter Nineteen

Today was the day. Efficient as always, Holly had found and vetted a skilled-nursing facility for Gordon. For better or worse, it was located less than twenty-five minutes away. Bringing Kade's financial resources to bear, Holly got him moved quickly.

Following their early morning spin class, Holly insisted on returning with Kade to her condo before she got ready to visit her father in his new location. Well, not get ready so much as dressed—Kade felt far from ready. Holly was uncharacteristically quiet as they worked through their well-honed routine to gather plates, glasses, drinks, napkins, utensils, and food from all corners of Kade's kitchen and set them out for a predawn breakfast.

Trying to pull Holly out of her doldrums, Kade asked, "Were you able to find any of those balsa-wood, toy stunt planes to send over to Creative Care?" She'd requested that Holly try to track down some of the old toys she and Cassie had played with as kids to send to the team.

Holly nodded. "Yep. Exactly as I remembered from my childhood. You gave me my first one, you know."

Kade didn't recall the gift. "Did I?"

"You and Cassie were babysitting me while we played in your yard. You gave me one. Mine flew farthest and landed in an oil pan where your dad was working on a car. It made a mess, and he started yelling and cursing. You took the blame and were banished indoors, and he sent Cassie and me home. I cried the whole way for getting you in trouble."

"I don't remember," Kade said. The times her father yelled at her were so numerous, she wasn't surprised this particular incident had slipped her mind.

"I was terrified of him," Holly said. "So were a lot of kids. But Cassie never was. That day she took me up to her room and gave me one of her planes to put together while she talked about your dad. To her, he was like a dog who barked at things that didn't exist. She said he didn't scare her because she didn't have to live in his head and see the world as the bad place he thought it was. She felt sorry for him. She said our job was to remind you of the far better sounds out there, of the many wonderful things to pay attention to, and that whatever world your dad saw out there wasn't what we knew."

"She never told me." Kade warmed at the thought of her childhood friend acting as a kind of guardian angel. "I always marveled at her ability to ignore him. She was never rude or impolite, but she also never backed down."

Conversation lapsed again as they started in on their fruit bowls and steel-cut oatmeal, the only sounds coming from silverware tapping softly against porcelain.

After wiping her mouth with her napkin, Kade said, "I'm anxious enough, you know. Having my loquacious friend go radio silent on me is killing all the nice endorphins I just released into my body."

Holly poured herself another cup of coffee and returned the carafe to the warmer. She backed against the counter and crossed her arms. "Why won't you let me go with you?"

Kade rose, slid an arm around Holly's waist, and rested her chin on her shoulder. "Because at some point I have to face him on my own. He can't hurt me unless I let him."

Holly pushed her back and held her by her shoulders. "True. But do you actually believe it, or are you telling me what I want to hear?"

Holly was her stalwart supporter, and Kade was indescribably grateful she'd somehow stumbled into the welcoming arms of the Keller family those many years ago, though after what she'd put them through, she'd never understood their devotion. Kade took

Holly's hands in hers and focused on them, afraid Holly would see right through her doubts should she meet her eyes. Although she wasn't sure how she'd deal with her father directly, she wanted to protect Holly from him. Based on the severity of his stroke, it was doubtful he'd be able to direct any churlishness at anyone any time soon, but she wanted to shield Holly from him nonetheless. All the Keller children had been at the receiving end of more than a few of Gordon's tirades, and Kade saw no reason to extend his influence to the present day.

"I want to believe it." Kade also wanted to believe Jen was right, that she somehow held the power to prevent her father from further inflicting emotional harm on her and those she cared about. They returned to the table and retook their seats. "Keep in mind I can leave any time."

"This isn't TV, Kade. Promise me you don't have your heart set on him saying something forgiving or heartwarming or even remotely human."

Kade stabbed a piece of melon. "You mean a camera crew won't be there to capture the joyful reunion, complete with maudlin voice-over?"

"Why are you doing this?"

"Because I'm a masochist?" At Holly's glare, Kade set her fork down. "Sorry. Not funny. I know you're worried about me. I promise that I think we have very little chance to reconcile. Here's the thing. If I do this and it turns out to be a mistake, at least I'll have made it based on being compassionate. I don't think that could ever be the wrong choice." Kade understood the breadth of Jen's influence in that moment, because she did not doubt her own words.

Holly pushed some berries around with her fork.

"Do you?" Kade asked.

"Damn it. No. But if you're going to do this, you're going in armed." Holly scooted her chair back and left the kitchen. She returned with the bag she'd dropped in the entryway and laid a gift-wrapped item on the table, leaving one in the bag. It was rectangular in shape and about a foot long. "Open it," Holly directed her, moving away their place settings.

Suspicion crept into Kade's consciousness since Holly was a bit of a practical joker, but Holly's demeanor was more solemn than usual, so she proceeded as requested.

Kade ripped the decorated paper and unearthed a brown box. After removing the cover, she pushed away the zigzag paper shavings that cushioned whatever was inside. It was made of delicately carved wood, cylindrical in shape, similar to but heavier than the cardboard inside a paper-towel roll. The base of one end was wider than the rest of the body, and at the opposite end was a dime-size hole. A kaleidoscope? She peered through the hole toward the light fixture above the table. As she rotated the base, gorgeous, colorful images, shapes that melded into others before disappearing and reappearing, greeted her.

"It's stunning," Kade said as she held it in her lap. She knew better than to remind Holly it wasn't her birthday. She wondered why Holly had bestowed such a gift.

"I want it to serve as a reminder that your father doesn't see you the way Cassie did or I do or Jen does or anyone else. He views things through a different lens. Everyone else sees the dynamic, boundless, beautiful person you are." She pointed to the kaleidoscope. "As if through that. Your father doesn't and can't. Don't ever forget it."

Kade studied her gift. She'd never thought her father might see things differently from others. Was her near-lifelong rift with him really so simple? Did their issues stem from him not seeing her for who she was? She covered Holly's hand. "This is easily the best present I've ever received. Thank you."

Holly smiled and gave Kade's hand a brief squeeze. "Well, don't judge yet, because there's one more." Holly delved into her bag and handed Kade a larger wrapped package. "Feel free to take this with you today."

Kade stripped off the gift wrap and laughed. This was much more up Holly's alley. It was a child's toy, a Viking set of a plastic sword, chest armor, helmet, and shield. "I'm suddenly feeling extraordinarily prepared for my visit."

"Kill two birds with one stone. You can protect yourself when you see your dad and wear it the next time you see Jen. Women love a gal in uniform."

"No doubt if she was wavering, this would seal the deal. But I thought you'd cooled on her."

"I don't blame her for wanting you to make some sort of peace with your father. Her heart's in the right place. I just wish he were."

"You wish his heart were in the right place?"

"No. I wish he were in the right place, geographically speaking. Siberia, for example."

❖

Kade didn't want to stare, even if her father wasn't paying attention to her. She moved to stand at the foot of the bed, into what she thought was his line of vision. "Hi, Dad. It's Kade."

His eyes shifted slightly, enough for Kade to think he'd understood her. His gaze passed through her line of sight, caught and held her eyes briefly, yet didn't settle upon her. During those few moments, she saw no emotion there, no recognition of her specifically.

She did stare then, not because of his distorted face, but because she was at a loss for what should come next. She looked to him for some sign of the steps she ought to take, some guidance for dealing with this incredibly uncomfortable situation. What now? What was she supposed to say to the man she'd loved and lost, the father who'd emotionally abandoned her before she left grade school? What was left to salvage?

Perhaps fueled by her self-preservation instinct, Kade felt a strong urge to remain physically distant from him. He'd never struck her—she wasn't worried about him in any physical sense, clearly not now, and not ever. At his worst, he'd grab her by the arm and pull her down the hallway to shove her into her bedroom before shutting the door. Hardly Father of the Year material and nothing she'd wish to emulate should she ever have a child. But for likely the same reason she found herself holding her arm across her torso in a self-protective gesture, she could not sit by his side. Glancing around the room, she searched for something else besides the heavy, square visitors' chair pushed back near the wall to the right of the bed. She spied a folding chair resting against the wall beneath the television set, and she took it. She unfolded it at the right corner of the bed and sat.

Seconds passed. Minutes. Flicking her eyes along the walls in search of a clock and failing to find one, she glanced at her watch. Time obviously passed slower here. Whether it was the facility, her state of mind, or the unsettled state between them, she wasn't sure, but the three minutes that had ticked by felt like thirty.

Gordon's eyes closed. Kade didn't know if he'd fallen asleep or was resting. After more minutes slowly passed, Kade asked, "Dad?" He didn't respond. "Gordon?" She asked another three times during several more minutes. Nothing.

"I'm not sure what I'm doing here, either," she said to the room. And then she began to slowly release words into the air, as if once she let them go, she could allow herself to leave as well.

"I don't want to be here, and you probably don't want me here. So it's a little crazy that I am. I guess I should start by saying I'm sorry this happened to you. We've had our issues, but I didn't—I'd never have wished this upon you or anyone.

"What else? Still single. Still gay—I know you like that one. I'm a venture capitalist now, writing checks with other people's money, spending most of my days in meetings. You'd hate that, being the outdoorsman you are. Oh—Holly Keller still works for me. She says 'hi,' by the way."

A teensy lie. Holly wanted to say a lot of things to Gordon, and 'hi' wasn't on the list.

"This place is supposed to be good, Dad. Reputable. Competent. Solid rehab program. The works.

"So. Not much more to report. I plan on popping by to check on you. Hope you're okay with that." Kade gave a hollow laugh. "Hope I'm okay with that. All right then." Kade stood, the blatant omission weighing heavily on her shoulders, holding her in the room. She sat back down.

"There's this woman." Kade sighed, rudderless. "This amazing, warm, gifted…" She stopped mid-thought. Why go there? He wouldn't want to hear it, and it's not as if she and Jen had a chance.

Still, she wanted to get everything on the table. She wasn't here as a doting daughter.

"You probably don't remember being moved to this facility or what the other one was like, but she thought you might do better in a place like this. She's also the one who suggested I visit you, against my better judgment. To what end, I have no idea. Baffling, I know, since she knows our history."

Kade shrugged and shook her head. "So. Now you know everything. We don't have to pretend this is anything else." Kade picked up the chair, folded it, and returned it to its place along the wall. She once again stopped at the foot of the bed, leaving the steady rise and fall of Gordon's chest the only movement in the room. It was mechanical. Emotionless. A body trying to survive. Kade recognized herself in those signs.

CHAPTER TWENTY

The following evening, Kade entered her father's room and took the visitors' chair this time, which was placed to his right, his good side. She dragged its massive weight closer to the bed, sat, and crossed her legs. She clicked off the television and set the remote back on the tray in front of him. With effort, she willed herself to touch his arm as part of her greeting and don a friendlier expression than the coolness she felt inside. Touching the stroke victim was recommended practice. "Hi, Dad. It's me again."

Gordon didn't move.

Kade used a direct approach, as she'd read about. "Look at me, Dad."

Gordon turned his head slightly and moved his eyes to hers.

"How are you feeling today?" The question sounded inane to Kade's own ears. What was he supposed to say? Not that he could say anything anyway, but whether the answer was "great" or "terrible," what was she going to do about it?

"Are they treating you well?" Again, Kade felt impotent. They couldn't communicate, and given their history, she wasn't sure that was such a bad thing. How could she possibly visit him at length, with any regularity? It hadn't been two minutes, and she felt drained.

Thinking of minutes, she opened the large shopping bag she'd set on the floor and held up two square boxes. "Wall clocks," she said, as she opened the boxes. "Cheapies from the office-supply store to start with, but you must be going crazy not being able to see the time whenever you want." From the moment she'd first stepped into his room, she knew Gordon Davenport wouldn't settle in unless he could constantly monitor the time. Once she popped the batteries in, she set about hanging them with adhesive hooks. The folding chair she stood on didn't allow her to hang them as high as she wished, but when she reviewed her handiwork, she was satisfied.

Another thought took hold as she scrutinized his surroundings. Cold. No warmth, no personalization of any kind. No photographs, no books, no plants aside from one plastic orchid. Two pieces of framed art seemed generic and un-Gordon-like, as if they'd come with the place. One way to give the room a decidedly Gordon feel was to have someone set up one of his beloved train sets. She'd contact the same company that had rigged the one in her condo and send them here.

She retook her seat by his side, and her gaze landed on his, fixated on the nearest clock. Less than ten minutes had passed. Oh boy, this was going to be fun. At least he'd noticed her contribution to his decor. No doubt clock-watching would be his preferred pastime until the train arrived.

When Gordon's eyes returned to hers, they softened. Rightly or wrongly, she took this as a sign she'd done something correctly.

She eyed his hand. She'd always thought he had strong hands, and this one at least—the right one—appeared the same as she remembered. She hadn't held it since she was a girl. Pushing past her distaste for him, she took it in hers.

"Odd twist of fate that I wish you could speak." She sighed. She wasn't here to make her father feel bad. She squeezed his hand. "Sorry."

Wait. Was that…? Did he…? "Dad. If you can understand me, would you squeeze my hand twice?"

He squeezed twice.

"Wow, okay. Wow. That's great. Um, let's try two squeezes for yes and one for no. Does that work?"

Two squeezes.

"We need to get you started on speech therapy right away. I'll talk to your doctor. Has anyone talked to you about speech therapy yet?"

Nothing.

She mentally replayed her question. Her research indicated that stroke patients often had difficulty comprehending complex ideas or ordering their thoughts. Should she simplify the question? Then she realized she ought to add one more concept. "Dad, give me three squeezes if you don't know an answer, okay?"

Two squeezes.

"Has a doctor been here?"

Three squeezes.

"Okay. It's only day two. But still. The sooner the better, from what I've heard. I'll get on them." Kade thought back to her running-at-the-mouthathon yesterday. Uh-oh. "Dad, do you remember my visit yesterday?"

Two squeezes.

Ugh. Had he heard her, or had he been asleep? She'd said she didn't want to be here. At the time, it was true. Was it still? Kade kept her hand on her father's, even though she felt like pulling away. Yes, it was true. Maybe a degree or two less unequivocal, but given other choices, pretty much anything she could think of, including getting a Pap smear or dental X-rays, was superior to sitting here with him. Still, she got a little excited at the prospect she wouldn't have to do it in silence or by performing monologues. But they had too much hurt between them, too many years of disappointment built on top of disappointment, for her to want to spend time with him.

What if she asked him the same question? She'd told him she thought he probably didn't want her here. Should she ask? If he said he wanted to be left alone, would she adhere to his wishes or show up despite them?

Jen's suggestion that Kade visit him was the only reason she was here, and it wasn't predicated on what either she or her father wished. Kade had sole control over whether to learn the answer, since he couldn't very well bring it up himself. As much as she feared yet another rejection, shouldn't she find out his preference? What if he did want her there, but only to relieve what must be nearly overwhelming boredom, making Kade as indifferent to him as any nurse? The answers could be incredibly painful, reopening wounds that had long since scarred over.

No. Perhaps one day soon, she'd ask. Today, she wasn't ready. Perhaps they could balance along the blade of polite, blunt-edged conversation long enough to one day tip the scales to a different answer, one that said they both wanted this time together. Today was not that day. Not for her.

❖

Jen didn't recognize the second car in Nana's driveway. It wasn't time for a shift change, so she wasn't sure what it portended. Laughter greeted her as she opened the front door. Nana and another gray-haired woman were seated at the dining-room table, shaking with glee. Upon seeing Jen, the woman immediately rose and moved toward her, smiling warmly and holding her arms out for a hug. "Jennifer Spencer. You're beautiful in the photos your grandmother sends me, but they don't do you justice. You've grown into a stunning young woman."

"Mrs. Talmadge?" What was Nana's former neighbor doing here? Jen returned the embrace. Mr. and Mrs. Talmadge had lived two doors down from Edna and Ben for many years until Mr. Talmadge's heart attack. After his death, Mrs. Talmadge had moved to Arizona—or was it Nevada?—to live with their son. "It's so good to see you." Jen pulled back and studied the woman, who was a good decade younger than Edna and several inches shorter than Jen. "You look fantastic." Mrs. Talmadge had large brown eyes and salt-and-pepper hair that curled slightly under her chin. Jen had always thought she was an attractive woman, and time had been kind to her. "What brings you to our neck of the woods?" Jen asked as she stooped to give Nana a kiss on the cheek.

"A lovely idea of your father's, actually. He asked if I could visit for a few days." Jen assumed her own confusion was obvious because Mrs. Talmadge continued as she retook her seat. "He had someone handle all the details so you wouldn't have to be bothered." Mrs. Talmadge smiled toward Edna. "He also explained how Edna was doing, and I was so delighted to learn she still lived in the old neighborhood. We were talking about old Mr. Stinkpot, weren't we, Edna?"

Jen appreciated Mrs. Talmadge's understated way of saying she'd been apprised of Edna's declining mental faculties, but she remained confused. Her father didn't have an assistant, nor had he ever suggested that Edna have a friend over, much less be instrumental in getting it to happen.

Edna snickered. "I'll never know what God-awful things he planted in that garden of his, but between that and the manure, it was like living next to a farm." She shifted her attention to Jen. "Do you remember Mr. Stinkpot?"

Jen smiled, pleased Edna seemed to be having a good day and enjoying her time with Mrs. Talmadge. She could hear Doreen in the kitchen and relaxed. All seemed well, if not as expected. She poured herself some iced tea from the pitcher on the table and joined them. "I do. The neighborhood kids used to take Cottonwood Street so we wouldn't have to bicycle past his smelly yard. What are your plans while you're here?"

Mrs. Talmadge eyed Edna fondly. "Golly. Whatever this troublemaker's up for, I suppose. Thought we might visit the Winchester Mystery House, or maybe the municipal gardens. Doreen's welcome to join us if she'd like." She turned to Jen. "You too, Jennifer. What do you think, Edna? Up for some adventure? Or would you prefer to stick close by?"

Edna tilted her head toward Jen and smiled. "This one's always on me about getting outside more."

"Can you join us?" Mrs. Talmadge asked Jen.

"Unfortunately, I have to work. But I'm jealous. It all sounds terrific. Where are you staying, Mrs. Talmadge? Here? Can I help you with any luggage or anything?"

Mrs. Talmadge waved a hand at Jen. "Heavens, no. I wouldn't want to put Edna out on my account. I haven't checked in yet, but I think she said it's called The Newcastle Inn. Downtown."

"She?"

"Oh, the nice woman who booked everything for me. Holly someone."

"Holly Keller?"

"Yes. That's right."

What the heck was Kade doing in the middle of this?

"I'm afraid I'm not clear on all the details, but I'm thrilled to be the beneficiary of all those extra mileage points," Mrs. Talmadge said.

Jen was confused again. "Mileage points?"

"Holly said your father had a number of expiring travel rewards and wanted to ensure they weren't wasted. He must have had a lot of points. Holly said everything's covered, and she even overnighted a Visa gift card for some spending money. So thoughtful."

Thoughtful, yes. Accurate, no. Jen's father had been the butt of countless family jokes over his fear of flying. When Jen's parents moved East to take care of her maternal grandparents, they drove across the country because of his refusal to board a plane. Holly had been spinning a yarn to Mrs. Talmadge. Jen wondered why. She gazed at Nana, whose expression gladdened Jen to the point of not caring. Mrs. Talmadge was here, and Nana was elated.

Jen laid her hand on Mrs. Talmadge's. "Promise to include me in your dinner plans during your stay, and promise you'll forgive me when I tell you about the time we left a dead fish in poor Mr. Stinkpot's azaleas."

❖

Kade had an immediate problem with her visit aside from her father's inability to communicate. The technology device she brought to aid conversation required her to sit close to him. Gordon's facial deformity didn't make Kade squeamish or bother her. Had he been healthy and talkative, she wouldn't want to be near him either. Physical proximity to him made her uncomfortable. He'd been a father and playmate when she was a child, happily tossing her into the air, carrying her on his shoulders, tickling or hugging her, yet he grew into a man who didn't show affection even if he'd felt it, which she doubted. Distancing themselves from each other physically had been the order of the day during her teenage years and the only way they managed to live under the same roof.

Now, a shared tablet was the sole tool they had to try to engage in any conversation, and Kade didn't delight in the prospect of sitting next to him for long stretches of time.

As she had the first day, she grabbed the folding chair, sensing it would make her feel less restricted than the heavy visitors' chair near his bed. She clicked off the TV, laid the tablet on her lap, and covered her father's hand. Cheating a little, she thought of Jen's beautiful smile, knowing the image would compel her to smile as well. It worked, and she brought her focus to her father's face.

"Hi, Dad."

Gordon shifted his eyes to hers and nudged her palm.

"It's good to see you," she said politely, if not truthfully. Placing the tablet on the bed between them, she said, "I've brought you something. It's a tool for us to be able to communicate better than we can on our own." Kade pushed aside the thought that they could have used something like it years ago.

She swiped the screen to bring it to life. "I've never used anything like this—well, a tablet, yes, this kind of software, no—so we'll both be figuring this out as we go along."

Frustration mounted as Kade sat with Gordon and opened the different exercises the software offered, hoping to land on one that piqued his interest. She found it difficult to explain simple technological concepts to him, regardless of the software company's reputation for ease of use. Gordon had spent his life outdoors, not behind a computer screen. No app could bridge that gap, at least not one she knew of.

For his part, Gordon was recalcitrant, which didn't help matters. Kade was used to his irritable demeanor, but after learning that some of his motor skills had returned, she'd hoped for solid progress. Today, he scarcely applied himself, if his restored ability to shake his head didn't count. She wasn't sure whether it was due to her visit, resentment about his condition, or something else. She was inexperienced with asking simple yes/no questions, and the most she could get out of him was that he wasn't in physical discomfort. But with the few swipes of his hand across the tablet, the only thing he did was return time and again to the home screen and tap the clock in the corner.

And then an idea struck her. Gordon was such a schedule hound, Kade wondered if he was telling her he wasn't in the loop about when the daily routines were supposed to happen and, as importantly, whether they were happening on time. Setting aside the tablet, she asked, "Has anyone given you your daily schedule?"

He shook his head, which in reality wasn't a shake so much as a slow turn of several degrees to one side and back again.

"Okay. I'll track down a nurse and make sure they share it with you. And I'll ask them to pay particular attention to arriving promptly at the times designated." If Gordon had a button to push, being off schedule would press it with the force of an explosion. "Keep in mind, Dad, some of the residents need more help than others, so sometimes the staff won't be able to keep to the schedule as much as you'd like. Okay?"

He nodded.

Kade wasn't convinced her father would handle disruptions to the schedule quite so easily when they actually occurred, but it wasn't as though he was in a position to do anything other than accept them. They'd had enough for the day, and Kade told him she'd return tomorrow. She consulted her calendar and specified seven o'clock. Hopefully he'd be more conducive toward his own therapy by then. She wondered whether his speech therapist was having better luck. It was doubtful those sessions could be worse.

CHAPTER TWENTY-ONE

When the doorbell rang, Kade practically jumped from her chair. It was approaching an hour since she'd called in her order to the Thai delivery place, and she was hungry. One of the downsides to takeout was the lack of attention to keeping within estimated delivery windows, like ordering new cable service. She opened the door, startled to see Jen holding a white plastic bag smelling of food.

"Looking for this?" Jen said as she brushed past Kade without waiting for an invitation. "I love being white-listed with building security."

Kade's hunger vanished. She closed the door and backed against it, staring at her visitor's departing form. She heard Jen calling out from the kitchen, "Hope you don't mind sharing." Kade couldn't move. She wasn't prepared to deal with Jen. She knew what her heart wanted, and every day the hold that her head had over her desires and actions grew more tenuous. Weak-willed had never been a term she would have used to describe herself before Jen, but she couldn't deny the degree to which Jen made Kade want to disregard every self-imposed boundary she constructed between them. Several moments passed before Jen returned to the entryway, grabbed Kade's hand, and tugged her toward the kitchen. "Come."

Kade parked herself with a shoulder against the wall while Jen opened the cardboard containers and began scooping rice, curry, and noodles onto two plates.

Jen asked, "What's that look for?"

"It's good to see you." And Jen was good to see, looking scrumptious in boot-cut, low-rise jeans and a casual, white button-down shirt that did little to hide the dark bra beneath, hugging curves Kade shouldn't be thinking about. Her hair was down and fell around her shoulders, perfectly framing her face as if she were starring in a shampoo commercial. Kade shoved her hands into her pockets to prevent herself from threading its soft strands through her fingers.

Jen stilled the serving spoon and met Kade's eyes. "Hungry, I see."

Immediately, Kade broke eye contact, having forgotten how well Jen could read her.

"I should be angry with you for the mixed messages," Jen said. "Setting boundaries and then crossing them by wooing me. But you don't even know you're doing it, do you?"

This confusing jumble of information was lost on Kade, who opted to open a bottle of chilled German Riesling for the to-be-determined occasion. "Wooing you?"

"I thought so," Jen said as she continued dishing. "Do you know who I met the other day?"

"Are we playing Twenty Questions?" Kade asked as she pulled wineglasses from the cupboard.

"Hunter, the shepherd mix."

Kade was unaware of what this tidbit meant. "As in German shepherd?"

Jen nodded. "Hunter was visiting Nana for the second time, his handler told me," Jen said as she began closing the containers. "He reminds her so much of her old dog Roscoe, she was beside herself with joy."

Kade busied herself pouring the wine since she had no idea what Jen was talking about. She hoped it would become obvious soon, so she wouldn't have to make a fool of herself by asking about something she was supposed to know.

"Hunter's a therapy dog whose owner takes him around to visit people who register to receive volunteer service animals. Lo and behold, Nana registered." The look Jen bestowed on Kade made it clear she knew Nana wasn't involved in that part. "Isn't that interesting?"

"Good for Edna," Kade said as she corked the bottle. "This, on the heels of my grandmother's dear friend visiting from Tucson. Another high note for Nana recently."

"This all sounds really great, Jen. I'm glad."

Amazingly adept at tracking down the napkins and water goblets, considering how little time she'd spent in Kade's kitchen, Jen set them on the table. "On top of that, Creative Care is already garnering interest from several of the VCs on our wish list that you've put us in touch with. Jeremy and I have our first meetings on Monday."

No longer on an uncomfortable subject, Kade closed the fridge and grinned. "Fantastic news. Yay."

"Know what else?" Jen asked as she dimmed the dining-room lights and turned off the bright kitchen ones.

Kade remained planted in front of the fridge, stilled by the gleam in Jen's eyes.

Resting the small of her back against the counter, Jen smiled in a way Kade could only describe as wicked. "Our food's going to get cold."

Kade swallowed with difficulty.

"Don't worry, Kade. I'm not going to throw myself at you."

Smiling slyly, Kade voiced her train of thought. "And here I thought I might discover a whole new meaning to the words 'special delivery.'"

Jen returned Kade's smile. Unhurriedly, she began to unbutton her shirt, offering tantalizing glimpses of trim torso beneath. "You're going to throw yourself at me."

Kade's eager eyes took in every inch of skin exposed by the ambient light, and the sound of her heartbeat began to crescendo in her ears. "Jen…" Oh, why was it suddenly so hard to speak? "Please don't do that."

"Holly did an admirable job of keeping a low profile, but I'm afraid it wasn't enough to remain incognito."

Kade shook her head, eyes trained on each button being unfastened. Jen was like a matador, waving a red cape that tantalized and stirred the bull. "I'm not sure I follow," she said, though she had a pretty good idea.

"You seem to understand far better ways to woo a woman than with chocolate or roses. Treat someone she loves with kindness."

Wishing she had something to grasp in order to keep her hands from reaching out for Jen, Kade wrapped her arms around herself. "I wasn't…I wouldn't use Edna or play with someone's emotions to get to you."

"I know. Your only objection to us is that you'll hurt me. Is that accurate?"

Objection. Yes. With Jen deliriously close, looking so edible, Kade found it difficult to recall why they shouldn't be together. Wresting her eyes from Jen's body to her face, Kade met Jen's gaze. She nodded.

"How? My company's already running out of money so you can't make it worse. You can't fire me since we both have a board seat and cancel each other out. You can't impact my marriage or relationship because I'm not in one. I'm in fund-raising mode, so I'm not doing anything adventurous any time soon." Jen slowly untucked her shirt until it hung loose and bared more flesh. "What else?" Jen's eyes sparkled with mischief.

"Jen, so help me God, if you don't cover up—"

"You'll do what?" Jen leaned back, resting her palms on the counter, parting her top. Black, lace-covered mounds of pale flesh rose and fell with each breath.

The matador's cape whipped around. Provoking.

"This can only end badly," Kade said, holding on to the last vestige of any argument against this seduction.

"The only way you can hurt me is to not touch me."

The thread by which Kade's willpower was hanging snapped. She strode over to Jen and slid one hand inside her shirt and around her waist, while, with the other, she teased a nipple through thin satin. Jen's arms immediately came around Kade's shoulders as she tried to pull Kade in for a kiss, but Kade kept their mouths millimeters apart. She wanted to savor the anticipation, to feel Jen's breath against her lips while she caressed the body she so craved. This close, she caught hints of apricot from Jen's shampoo. Her eyes latched onto Jen's blue ones, seeing desire there and an intoxicating mix of confidence and vulnerability.

The hitch in Jen's breath from the light graze of Kade's thumb was the death knell to holding out longer. With one sweep of her arm, Kade shoved aside everything from the edge of the counter. Then she lifted Jen onto it, stepped between her legs, and pulled her head down for a demanding kiss.

Jen threaded her fingers in Kade's hair until she was cupping the back of her head, matching her abandon. Wet heat blossomed in Kade's mouth as she welcomed Jen's tongue inside. Kade slipped both hands inside Jen's shirt, splaying her fingers across her bare back and hugging her more tightly against her. All other thoughts faded from her mind. Only Jen existed, and she couldn't get close enough.

Kade made short work of Jen's front-closure bra, freeing the ample flesh and breaking their kiss to draw a breast into her mouth. She gently scraped the nipple with her teeth, arousal shooting through her at the sound of Jen's gasp.

She wanted to taste more of Jen, but as she released the button on Jen's jeans and slid the zipper down, she realized she should have freed Jen from her pants before setting her onto the counter. Not that she had a ton of experience trying to take advantage of women in her own kitchen—though Thai food would forever hold sentimental appeal.

Kade kissed Jen and saw a glimpse of a smile, as if Jen was cognizant of the access restrictions Kade faced. "Although you would definitely be the sexiest thing I've ever eaten in here, I'm inclined to move this to the bedroom."

Jen slid off the counter and took Kade's hand. She marched them straight into the master bathroom, removed her footwear, and started the shower. Turning around and swiftly tugging Kade's shirt over her head and off, she asked, "I take it you're okay delaying dinner?"

"You know what they say," Kade replied, as Jen moved to the waistband of Kade's slacks.

Jen unbuttoned and unzipped, slid her hands into Kade's bikinis, and worked the clothing off her hips. "What do they say?" Although she was standing before Jen in only her bra, the way Jen was devouring her with her eyes bolstered Kade's confidence. "Life is short. Eat dessert first."

Shrugging off her bra and shirt, and shimmying out of her remaining items, Jen cocked her head toward the shower. "Dessert might get wet." Splendid in her nakedness, Jen entered the stall and dipped her head back to let the water saturate her hair and cascade down her body.

Breathtaking, Kade thought. She swiftly removed her bra and stepped into the shower, feeling for the handle and closing the glass door behind her. "I certainly hope so." Her voice sounded lower to her own ears. It had a needy, desperate edge.

Jen slowly turned in a circle as she leisurely palmed her torso, sides, and arms. Brazenly raising a leg and assuming a wide stance on the small shower seat, Jen moved out of the spray until her back rested against the tile, giving Kade access to more than the water. She met Kade's gaze and continued caressing herself, one hand running across her breasts, the other along her inner thighs. Her lips parted slightly and she leveled Kade with a lustful look, demanding participation.

Emboldened and completely turned on by Jen's wantonness, Kade advanced, quickly ducking under the showerhead. Then she launched herself at Jen, pressing her against the wall, plundering her mouth with her tongue and swiftly entering her. Jen broke the kiss to cry out, wrapping her arms around Kade for balance. Kade swallowed Jen's cries, needing to be inside of her, surrounding her, part of her.

And still there was too much distance for Kade. Abruptly she dropped to one knee and put her mouth to Jen's center, devouring her. She sheathed her fingers into Jen's slick heat and stroked her as she continued to work her with her tongue, spurred by the wet warmth evidencing Jen's desire.

"Yes, Kade. Oh, God. More." Jen's moans were joyful music to Kade's ears, and she increased speed, pushing Jen farther, higher. It wasn't long before Jen's muscles convulsed around her. She eased slowly to her feet, worshipping Jen's body with her mouth and hands as she rose, enjoying the slight tug of Jen's hands in her hair, urging her upward.

Upright once again, Kade was enveloped in Jen's arms and met with a passionate kiss. The feel of their warm, wet skin against each other was exhilarating, and the shower quickly vaulted to her favorite area of the condo.

As they toweled themselves dry, Kade couldn't take her eyes off Jen. She wanted to ask what had possessed Jen to come on to her in such a decisive way. Was Jen simply needing an outlet, a way to keep her mind off her grandmother's situation and the challenges facing Creative Care? Or was it more than that? Nothing had changed between them, had it? Kade still couldn't give Jen more of herself. Yet she just had. She hadn't skipped a beat. She wanted Jen as much as Jen seemed to want her. Why had she given in so easily? So completely? Why didn't she have the willpower to keep Jen at arm's length?

"Hey." Jen's voice brought Kade back to the moment. Jen threw a towel over Kade's shoulders and held her by it. "Stop it."

Kade wrapped her towel around Jen and her arms around the towel to keep Jen warm, though the steam in the room was sufficient. "Stop what?"

"Overanalyzing."

Kade rested her forehead against Jen's and closed her eyes. She couldn't deny how good she felt, how she wanted to be closer. She pulled Jen to her, letting the towel drop, relishing the feel of their bodies intertwining, of Jen's arms coming around her.

She was falling in love and completely unprepared for dealing with it.

To her shame, her emotions threatened to overwhelm her, and tears welled in her eyes.

Jen cradled Kade's head and tenderly kissed Kade's wet eyes before wrapping her arms around her again. "I've got you," she said softly.

And Kade felt it, felt that Jen would hold her up and not let her fall. She wanted to ask why Jen cared, why she was here of her own volition, what she saw in Kade that Kade couldn't see. Yet as she looked into blue eyes shining with adoration, she wondered if it was better not to know, not to understand. The magician's magic was more awe-inducing when you weren't informed of the inner workings of the trick.

She unleashed the tiniest shake of her head as she stroked Jen's cheek, amazed and grateful to be sharing this moment with her.

Jen kissed the hand caressing her face. "It's reciprocal, you know. I see the same thing being reflected back to me."

Kade tilted her head, not following.

"What you're seeing is how being with you makes me feel," Jen added.

Jen's face was so earnest, Kade almost checked her immediate inclination to doubt. "How can you mean that?"

"How can I not?" Jen turned Kade around to face the mirror and scooped a towel from the floor to wipe away the steam. Standing behind Kade, looking over her shoulder, she asked, "Who's the prettiest brunette in this room?"

Kade laughed and turned her head. "I'm the only brunette in this room."

Jen used her index finger to push Kade's chin back around so they were once again seeing themselves through the mirror. "Answer the question."

"I am."

"Don't look at me. Look at you. Who successfully started and sold two companies in her twenties?"

"I did."

"Who came to my house to check on me and help me with my fund-raising deck?"

"I did."

"Who gave my grandmother the incredibly thoughtful gifts of inviting a friend and companion animal over?"

Kade wasn't about to take credit. She turned her head as far around as she could. "Who didn't even bother asking if you needed help with anything?"

"I'm asking the questions. Who singlehandedly jump-started Creative Care's referral program?"

"Who rushed to judgment when you couldn't make it to those meet—"

Jen clasped her hand over Kade's mouth. "God, you're terrible at this." Jen slid an arm around Kade's waist and brushed Kade's hair off a shoulder with her other hand. She dropped kisses along the exposed skin. "Who gave me an incredible orgasm a little while ago?"

Kade angled her head to allow Jen greater access. "I did."

"Mmm-hmm." Nuzzling at the crook between Kade's neck and shoulder, Jen said, "Move your eyes to me and ask me how I'm feeling."

"How are you feeling?"

Jen smiled. "I'm happy."

Kade returned Jen's smile. "It looks good on you." Kade liked the way Jen's statement made her feel. Jen's happiness mattered.

"It does. Now look at yourself while I say it again."

It wasn't easy to not make eye contact with someone speaking to her, but Kade acquiesced.

"You make me happy," Jen said.

"I'm glad."

"Do you see that? Your expression closes slightly, like the tone of your voice. They both stiffen. You're not comfortable hearing me say that, and you're not glad."

Kade couldn't disagree. Part of her wanted to be able to make Jen happy, yet another part wanted Jen to find happiness with someone else.

Jen turned Kade around and cradled her face in her hand before kissing her. She slid her other hand down Kade's back and cupped her ass, pulling their bodies together. As always, Kade immediately responded, holding Jen to her and savoring the press of breast to breast, thigh to thigh, belly to belly. Jen gently nibbled Kade's bottom lip before releasing her and shifting her to once again face the mirror. Kade could see as well as feel the more rapid rise and fall of her chest before her breathing returned to normal.

"Now," Jen said as she threaded her fingers in Kade's damp hair and massaged her scalp. "Close your eyes. Think of my mouth on yours, my hands and tongue worshipping your body, the sound of my voice instructing and cherishing you, hours of uninterrupted time together."

"Mmm." Kade heard herself moan in appreciation of her imagination's visuals and Jen's seductive murmuring.

Jen's arms encircled Kade's waist, and she kissed the back of her neck. "Open your eyes." Kade found Jen's eyes in the mirror. Jen said, "Now look at you." Kade met her own gaze. She watched and felt Jen kiss her temple, then her cheek, then below her ear. She covered Jen's arms with hers. Jen continued. "*That* is how being with me makes you feel. *That's* what I see when I'm sharing myself with you. Amazing, isn't it? Look at you. You're luminous. Breathtaking."

Without a doubt, Kade felt treasured. She didn't understand the logic behind the feeling, but it was unmistakable. Jen rested her chin on her shoulder, tenderness exuding from her gorgeous blue eyes that met hers once again via the mirror.

"Do one thing for me?" Jen asked.

"There are few things I wouldn't do for you, if I could."

"Don't laugh at what I'm about to say, because I've never been more serious. Got it?"

Kade nodded, surprised by the sudden solemnity of Jen's tone.

Jen pointed to their images before wrapping her arms around Kade. "Say this with me. 'I deserve to be loved.'"

Jen's earnestness stripped Kade of her tendency to deflect, and she stifled the sarcastic reply on her tongue. Holy cow. Jen actually expected her to say the words genuinely.

Kade's features quickly blurred through her tears. She opened her mouth to speak, but her throat closed, and she dropped her gaze.

"Tall order for you, I know. But it's true. You do." Again Jen kissed her temple. "You may be the boss, but I'm giving you homework. Next time I see you, I want to hear you say it, and I want to hear in your voice that you believe it."

Why were the words "next time" sending a thrill along Kade's spine? Why was she struck by hope? Why was she feeling a shade optimistic she might somehow break the cycle of hurting people she cared for? Was she so desperate for the possibility of a future with Jen that she was willing to cast aside her certainty of causing Jen pain when all facts dictated its inevitability?

Kade turned in the circle of Jen's arms and faced her. "Say that again."

"You deserve to be loved?"

"No. *Next time*. Say *next time*."

With a kiss to her nose, Jen said, "Next time I see you."

"I don't want to aim for deserving to be loved. I want to aim for deserving to be loved by you." Kade brushed away a renegade tear. "I want there to be a next time. And a time after that."

Kade was heartened by the obvious pleasure in Jen's expression. She didn't understand why Jen felt she was worthy of love, but she no longer wanted to be the one providing arguments against her own best chance for happiness. She might never be able to look Jen in the eye and repeat the words asked of her—after all, she'd been telling herself the opposite her entire adult life. But if anyone merited a Sisyphean undertaking, it was Jen. "Tell me I have a chance."

Jen held up her thumb and forefinger millimeters apart to indicate Kade's chances, but her smile belied the gesture.

Kade kissed her soundly. "I'll take it."

Jen walked back and forth along Kade's small veranda, talking on the phone to Nana, wearing the same white, long-sleeve shirt she'd arrived in over lacy, black bikinis. Kade was certain it was among the top ten most magnificent visions she'd ever seen. Tasked with scooping sorbet into two mugs, Kade was failing spectacularly, unable to take her eyes off her. Dessert melted slightly with each passing second.

Jen ended the call and slid the door closed behind her. She sat on a kitchen stool, planted an elbow, and rested her chin in her palm.

Her expression was open and content. Kade had never seen anything more beautiful. Warmth emanated from Jen's eyes and coursed through Kade like a shot of fine whiskey.

"How is this going to work?" Jen asked.

Kade looked down at the now-runny strawberry sorbet. "You mean, do I have any straws?"

"No, silly. I mean, how do I see you? Do I have to book appointments?" Jen's tone was light. Teasing.

"I'm not exactly an expert, but I think they're called dates." Kade covered the container and returned it to the freezer, removing a pint of lemon sorbet in its stead.

"Does this mean we're dating?"

Kade frowned. Dating sounded far more casual than what she wanted with Jen. Selfishly, she wanted Jen to herself. But maybe she was alone in that desire. Focusing on dishing out the frozen dessert, she said, "Sure."

"Sure?" Jen's tone wasn't.

"Sounds good," Kade said as she dropped a spoonful of sorbet into a mug. Not wanting to sour the mood, she added, "Let's pick a night."

No, no, no. She was doing it wrong, sensed an unwanted shift in her own demeanor. Jen deserved better. Kade set the spoon down and met Jen's eyes, more guarded than they'd been moments ago. "Damn it. Yes. Yes, I'd love to date you." She moved behind Jen and put her arms around her, entwining their fingers. "Sorry my hands are cold." She dropped a kiss below her ear and pushed past the fear of rejection. "What I really want is to see you exclusively. If that's not what you want, I'll take what I can get. But I'm telling you now, the idea of dating you doesn't come close to capturing how I feel about you."

Jen turned in Kade's arms and cupped her chin. "That wasn't so hard, was it?" She gave Kade a quick kiss, her smile flooding Kade with relief.

"Are you kidding? I've just aged ten years. We're definitely into May-December romance territory now."

"Nana has a spare walker you can borrow."

Kade patted Jen's nose with her index finger. "And here I thought you were the nice one."

"Does that make you the naughty one?"

Kade released Jen, lidded the sorbet, and returned it to the freezer. Dessert, of the frozen variety, could wait. She extended her hand to Jen with a prurient smile. "Let's find out."

Later, as they lay in bed talking, with Kade on her back lazily caressing Jen with one hand, and Jen lying half on the sheets, half on Kade, Jen asked, "What changed your mind? About us?"

Kade knew what she was asking but replied with, "The sex." This was followed by "Ow," as she rubbed her upper arm where Jen had swiftly pinched her, waiting for the real answer. "I don't think I have. I'm still afraid of hurting you, selfish for wanting this."

"It's only selfish if you're primarily concerned with yourself, which is never the case with you."

Stifling a self-deprecating reply, Kade tried to answer honestly. "You rub off on people. On me. In a good way. The person I am when I'm with you…I'm intrigued by her. She—I should say, I—see things in a more positive light. If I can be the person you seem to see, the person I want to see, I'm hoping it outweighs my selfishness in proceeding with us despite my fears."

"The greater good?" Jen asked, humor in her voice.

"Laughing at me?" Kade replied lightly.

"It's sweet, your answer. And funny. A little funny."

"How so?"

"For an intelligent woman, you can be very thick." She rested her palm over Kade's heart. "Those things you like about you? They're already here."

Kade cast a doubtful scowl. "Hibernating?"

Jen laughed, a sound lovelier than any symphony Kade had ever heard. "You're a woman of action, Kade. Nothing about you could remain dormant for long. I think circumstances beyond your control have shaped the way you see yourself. I simply provide you with an alternate lens." She kissed Kade softly. "An accurate one."

The comment mirrored Holly's so closely, Kade wondered if she should give more credence to it than she was inclined to.

"What are you thinking?" Jen asked, slowly caressing Kade's cheek with her fingers.

"Holly said something similar." With a quick kiss, Kade rose and went to fetch the kaleidoscope. She handed it to Jen and turned on a reading light. As Jen studied it and peered into it toward the light, Kade said, "She gave me this before I visited my father in his new place. Said the way he sees the world, and me, isn't how others do."

"What a beautiful gift and sentiment."

"Yes."

Jen set it down and shifted onto her stomach before gently tapping the side of Kade's head. "Are we getting through?"

Kade took Jen's hand and kissed the nudging finger. "I'm glad to have people in my life who are trying."

Jen propped herself on her elbows. "That is an evasive, bullshit answer."

Kade laughed. "I love how you talk to me. So deferential."

"Respect is earned, sunshine."

Leaning in for a gentle kiss, Kade said, "I've been called a lot of things. Sunshine isn't one of them."

"A new day is dawning."

She traced her fingers across Jen's lips. "I like how it's starting."

"Me, too."

CHAPTER TWENTY-TWO

A call from Kade interrupted Jen's busy Monday morning. She left her cubicle to take it in the conference room.
"Hey, you," she said by way of answer.
"Have dinner with me tonight," Kade said.
Jen chuckled. "We just had dinner last night."
"I love how nothing slips past you."
"How is it that your schedule is suddenly so flexible? I would have thought you already had plans tonight."
"I do most of my research in the evenings. This is no different."
"Oh? What are you researching?"
"Your body."
Jen blushed. Although alone in a closed conference room, she dropped her voice. "Kade. I'm at work."
"And I'd like to get back to my research."
Jen chewed her lip. The idea of seeing Kade and the explorations they could undertake brought more heat to her cheeks. Tempting, though tough to pull off tonight. She had massive amounts of work to get through—not the least of which was a follow-up call with Roger Daniels from Matlock Ventures—and wanted time to visit with Nana. Had Kade not brought up Matlock's interest in Creative Care because she wasn't aware Roger was pursuing it or because she didn't want to get Jen's hopes up if things didn't pan out on that front? In either case, they wouldn't have much to discuss if it was a dead-end, and she'd find out soon enough.

She couldn't think of an easy way to carve out a scheduled, sit-down dinner. She'd be fortunate to grab something to eat on the way home. "These are probably among the worst words you ever want to hear, but can we play it by ear? I don't think I can confidently specify a dinner time tonight, and I'd hate to be late."

"Hmm. How about this? I'll order takeout. You'll drop by whenever you can, and I'll have a glass of wine with your name on it for you to consume while I reheat your dinner. No expectations, and if you can't swing it, no problem, though I'll probably call to check in."

"Who are you, and what have you done with Ms. Davenport?"

Kade laughed, sounding as carefree as Jen had ever heard her. She hoped to make time for Kade tonight if only to hear it again.

"Whoever you are, you have yourself a deal," Jen said.

"Excuse me," Kade said as she approached the nurses' station. She'd briefly popped into her father's room and couldn't locate his computer tablet, and Gordon wasn't able to help. A kind-faced, forty-something nurse glanced up and removed her reading glasses.

"Yes?"

"What happened to my father's tablet?"

"Who's your father?"

"Gordon Davenport. Room four-ten."

"One moment." The woman donned her glasses and consulted her computer screen, bending forward so much that Kade wondered if her glasses were the Clark Kent variety—worthless save for hiding an alter ego. "Oh, yes, it's in one of the security lockers. I can have someone fetch it for you if you'd like."

"Why isn't it in his room?"

"Theft prevention. Residents' valuables remain secured unless checked out."

"I bought the tablet specifically to assist in my father's rehab. He'd make more progress if it was available to him whenever he wants it."

"I'm sorry, ma'am. It's policy."

Kade pondered this information while the nurse dialed someone and instructed them on retrieving the device. This facility had state-of-the-art equipment in its gym as well as physical, occupational, and speech therapists to help expedite patient recovery. Why wouldn't they have rehabilitation tools in all the rooms for those who were homework-inclined? Retractable folding wall- or bedframe-mounts could store them out of the way when not in use, and the loaded software could be centrally administered to prevent illegal, harmful, or other non-rehab-specific activities.

As Kade waited, the nurse doffed her glasses and asked, "Has he been receptive to using the tablet?"

Kade nodded. "So far. That's why I think it should be kept beside him."

The nurse smiled. "You must have a special way with him. His speech therapist says he hasn't shown much interest in working with her. But it's early going. Many residents require time to adjust to needing care."

This was news. Aside from the first day, Gordon hadn't hesitated when she used the device with him. She'd brought him here to improve, not while away the days. After an aide approached and handed her the tablet, Kade told the nurse, "I'd like this to remain in his room at all times. I'm happy to sign a waiver stating that I won't hold the facility liable if anything happens to it, be it theft or damage."

"You'll have to speak with one of our administrators."

Kade opened her purse and extracted a business card. "Fine. Please have someone contact me as soon as possible. I'll be here for another hour. After that, I can be reached at this number." Kade scanned the woman's nametag. "Theresa, how many people here are recovering from a stroke?"

"Forty out of our hundred and sixty beds are for stroke and cardiac patients, so at least twenty at any given time."

"Couldn't all of them benefit from having therapeutic tools of some kind next to their beds, versus waiting for their daily gym session?"

"Many of them could, yes."

"The sooner they get help, the better their chances for recovery. Isn't that right?"

"Yes."

An idea was germinating. There had to be a far better way to get rehabilitation technology into the hands of stroke victims, which according to her limited knowledge numbered eight hundred thousand Americans annually. Kade thought back to the first facility her father had been transferred to from the hospital, the one Jen had visited with her. It was a place for people with scant financial resources, and if it offered any rehabilitation services, which Kade couldn't recall, she was sure the technology would be outdated. Successful recovery tools shouldn't be limited to those who could afford it. They should be available to those who needed it.

Kade returned to her father's room and stood inside the doorway. Having been on a mission to locate his tablet earlier, she hadn't taken the time to appreciate the train now traveling around the perimeter of the room.

Gordon was watching it move steadily along its tracks. The train passed a water tower, bridge and railroad crossings, a forest, a coal mine, a hot-air balloon, and a circus with moving rides, including a Ferris wheel, merry-go-round, and a roller coaster, all with working lights. Gordon's room was small, which limited the scenery options, but the workers she'd hired had made the most of the space.

Kade observed Gordon for several minutes before making her presence known. He seemed content and engaged, the train providing a link to his life before his stroke. Kade wasn't familiar with what his world was like before he wound up here. But as she looked around at the miniature scenery and saw the satisfaction in his eyes, she realized this was his home now, for however long he needed to be here. It was a rehabilitation facility, not hospice care. It was a place for living, designed to assist the residents in their journeys to recover at least some degree from their ailments.

Kade was somehow helping him do that, helping him live whatever kind of life he would now have. Clocks and a train set. Simple things that made life worth living for this man.

Yes, he was a man for whom Kade had unresolved, mixed feelings. She could have refused to transfer him to this facility or withheld these small pleasures in order to force a conversation about Cassie's death, but chances were remote that such a discussion—which Gordon was physically incapable of having at present—would have led to his apology or an understanding between them. It hadn't over the course of years and was no more likely now.

But what kind of person would she be if she had the power to bring him comfort and help him improve, yet made their delivery contingent upon him telling her something she wanted to hear?

She'd be like him. Petty at best. Contemptible at worst. She shuddered. She could never require that they resolve their differences before she treated him with simple decency.

A thought occurred to her. Why would she treat herself less favorably than this ill-tempered man? Why withhold from herself small things that could make her happy? Gordon was hardly the most deserving person Kade knew, yet even he ought to be surrounded by meaningful things. Was she less worthy of happiness than her father? Was she less deserving of taking restorative steps to return to the land of the living?

These and similar questions began to swirl in her consciousness, taking up residence. They occupied the same space as her anger toward Gordon, forcing it to shrink, reducing its power.

Could she one day lay to rest her animosity toward her father? She didn't have much faith in the possibility, but she also didn't have as much negative power whirling within her. She was certain of it. On a storm index, the ferocity of Kade's bitterness had already diminished a category or two.

Was this the direction Jen had anticipated things going in when nudging Kade to spend time with Gordon? On one hand, it seemed unlikely Jen could have been so unreasonably optimistic after learning Kade and Gordon's history. On the other, here Kade was, feeling less ill-will toward him.

As she was beginning to learn from being in a relationship for the first time, optimism didn't have to be part of her natural disposition for her to start thinking positively. It all seemed to stem from Jen. Kade had never seen her future look so promising.

❖

After eight, while relaxing on her veranda with a glass of wine, Kade decided to call Jen and get an update on her chances to see her tonight.

"Kadrienne." Jen answered in a gravelly voice as if she'd been chewing on rocks.

Full name and tone of voice said Kade was in trouble. Holly used both on her all the time, but it was a first from Jen. "What's wrong?" Kade asked, sitting up straight.

"Did you perchance express to anyone within Matlock that you had doubts about my ability to lead my company?"

Kade's stomach clenched. "What happened?"

"Answer the question, please."

Kade took a deep breath. "I was on the fence once. You know that. I never said I believed you weren't up for the job."

"Never said it or never believed it?"

"Jen, it's my job to thoroughly evaluate the strengths and weaknesses of every CEO I work with. What's this about?"

"I would hope that if you have reservations about my effectiveness as a leader, you'd have told me personally, so I could address whatever was at issue."

"I have. I did."

"So this is about you thinking I haphazardly flaked on our meetings? I thought we went over this."

"I don't even know what you're talking about. Please tell me."

"Check your inbox." An absence of ambient noise signaled the call had ended.

Kade's phone notified her of an incoming message. When she opened the app, she found an email from Jen.

Subject: Term Sheet.

Our first-term sheet, attached. –Jen

Kade clicked open the file and scanned its contents. It was from Matlock Ventures, and if signed by Creative Care, the company would be agreeing to immediately begin an executive search for a new CEO post-funding.

Essentially, if Jen accepted Roger's offer, she would be fired.

"God damn it! What the…" She entered the kitchen and managed to set her phone on the counter, when what she really wanted to do was throw it. "Fuck!"

Furious with Roger for blindsiding her, she tried to move past the anger enough to think. This couldn't be happening. Surely Roger would have given her a heads-up? And why would he include such a stipulation in the first place? Jen was living the quintessential example of someone who would benefit from the platform Creative Care was building. She offered prospective investors a hands-on, personal view of both the problem and the solution. And she'd engendered loyalty in her team not only by highlighting the real-world importance of the issue Creative Care was solving, but by caring about their well-being as individuals with lives outside of work. It was who Jen was as a person.

Her failure to mention these facts to Roger hit Kade like a punch to her gut.

She needed to see Jen. Explain. Apologize.

She headed to her car, calling Holly as she walked out of her condo. "Find Roger and get me his first available appointment. I don't care how early or late."

Most of the people who lived on Jen's street parked in their garages or driveways, which made cars on the street stand out. Jen could tell as soon as she turned onto her block that a vehicle was stationed in front of her house.

Surprises seemed to be the order of the day, and seeing Kade waiting for her tonight wasn't worse than finding out a top-tier VC firm thought Jen should be fired, but not by much. Jen didn't have any kind words for Kade at the moment, and she tried to live by the maxim, "If you can't say anything nice, don't say anything at all." She clicked open the garage door and pulled in without waving or rolling down a window, hoping Kade would get the message. But before she could click it closed, Kade was inside the garage, standing beside her car as she opened the door.

"Jen, please."

"I have nothing to say to you. Please leave."

"Let me explain."

"It's pretty self-explanatory."

"I didn't know what Roger Daniels had planned."

"Stalking doesn't become you, Kadrienne."

"Please don't call me that."

Jen threw up her arms before crossing them. "Why? Too impersonal? I'll tell you what's impersonal. Taking a call from a VC and having him walk me through a term sheet that stipulates my departure from *my own company*. A company I…"

She stopped short. What good would it do to list everything Creative Care meant to her? She'd started the company from nothing, initially bootstrapping it with a second mortgage and building it by working her ass off for the last two years. Its mission actually meant something to her and could make a difference to people like her who struggled to find quality, affordable home care for someone they loved. Now she was supposed to simply sign on the dotted line and walk away as if she hadn't put her heart and soul into every aspect of the operation?

She stared at Kade, a woman in whom she'd put her trust, shared private misgivings and concerns about the company. How much of what she'd told Kade in confidence had found its way into Roger's offer?

No. This was Kade, one of the most honest people she knew. She wouldn't have revealed information disclosed off the record.

Yet business took precedence for Kade. If a senior partner of the firm it had taken her own sweat equity to break into had solicited her feedback, would she have remained mute about her concerns? How else could Jen explain the highly irregular term-sheet stipulation?

The fact that she was even questioning Kade's integrity and motivations meant they shouldn't be talking. But being mindful enough to understand this notion conceptually didn't mean Jen was above taking pot shots, no matter how much she knew she'd regret them later. The wound was too fresh and too deep not to flinch.

"Don't worry about it. It's only my company, my job, and my passion at stake. No big deal. If you'll excuse this incompetent fool, I'm calling it a night."

The automatic light from the garage door opener wasn't bright, but she couldn't mistake the hurt in Kade's eyes. Jen took no satisfaction from it. She was lashing out like an injured animal but couldn't stop herself. She was overwhelmed and disheartened by the prospect that the only way Creative Care could continue was if she walked away from it. Her baby. Her dream. Emotionally battered and discombobulated, she found herself laying the blame at Kade's feet.

Kade's trembling jaw was the only communication she seemed capable of making in light of the distance now stretching between them like an ocean.

Jen took the single step up to the back door leading to the laundry room and turned to Kade. "You were right, Kade. Congratulations. You hurt me. But if you don't mind, let's skip the I-told-you-so." She touched the button to close the garage door before slipping inside the house, forcing Kade to head swiftly for the driveway.

As the heavy door swung closed and snapped securely into place, Kade sensed she was being locked outside of Jen's heart. The ensuing darkness felt reminiscent of the cloak of dread that had covered her as she watched the snowmobiles head up the mountain in search of Cassie.

This is what Kade had feared from the beginning. She'd gone ahead and done it again in colossal fashion—wounded someone she loved. Nothing like taking aim at the center of someone's universe, obliterating it, and tipping your hat to let them know it was your doing. Having come here to explain, she'd fallen silent. What could she say? She had no excuse. Unless and until she had an alternative opportunity for Creative Care, she had nothing to offer.

Her desire to take Jen into her arms and whisper promises she had no right making would be as welcome to Jen as Roger's precondition. A yearning to protect Jen surged through her like wildfire—how ironic that the sole thing Jen needed defense from was Kade.

She had to leave Jen alone. She'd known it all along.

CHAPTER TWENTY-THREE

Holly was typing away on her laptop at Kade's conference table when she arrived at the office the following day. "Roger's out this morning, but he'll swing by after his eleven o'clock, sometime around twelve thirty. What else do you need?"

Kade sat at her desk and brought her laptop to life. "I expect Jen Spencer or Jeremy Corbin will want to set up a board meeting in the next day or two. I don't care if I have to cancel a meeting with the president, book the first time that works for them."

"Will do. Want to fill me in?"

Kade met Holly at the small table and apprised her of Matlock's term sheet and stipulation. "The financial terms are reasonable and competitive, but it's not the right call for Creative Care. Jen needs to be at the helm."

"Does she know you feel that way?"

"Doesn't matter. Had I not expressed my doubts to Roger early on, he would never have included his requirement. She knows that."

"What do you intend to do about it?"

Kade smiled mirthlessly. "There's no coming back from this. That company means the world to her."

"So do you."

Kade thought back to their recent night together and all the hope it had inspired. Hope had been like a powerful drug that had caused Kade to willingly ignore her own internal warnings because being with Jen felt magical, otherworldly. Jen was the forbidden fruit Kade couldn't refuse, and now she needed to pay the price of indulging in her heart's desires.

Holly's voice brought her back to the conversation. "Yes, she's going to be hurt. Yes, she's going to be mad. Who wouldn't be? But she'll get over it. Kade, this is business, your forte. Make it right."

In terms of their relationship, Jen was clearly uninterested in explanations, but Kade needed her to know where she stood on the term sheet. Jen respected her opinion when it came to business matters. The least she could do was share it. She couldn't make things right between them, but she could bring her resources to bear on behalf of Creative Care.

Wheels were already turning in a new direction. Kade felt them churning as she studied her friend, a talented assistant with a bright future. Kade knew Holly's loyalties but owed it to her to offer options. A number of Matlock's partners had expressed to Kade how impressed they were with Holly's efficiency and professionalism. They never knew that to Kade, Holly was far more than a competent assistant. "Matlock's a top-tier firm. Are you interested in working for anyone else here?"

"Besides you? You know better than to ask."

"My days might be numbered."

Holly closed her laptop, arched an eyebrow, and gave Kade her undivided attention.

"I might do something really crazy in the next twenty-four hours," Kade said.

Holly grinned. "I like it already."

Roger's rap on Kade's door brought her head up from her screen. "Got a minute?" he asked.

She rose and indicated that they sit at her conference table. "Thanks for fitting me in today. I was hoping to discuss the term sheet you sent to Creative Care."

"I realize it's not typical."

"No. And I don't want to jump to conclusions, so may I ask what convinced you that Jen Spencer isn't the right person for the role?"

He crossed his ankle on his knee and nodded slowly, as if carefully considering his response. "I gave her the benefit of the doubt you expressed, Kadrienne, and I appreciated her warning at the start of our meeting that she might have to take a phone call. But I was troubled when a call came in such that she left halfway through and had the CTO, Jeremy Corbin, pinch-hit. It was a clear signal of priorities and intentions. Like you, I agree with the fundamentals and like the prospects of the business. I think we can find someone with a strong health-care background to lead it."

"She's proved that a health-care background isn't a requirement for the job."

"She's also proved Creative Care isn't her top priority, and I'm not interested in investing in that situation."

"You're putting me in a difficult position. As a board member, I have to do what I think is best for the shareholders, not Matlock."

"You must also put the interests of the shareholders over any personal interest. Is there something I need to know?"

Kade always appreciated Roger's intelligence, and he was clearly seeing there was more at play than she had shared. "I'm not a fan of ultimatums, Roger, and I imagine you aren't either. But I have to ask. If my staying at Matlock Ventures was predicated on you revising that term sheet to remove the stipulation about the executive search, would you revise it, leave it as is, or would you pull it altogether?"

"I value your work here far more than our investment with one company."

"I appreciate that."

"But you realize once Matlock has a board seat, I can't make promises about the longevity of the management team. Plus, I've already shown my hand. Even if I revise the term sheet, Jen knows she's on the hot seat."

"Yes. And I realize if you withdraw your offer, it wouldn't help the company's prospects."

"No. Are we losing you over this, Kadrienne?"

Kade valued her relationship with Roger and saw no reason to prevaricate. "I don't know. You've done nothing wrong, so it feels unfair and disloyal to be irresolute."

"Had I known Creative Care was special to you, I'd have consulted you. I thought I was making it easier on you by not involving you and not having you risk your objectivity."

Kade shook her head and sliced a palm through the air to cut him off from the idea that any of this was his fault. "You acted fairly based on the information you had. And I appreciate you trying to keep me out of it." She smiled. "Unfortunately, I'm completely in over my head when it comes to my involvement with that company and its founder. Nothing you can do could change that."

"I'm sorry if my offer has put you in an uncomfortable position."

"You couldn't have known. The thing is, I've been considering starting my own firm and fund, and for whatever reason, this feels like the kick start I needed."

Roger smiled knowingly. "'For whatever reason?'"

Kade felt heat in her cheeks. "Regardless of where we go from here, I don't want you to think I'm ungrateful for the opportunity you and the other partners have given me."

Roger stood and extended his hand. "You've been an excellent addition to our team. Whatever your future holds, and I hope Matlock holds it, you'll always be welcome here."

Kade shook his hand. "Thank you for understanding what I don't even know myself."

"Don't you?"

Kade laughed. "Not in a million years. I'm so far in the dog-house, the postal service will start delivering my mail there, and the city will charge for utilities."

Roger grinned. "Sounds like my first marriage. I preferred to call it my man cave."

Jen watched as Jeremy led Kade to the conference room and commandeered it from two employees working through an issue on the whiteboards. It wouldn't take long for him to come collect her, and Jen wished she could prolong the wait. She still hadn't figured out how to strike a balance between standing up for herself and giving Kade the benefit of the doubt. As she tracked Kade's movements, she also hadn't figured out how to immunize herself from the effect of seeing her. Feelings of hurt and anger couldn't extinguish the rush of pleasure she experienced whenever Kade was near, and part of her hoped they never would.

Jeremy beckoned, and Jen followed. She took a seat several places away and on the other side of the table from Kade. Jeremy was the first to speak. "I'd like to start."

"Please," Kade said.

"I want to understand what exactly your role was in coming up with these terms and where your no-confidence vote in Jen stems from." If Jen had a pompom, she'd have cheered.

"Fair enough. Our firm requires that a different partner, in this case Roger Daniels, manage a potential investment in a company that another partner is a related party to. I've had no role whatsoever in coming up with Matlock's term sheet. Jen's email was the first I heard that Matlock was making an offer, let alone knew the details of."

"So how has Roger decided Jen should be replaced, if you've had no role whatsoever?" Jeremy asked, adding a disbelieving emphasis to the final word.

Jen laid a hand on Jeremy's arm in a silent request to dial back his aggressiveness.

"I understand where you're coming from, Jeremy, which is why I'm here. I have nothing to hide. Before Roger decided to take an active interest in Creative Care as a potential investment, he asked for my thoughts on the leadership team. I told him I was on the fence." Kade looked at Jen. "The conversation occurred the same afternoon the team was at Disneyland, the same afternoon Jen had just stood me up on back-to-back meetings with potential referral partners I'd introduced."

Kade turned to Jeremy. "I've since come to learn the underlying and completely understandable reasons for all of those things, but at the time, the excuses I'd received were lacking, in my opinion, which is why I told Roger I was undecided. I hadn't drawn any conclusions about Jen's leadership one way or the other and, in fact, mentioned I found it difficult to judge because our styles are so different."

"You can say that again," Jeremy said disdainfully.

"Jeremy," Jen said, shushing him.

"Roger Daniels is a self-made man who makes his own decisions, though clearly my feedback influenced him. I hope you can both at least understand where I was coming from at the time. But I'd like to move on, if I may. My advice? Don't sign this. Try to get more term sheets ASAP. Jen, work with Holly. I've already spoken to her, and she's expecting to help you schedule some meetings, so share your calendar. A number of VCs excluded from your wish list are worth talking to, some of whom I know well. I'll make as many introductions as I can. Put a bulletproof backup plan in place for your grandmother's care over the next few weeks, and I'll personally cover any difference in cost." She pointed at Jen. "You have issues accepting my help. Set them aside. This is too important." Then she looked between them. "Make sure to customize each pitch to the VC you're meeting with and let them know you already have a term sheet. They'll move faster."

Kade focused on Jen, and Jen had to force herself to listen to her words instead of be mesmerized by her body language. Her elegant pantsuit gave her the authority of a woman in uniform, and her directness was an aphrodisiac. She was subtly commanding, all the more powerful for her lack of decibels. Jen schooled her expression and her breathing by focusing on her anger. She wasn't about to fall at Kade's feet simply because she was receptive to the message and appreciated the appearance of the messenger.

Kade continued. "Also, use Matlock's stipulation to your advantage. You're the face of Creative Care and the perfect use case. Use it. You're pursuing a career while trying to ensure that your grandmother's care is never compromised. And in doing so, your own job is now at stake. Remind these VCs that, unlike them, you can't just write a check to cover the need. This is exactly why Creative Care makes sense. Millions of people are in your position, and Creative Care is solving their problem. Caring for an elderly relative while pursuing a career shouldn't be mutually exclusive. Leverage Matlock's term sheet to get others. Any questions?"

Jen and Jeremy looked at each other for several seconds, shook their heads, and returned their attention to Kade.

"Great. Thank you both for your time." Kade stood, gave them each a brief nod, and left. Jen wrested her eyes away from her departing figure.

"I can't believe I'm about to say this, but I agree with her," Jeremy said once he and Jen were alone. "We're not signing that term sheet."

"I don't know. If people like Roger Daniels are deciding I need to go, I have to be open to hearing it."

"Bullshit."

"I'm serious. He and his firm are extremely well-respected."

"Screw those Matlock people." Jen must have given away something in her expression, because Jeremy blushed. "You know what I mean," he said.

Jen laughed, the levity a welcome diversion from the sober discussion. She dropped her head in her hand and covered her eyes. "Oh my God. That woman. I'd love to."

Jeremy tossed a dry-erase marker at her. "Scoundrel."

Jen pretended to fan herself. "She's so damned hot when she gets all business-like. Good God. If I wasn't so upset with her, I'd be majorly turned on right now."

"La la la. Not hearing this," Jeremy said in a singsong manner, covering his ears with his hands.

Jen smiled sadly. "I do enjoy working with you."

Jeremy sat up straighter and said earnestly, "Don't strike that tone. We'll find another investor."

"There's a very real possibility this is the only term sheet we'll get. Even if it isn't, it may be the only one we get from a tier-one player."

"Doesn't matter."

"It's a solid valuation from a well-respected firm. Creative Care's mission would move forward and your stock would continue to vest, both of which are important to me."

"We're not signing."

"Only to lose everything? Jer, we've come too far."

"We're not going to lose everything. We do what she says. Use Matlock's offer as an asset."

Jen rapped her fingers on the table. "Easy for her to say. She's not the one whose reputation is at risk. Only a handful of folks know that Matlock's offer requires my departure. I'm not inclined to advertise that information to every VC we meet. I made a calculated decision not to use family as an excuse when I've had to leave work. Now I'm suddenly going to tell everyone? I don't think so. You know the biases female entrepreneurs face. Why would I make it harder on myself?"

"Because Matlock's term sheet underscores that bias. Your job's in jeopardy because you're being responsible about your grandmother's care. That's unacceptable by any standard and doesn't make you look bad. It shows why Creative Care will be successful."

Jen pursed her lips. "I don't like it."

"Let me ask you this. Did you believe her about not knowing what Roger was up to?"

"I might not always agree with Kade, but I never doubt her veracity."

"Then it's clear she believes you should be running this company, and I agree. I wasn't expecting much from this meeting, but I'm impressed as hell. This is a woman with more startup experience than almost anyone in the Valley, and she's recommending you leverage Matlock's term sheet during our pitch. What do we have to lose?"

"You mean besides our only offer, our company, and my prospects in Silicon Valley?"

"Yeah, besides that."

"Remind me again why I enjoy working with you?"

Jeremy opened his laptop. "Because while I'm busy paying attention to what our board member is saying, you can ogle her."

"That works."

Chapter Twenty-four

It was another long day involving attorneys and paperwork. As they had for years, Kade and Holly worked together like the movement inside a Swiss watch. Holly handled most of the details with counsel, consulting Kade whenever a major decision needed to be made.

Wading through hundreds of pages of formation and partnership documents was no one's idea of fun, and Holly signaled they needed a break.

"We're not naming your firm Time Honored Ventures, by the way," Holly said, getting up to stretch her arms and back.

Kade rolled her head side to side, appreciating the opportunity for a breather. "What's wrong with it? It sounds classy and prestigious."

"I would have gone with stodgy and pretentious. You're building an organization to support female-led businesses, yet you're practically calling it Old Boys' Network. I thought you wanted to create something new and different."

"We still have to demand the highest degree of professionalism, even if we're affirming that family and entrepreneurialism aren't mutually exclusive."

Holly peered at the various snacks they'd set out in the boardroom of Kade's condo. "On one hand, you're telling women they won't be vilified, judged, questioned, or punished for prioritizing family over work, and on the other you're scaring them off before their first meeting."

"Fine. What would you call it? Estrogen Ventures? Kumbaya Capital?"

Holly laughed. "I love how absolutely devoid of hyperbole you are." She snatched some cashews from a bowl and popped one into her mouth. "Davenport Ventures."

Kade rolled her eyes. "Talk about pretentious. Should I wear a tiara around the office, too? Put a sign on my door: PLEASE GENUFLECT BEFORE ENTERING."

Holly laughed again. "You, my friend, have broken through a glass ceiling few have shattered. This is a crappy industry for women, which is why your idea for a firm prioritizing female entrepreneurs rocks. Your reputation is unparalleled. It's not a bad thing, Kade. Your name means something in the Valley. Use it to your advantage." She munched on another nut. "How many prospective investors have you talked to about your new venture?"

"About a dozen."

"And about what percent have expressed interest in funding you?"

"A hundred."

"I rest my case." Holly returned to the document on her screen, and Kade followed suit. Another hour passed in silence before Holly closed her laptop and sat back, arms folded. This gesture spelled more dissatisfaction, so Kade patiently waited for whatever reproach was on Holly's mind this time.

"I strongly disagree with your appointment of Charles to the Creative Care account in the event Jen accepts your offer," Holly said.

"His doctors have given him the green light, and he's game. He promises he's up to the task." Charles had already retaken his seat on Creative Care's board, and when Kade had informed Holly of her desire to make Creative Care her firm's first investment, Holly hadn't expressed concern at her idea of asking Charles to be her proxy. Since Charles wasn't affiliated with Time Honored Ventures, the term sheet stipulated the special arrangement Kade had worked out with him, keeping him on the board in lieu of her. "Do you think it's too soon?"

"No. I think it's cowardly of you to shove off your responsibilities onto him."

"I'm doing no such thing. Jen doesn't want to have anything to do with me. There's no way she'll accept an investment by me unless she never has to see me."

"You don't know that."

Kade returned her attention to her screen. No point in arguing about it. Her calendar notification sounded, reminding her to pack up to visit her father. Saved by the bell.

"You're doing it again," Holly said.

Kade sighed and asked the question expected of her, though she had no desire to hear the answer. "What am I doing?"

"Erecting barriers. Keeping people away. Deciding for others that you're not someone worth getting close to."

Kade closed her laptop. "We're not talking about people. We're talking about Jen, someone who has every right to be disappointed in me. She has a good relationship with Charles, and they respect each other. I'm trying to take her feelings into account."

"You don't think you deserve another chance, so you're not even going to try."

Kade tried not to show how deflated the subject made her feel. She slid the computer into its protective sleeve. "It's not up to me."

Holly shot to her feet and shouted, "It is up to you!" Holly closed her eyes briefly and pinched the bridge of her nose, clearly upset by her own outburst. "You're giving that prick of a father of yours another chance, but not you."

Kade didn't agree that was what she was doing. "Even if that were true, I don't understand why that's a bad thing."

"Extend yourself the same courtesy, and I'm fine with it."

"I need to go."

Holly made a shooing motion with her hand. "Yes, go. Hide behind your rigid rule-following. God forbid you're late."

Kade set the carrying case down and folded her arms. "Just say what's on your mind, Holly."

"If Cassie could somehow come back to us, would you stop spending time with her because you were afraid you might hurt her?

Is that how you'd treat her? Is that how you'd show her how much you care? By keeping your distance?"

"Well, she's not coming back to us, is she? I made damn sure of that." Kade grabbed her laptop bag and purse, and headed for the door.

"And now you're making sure Jen doesn't either."

Kade heard this parting shot and refused to respond. Anger infused each step as she stalked to her car. What the hell was Holly's problem? What kind of inane question was that to ask about Cassie? Holly well knew how Kade felt about losing her. Why rehash it and put her on the defensive?

And what was that crap about making decisions for Jen? Jen had been unmistakable in terms of what she thought of Kade's betrayal. Kade was doing her a favor by not standing in the way of what could potentially be a solid investment for Creative Care. The company would get the funding it needed to continue executing its mission, Jen would remain in charge, and Charles, a reputable and active director, would continue providing guidance along the way.

She wasn't hiding behind anything. Previously she had, but once Jen had convinced her to give their relationship a chance, Kade was all-in. Not that they'd had time to explore it before she obliterated it.

She threw her things into a heap on the passenger seat and strangled the steering wheel. How ridiculous to even float the fantasy of Cassie being alive! If she were, Kade would throw her arms around her and never let go. She wouldn't—couldn't—distance herself. Cassie wouldn't let her anyway.

She flexed her grip and thought of her old friend. Yes, she'd hold fast to Cassie. Never let her out of her sight. Lock her in her condo with specific instructions to the security team.

Kade smiled as she imagined the look on Cassie's face. Cassie would hate every second of being hemmed in. Nothing could ever contain her unapologetic zest for life, and Kade wouldn't want to try. It was what Kade loved in her friend. And Cassie brought it out in Kade, a side of herself she'd almost forgotten.

Cassie had never accepted Gordon's ever-tightening control over Kade. She was Kade's pressure valve, granting her release from Gordon's demands and freedom to simply be a playful kid who enjoyed life.

Kade was so far from being the girl she once was, the girl Cassie spent every day with, she wondered if Cassie would even recognize her, let alone want to spend time with her.

Zero point two seconds was as long as it took for Kade to reach the sad conclusion.

She covered her face with her hands, trying not to lose her composure in the parking garage. She needed to get going or she'd be late. Though why would it matter if she was? If the person who was always so concerned with showing up on time was the one neither Jen nor Cassie would want to be around, what was the point of showing up at all?

She dropped her head back against the headrest, closing her eyes. She knuckled away a tear that managed to spill. A shadow fell across her windshield, and she cursed herself for not having left the garage sooner. Hopefully whoever it was wouldn't pay close attention to the woman in the sleek sedan on the verge of a breakdown.

Her door opened, and Holly squatted on the pavement beside her, placing her palms on Kade's left thigh and looking up at her. "I don't bring her up in order to wound you. Or me."

Kade covered Holly's hands and laid her head back again. "I know."

Holly entwined their fingers. "The best way to honor my sister is to care for and nurture what she loved."

Kade opened her eyes and glanced down at Holly, curious to learn more.

"You," she said with a sad smile.

Fresh tears flooded Kade's eyes.

"I can't…for the life of me, I can't figure out how to get you to do it, but I'm not going to rest until I do."

This remark elicited a small smile from Kade. "Thankless job."

Holly's smile turned bright. "Not on your life." She stood and moved out of the way of the door. Kade started the engine and rolled the window down. "Tell the Grinch I said 'hi,'" Holly said with a wink.

CHAPTER TWENTY-FIVE

Day after day, Kade's father had been making steady progress. Working with him each day to improve his cognition, memory, reading, attention, and comprehension skills had given Kade a strange sense of accomplishment. Speech still eluded him, but he was a willing and engaged student, rarely pushing the tablet aside in favor of rest. In the short time he'd been at this facility, color had returned to his face, and a small spark had appeared in his eyes whenever she visited.

Therefore, Kade wasn't expecting the dramatic decline in his overall appearance when she visited after only a few days away. His pallor was back and his cheekbones more pronounced, as if he'd skipped a good number of meals, which seemed unlikely in a facility that prepared and delivered the food. Gordon nodded when she asked if he was feeling okay. She resolved to speak to a nurse as soon as she finished working with him. Additionally, his train set had been removed. She asked Gordon if it had been at his request; it hadn't.

Ten minutes after her arrival, a nurse entered Gordon's room. The fifty-something bottle brunette smiled as Kade asked if she'd visited Gordon before. When the nurse said she had, Kade asked about his missing train.

"Sorry, ma'am. It was deemed unsafe and dismantled. Our residents' safety is our priority."

"What was unsafe about it?"

"I believe it was difficult for the cleaning staff to work around."

"So was it unsafe or merely inconvenient?"

"Sorry, ma'am. I know it was for safety reasons. Let me find my supervisor for you."

While Kade waited, she continued working with Gordon.

Shortly after the first nurse left, another one returned in her stead. The late-twenty-something redhead with blue eyes and freckled cheeks asked Kade if she was Gordon's daughter. Once Kade confirmed, the nurse asked if she could observe Kade and Gordon as they worked through his tablet exercises. Gordon seemed okay with the request, and Kade didn't mind but informed the nurse she'd like to speak with her once they finished.

Perched on one of the folding chairs, the nurse watched in silence. At first slightly disconcerted by having an audience, Kade quickly forgot about her as Gordon took his time working through the questions provided by the software, and she helped guide him when he seemed stymied. After about ten minutes, the nurse excused herself and told Kade she'd be right back.

Carrying a food tray with her when she returned, the nurse set it on Gordon's rolling table before retaking her seat. Once Kade wrapped up the exercises with her father, the nurse asked if she'd mind helping feed Gordon his snack, though she insisted she'd be happy to do it if Kade preferred.

Even a week ago, the idea of the intimate act of feeding her father would have made Kade blanch. But his gaunt face and acceptance of her assistance with his mental exercises made her more receptive to the idea. It meant staying longer than the hour she usually allotted, but work was the only thing she'd be returning to at home this late in the day. And this seemed more important.

Though the process was slow and at times messy, with Gordon chewing the fresh orange slices before pulling them fully into his mouth such that the juice dribbled down his chin, Kade took some comfort in the fact he so willingly accepted her help. She half expected him to demand that the nurse feed him. Dabbing the edge of a napkin into Gordon's water glass, Kade cleaned off his mouth and chin. He didn't fuss.

Kade bid Gordon good night after informing him she'd return tomorrow. She followed the nurse out of his room and into an office. Kade said, "He looks much worse off than he was even four days ago. What's happened? And why has his train set been disassembled?"

"It's been four days since you last visited?"

"Yes. But I was here daily prior to that, and he was improving."

"In the short time you were here this evening, you've been able to do what our nurses and therapists haven't in several days. He's refused both food and therapy."

"But he's been able to swallow since he was moved here."

"The only time you've not visited daily has been these last few days?"

"Yes, but what's that got to do with his health?"

"Ms. Davenport, I wanted to observe you with your father because you seem to be the cornerstone to his rehabilitation. I've had a chance to watch him interact with a number of staff members since his arrival, and after seeing him interact with you, there's simply no doubt he is very much motivated by you."

Kade stared at the redhead before laughing derisively. "Look, Ms..." Kade flicked her eyes to the woman's name badge. "McCutcheon."

"Erica."

"Erica. My father and I have scarcely spoken in years. His stroke is the only reason I'm in his life these days, and he's probably cursing every God there is that I've been thrust back upon him. In all likelihood, he's probably so pliable with me because he'll do anything to expedite my departure."

Erica smiled in a way that made Kade believe she hadn't understood a word. "You said you noticed improvement from his arrival until today, which is several days since your last visit. Correct?"

Kade nodded, irritated that the conversation had devolved into restatements of things already said.

Erica continued. "We've found he's very uptight about his schedule. Had you informed him you wouldn't be returning until today?"

Kade frowned, swallowing the excuse she was about to offer. No one knew the importance to Gordon of adhering to schedule more than Kade. Until recently, she'd visited each evening. When she'd last visited, although she hadn't told him she'd return the next day, she could understand having implicitly set that expectation.

"In the last three days, your father has obstructed all staff attempts to feed, clothe, bathe, or provide any therapy for him, which started the day after your last visit. Prior to that, he was the ideal resident. Aside from loss of appetite, his doctors have confirmed that his physical health hasn't deteriorated. During this time, the only thing that's changed in his routine is you."

Feeling defensive, Kade said, "The far more likely explanation is that his train set—"

Erica held up her hands as if to suggest she wasn't trying to make accusations. "Ms. Davenport, I've—"

"Kade. Please."

"Kade. I've been at this for longer than it might look. All it took was sixty seconds to see the intensity of his expression as he works with you on his exercises, the way he focuses on you after he responds to a question, and the gleam in his eyes when you voice your approval, to know how important you being there is for him. As someone interested in his care, I don't need to know what's happened in his past as much as I need to understand what impacts his present, and you do, very positively."

This was more information than Kade could absorb. She stood and thanked Erica for her time. Before she'd opened the door wide enough to secure her escape, Erica said, "I'll see about his train set, but please. Return tomorrow as you told him you would. I think you'll see all the proof you need."

Kade wasn't sure she should drive home. Would she be able to safely negotiate traffic when she couldn't focus on anything except the voices arguing in her head? Estranged from her father for years, now she was suddenly the impetus behind his rehabilitation? Did that mean she could essentially kill him if she walked away?

No, no, no. This couldn't be happening. The nurse was wrong.

As Kade headed for the exit, she paused in front of the facility's beauty shop, gray wigs on two plastic female heads catching her attention. She silently questioned why neither dummy sported blue hair, which seemed to be in fashion here. A sign indicated the shop was closed, and the lights were off except for the recessed lighting above the display window, but the door was slightly ajar, luring her in. She pushed it open and called out. No one answered. She took a seat in one of the hydraulic styling chairs and looked around the small salon, noting the implements, wondering if it should be this easy for certain of the residents to access sharp scissors. Wondering whether, in her present state of mind, it should be this easy for her.

In the best of health, Gordon was scarcely capable of having a conversation that would bear emotionally satisfying fruit. In his current condition, it was impossible. He suffered from both aphasia and dysarthria, so it was difficult for him to understand words and meaning, and the damage to his nervous system made it tough for him to speak. His ability to follow or convey long, complex ideas was severely compromised. If she forced a conversation, she'd never know precisely how much he comprehended or the degree to which his responses accurately communicated his thoughts.

For half her life, Kade had wanted to mean something to her father. Now that she might be a blip on his radar screen, she couldn't do anything with the information.

She stared at the mannequin head with the schoolmarm hair style that completely contrasted with the youthful face, as if dressed for a costume party. It made her think of Jen, someone wise beyond her years.

I want you to be you, Jen had said. What did it mean? The statement contained a kernel of something that had touched Kade at the time and never really ceased. Something inherently hopeful lurked within it, something profoundly simple. But *who* was the *you* she was supposed to be?

She had no idea. Unsure of how she could be more *you*, she considered how she could be less of the current, adult Kade, and more of the kid version she used to be, the Kade whom Cassie had loved.

She could start by unraveling several lengths of coil that she'd wound tightly over time to adhere to Gordon's disciplinary demands in the hope of salvaging what they used to have. He had required everyone to adhere to a strict timetable, born from his guilt over failing at his job. She'd taken on his guilt, worn it like a prosthetic all these years. No longer the youngster who longed for attention and approval, perhaps she could excise it.

But how much of the girl remained inside? How much of what Cassie had been drawn to for all those years was fundamentally intact? Was that the person Jen saw in her?

Had seen. She corrected herself. The only thing Jen saw in Kade these days was betrayal.

Focus on what you can control, she reminded herself. It was a piece of advice she gave entrepreneurs in her book. For all her obsession with time, Kade couldn't turn back the clock to a period before she'd hurt Jen.

Jen.

What would Jen do?

She shifted her gaze to the mirror.

Forgive him.

Kade arrived at the conclusion in a millisecond. Unequivocally, it's what Jen would do.

But she wasn't Jen.

The man in room four-ten didn't deserve forgiveness. *Yet forgiving a saint doesn't take much. The hard part lies in forgiving someone for the actual harm they've done. Things that don't matter don't need to be forgiven.* She didn't have to deny the seriousness of the pain he had inflicted or give him license to mistreat her in the future. She didn't even have to feel forgiving in order to forgive. Nor did she have to self-righteously announce to him that she forgave him. It needn't be an exercise in manipulating him into feeling guilty. In fact, it would have nothing to do with *his* action or response. *She* would be making the conscious, deliberate decision to release her resentment toward him.

Maybe she could see it as a weight being lifted off her. Learning his motivations regarding her wasn't necessary in order for her to act.

Was she ready to take this step? Forgive Gordon for the emotional injury he'd inflicted?

She wasn't sure. But she couldn't let Gordon shackle her any longer. In all these years, time—the keeper she'd so meticulously respected—had not healed the wounds. She needed to try something new.

Kade left the salon and returned to Gordon's room. His eyes were closed, the overhead lights off. The lamp on the corner table was on, as usual, and her eyes seemed to settle, as if appreciating that they were out of the brightness of the hallway.

The room was quiet and Gordon rested peacefully, his mouth hanging open. It seemed simple enough to speak the words or think them, to accept the serenity of the moment and move forward.

Yet something was missing. The way Jen described it, forgiveness was, at least in part, an act of self-love. If she could forgive Gordon but not herself, it would be a hollow gesture, like having a puppet absolve him. If she were truly to forgive him, wouldn't she need to be able to forgive herself as well? She wasn't sure she could. Stepping free and clear of her role in her family's disintegration and Cassie's demise seemed wrong and unjust. Cassie could never again be carefree, so why should Kade?

She noticed Gordon's tablet. The installed software contained comprehensive how-to guides. The man lying next to it didn't come with a knowledge base. He was a human being, fallible, damaged. No different than Kade. She didn't have a set of instructions to work with when it came to forgiveness.

All she could do was ask herself an important question: could she continue to deny him the one thing her ten-year-old self had wanted him to give her?

He had been cruel not to forgive her all those years. Not to forgive him, regardless of reason, would be no less callous.

Gordon's breath caught. He cleared his throat and closed his mouth without waking. With the recent weight loss and the condition of his overall health, he seemed smaller than the man who had disciplined her in her youth. Fragile, not unlike the psyche of a ten-year-old girl.

Kade was a lot of things and failed on many fronts. But she wasn't cruel.

She walked to the bulky visitors' chair to the right of the bed, curled into it, and closed her eyes. She would stay until breakfast and help feed him or get kicked out for breaking visiting hours' rules. Either way, she would awaken to a new dawn, one in which Gordon Davenport received the absolution he never gave his daughter.

Chapter Twenty-six

Jen couldn't believe the words on her laptop screen. She'd opened an attachment from kdavenport@thv.com, an email address she didn't recognize, and simultaneously wondered whether her antivirus software was up to date. It seemed as likely to be from Kade as an actual Nigerian prince contacting her for assistance with transferring millions of dollars to her if she would kindly provide her bank account information and Social Security number.

The subject said *Term Sheet*, and the message body was nondescript.

Jen, I hope all is well. Please let me know if you have any questions regarding the attached. –Kade

It was an investment offer—a generous one—from Time Honored Ventures, a firm she'd never heard of and didn't recall meeting with. She looked at the signature, which she had seen on Creative Care documents and which confirmed the identity of the sender: Kadrienne Davenport. This didn't make sense. Kade was a partner at Matlock Ventures. What was her signature doing on a non-Matlock offer?

She reread the document. Charles Jameson would be THV's choice for the board seat created by the financing round, representing the investors. Jen shook her head, confused. Why would Kade be looking to invest in Creative Care via a company Jen had never heard of? And if it was a bona fide offer, why wouldn't Kade take the board seat?

She backtracked through what she thought she knew. Charles had been back at work for a week, and Jen had already caught him up on the term sheets they'd received. True to her word, Kade had made a number of introductions between Creative Care and VC firms in its industry. Initially reluctant to take Kade's advice with respect to sharing her story about Matlock's term sheet and her difficulties covering gaps in Nana's care, Jen had become a believer. Results from implementing the strategy had immediately borne fruit, as the half-dozen initial meetings had all yielded requests for second meetings. Creative Care was now in the enviable position of comparing three competitive offers—make that four—two of which were from top-tier VCs.

Jen missed Kade. They hadn't communicated on a personal level since the day of Matlock's offer. She hadn't meant to punish either of them by taking a break, but she'd needed time to heal. Having been in the unhealthy headspace of questioning Kade's loyalties and values, Jen knew a little distance would give her perspective. It would also minimize the chances she'd say something else she'd regret. She'd dealt Kade low blows, packing words more harmful than punches, and she felt terrible. Kade deserved better.

Unable to directly share recent successes with Kade, even work, which challenged and gratified her, lacked its usual luster. Jen felt the sense of loss more acutely once Charles retook his board seat, even though she liked and respected him. Prior to his health scare, Charles had been an active, engaged director, but Kade's commitment to the company and the advice she gave Jen time and again had proved her indispensable. No offense to Charles, but to Jen's mind, there was no comparison.

As interim director, Kade had been apprised of two of the term sheets that had come in subsequent to Matlock's, so she knew Creative Care had solid options and wasn't facing a shutdown. Was this some sort of over-the-top and unnecessary make-good for Kade's conversation with Roger? No. Kade wouldn't offer to invest simply because she felt guilty. Her professionalism dictated she would only invest if she was serious about the company's prospects. While Jen surged with pleasure knowing that, with all the prospective investments Kade could make, Creative Care was at the top of her list, the gratification immediately ebbed at the thought that Kade was obviously wary of communicating about anything but the briefest work-related issues.

Jen was responsible for Kade's caution. She hadn't treated her fairly, hadn't taken time to consider things from her point of view. In fact, THV's term sheet solidified what she already believed from what Kade had told her. Roger hadn't informed Kade of his plans to pursue an investment in Creative Care. And as Kade had pointed out, Roger made his own decisions. Yes, he would have taken Kade's feedback under advisement, but Jen's abrupt departure during their only meeting must have also concerned him. By making this offer, Kade was backing up everything she'd said: Roger's offer had blindsided her as much as it did Jen, she believed in what Jen was building, and she had confidence in Jen's leadership.

Kade hadn't failed Jen by responding to Roger's inquiry in the only way Kade would: honestly and fairly, based on the information she'd had at the time. Jen had let Kade down by not telling her why she was struggling to adhere to their scheduled meeting times.

She owed Kade an apology. And unlike Kade, she wasn't into self-denial. Being with Kade brought her joy, and she had no desire to prolong her misery by staying away from her.

All the paperwork was complete. With a few strokes of her pen to execute the documents, Kade would be starting and managing a new venture-capital firm. A drum of excitement beat through her. She would be helping female business owners and executives pursue their dreams on a level playing field. Years ago, when she was a fresh-faced college graduate forming her first company, a VC firm like this didn't exist. She'd been fortunate in a way. She hadn't been forced to choose between her family and her company. Work had dominated her life then as it did now.

These days, however, she wasn't feeling particularly lucky. As elated as she was at the prospect of putting women on a more equal footing in the Valley, she'd subordinate work to family in a heartbeat if it meant Jen was sharing her life. She wouldn't hesitate to put this endeavor on hold for Jen, temporarily or permanently.

Something undefinable was delaying her, keeping her from signing, nipping at her brain like a puppy at her heels, harmless yet insistent. Glass of wine in hand, she walked barefoot through her condo, trying to figure out what was pawing at her. The kaleidoscope Holly had given her caught her attention, so she scooped it up as she meandered.

She sat cross-legged on the dining-room floor, next to a section of train-set scenery involving a logging town. The train passed by every few minutes on an exact schedule, the synchronized timepieces surrounding it marking its feat of precision. A child would love this room, she thought as she watched the cars roll along. She never had.

Setting down the wine, she looked through the kaleidoscope lens. The colorful images were bold and beautiful, like stained glass. She recalled Holly's words about the lens through which Gordon saw her causing him to see things differently. It was a lovely idea, she thought as she looked around the room, as she took the pulse of her life to gauge its health and asked herself whether her own vision of it was distorted or clear.

This room contained artifacts of her childhood, none of which she reminisced about fondly. She'd always thought she'd glean answers from them over time, but that had never materialized. Clocks and train sets made Gordon happy, not Kade. More than that, they made her unhappy.

"You killed her." His words had plagued her for years. But hadn't she assigned herself the blame before he'd ever said it? Yes, he'd squeezed citrus into the gaping wound, but the injury had already been bone and soul deep, taking root the moment she'd noticed the rescue team head up the mountain.

Another sip of wine, another intake of her surroundings. Her father hadn't lined her condo with timepieces, either. Nor had he installed a train set inside its walls or converted a family room into a boardroom. Nor had he moved her into this residence, largely devoid of warmth, lacking in details to welcome guests.

Kade had done all those things exactly for the reasons Holly identified—erecting hurdles designed to prevent people from getting too close, constructed to protect them from her. Far from caring for the girl Cassie once loved, she was punishing her over and over.

Slowly, she twirled the kaleidoscope in her lap, trying to see things differently for once. She thought of Holly's words. *If Cassie could somehow come back to us, would you stop spending time with her because you were afraid you might hurt her?*

Not a chance. Kade could never punish Cassie for her enthusiastic love of life or ask her to live less. Smaller. Protected. No. Cassie needed to be free to play, explore, adventure, and she reveled at bringing out that same spirit in Kade.

Kade needed to return to living, to following Cassie's example of how to do it. She wasn't sure how she'd manage, but it was essential. Leaving this mausoleum would be a start.

There was the "us" in Holly's question as well. Holly had been a child during Kade and Cassie's teenage years. At those ages, the difference was significant. No more. Holly was a grown woman who would delight at having Cassie in her life. Moreover, Kade realized, at this point Holly had been her friend longer than Cassie had. Holly and Cassie were fairly different personality types but very similar when it came to Kade, both looking after her in ways she'd never deserved, without reservation.

She and Holly didn't have the all-consuming type of friendship she had with Cassie, but they had each other's back, made each other laugh, and were consistent sounding boards in each other's lives. Having Holly as her assistant added an odd dynamic to their relationship, requiring a layer of distance on one hand and complete transparency on the other.

They didn't often speak of Cassie, given the years that had passed. The one-two punch of Jen's resemblance to her and Gordon's stroke had brought Cassie to the forefront of their minds again. And so Kade didn't usually compare Holly and Cassie. One was the friend of her youth, the other the friend of her adulthood.

Both meant the world to her, and as she studied the kaleidoscope, she realized why she hesitated to sign the paperwork.

Kade had been doing a terrible job of expressing to Holly how much she appreciated her. Holly knew how much Kade had loved her sister, but did Holly understand how much Kade loved her? Had Kade ever told her?

It was far past time to let Holly know what she meant to her, and Kade had an idea that would leave no doubt.

She returned the kaleidoscope to its shelf, feeling better for having a plan for Holly. Too bad she was bereft of one for how to rejoin the land of the living. Her only ideas on that front revolved around Jen, a dead end.

She took another sip of wine and slid onto a stool in the kitchen, where she had pleasant memories of happier times with Jen. They could have been good together, couldn't they? If she hadn't screwed up?

Having Jen love her—and she'd glimpsed that love—eclipsed everything else. Jen was an anti-gravity phenomenon, repelling forces that dragged Kade down. More than buoy her, Jen made her feel she could climb higher. Soar. How was that possible when she'd asked Kade only to be herself?

No, that wasn't the entire request. She'd also asked Kade to turn inward, to find the woman—or was it the child—inside her and tell her she was worthy of love. Convince her of it. Repeat it until it was second nature, as easy to believe as knowing her name.

A daunting demand. Kade understood that if she couldn't love herself, she had no right to expect anyone else to love her. But making it a reality seemed akin to landing on the moon. How could she not only begin to believe she was lovable, but do so in time for Jen to give her another chance? Might as well pack it in now.

Kade smiled as an image of Holly popped into her head, scolding her for exaggerating. Baby steps, she reminded herself as she sipped her wine. If she were counseling the CEO of a startup, she'd suggest breaking things into small, achievable pieces. When fund-raising, tech firms needn't have solved all their challenges in order to raise money. They needed the money to execute on the company's vision. Only the idea needed to be solid.

Kade could espouse the idea of loving herself. She didn't have to start shouting from rooftops how wonderful she was. She didn't have to completely believe she deserved love *today*. But she did need to start taking steps in that direction, and she had to do it on her own.

Though the first step wouldn't be easy, the only way to arrive at the destination was to begin the journey.

She walked down the hall to the master bathroom and looked in the mirror. Memories of Jen standing with her arms around her, the sound of her voice telling Kade she deserved to be loved, permeated and warmed her. Another image of sorts stood behind her, Cassie repeatedly moving her hand in a forward rolling motion, as if telling Kade to get on with it so they could go outside. Both women had something to impress upon her.

It was time to listen.

Focusing on her own solemn eyes, she contemplated the words required to close this chapter of her life, reminding herself that she didn't have to deserve the gift of compassion. Heeding her friends' messages made Kade feel less alone in the empty room.

"I forgive you," she said to her reflection.

I love you was on its heels, but as the words streamed by her mind, she let them scurry away. She wasn't ready yet. Instead, she took a deep breath and repeated, "I forgive you."

It was a start.

CHAPTER TWENTY-SEVEN

K ade was anxious. She was about to give the pitch of her life. But a PowerPoint presentation wouldn't accompany this one. She'd be speaking from her heart, which wasn't her strong suit. Trying to persuade Jen to sign up with Time Honored Ventures was a work-related task, the likes of which she could perform handily. But it was something else entirely to convince her to forgive Kade and risk getting hurt again. Kade had to try.

She hadn't informed Holly of her forthcoming meeting because she didn't want to add to her already sky-high performance anxiety, something she never experienced at work. Holly would want to provide suggestions of what to say, and Kade wanted to succeed or fail in her own words. In an utterly gutless move too embarrassing to think about, however, Kade had scheduled Holly to drop by THV's temporary office shortly, a backup plan in case things with Jen nosedived.

"Come in," she said at the knock on her door. She'd left it open wide enough for Jen to enter, an attempt to avoid any awkwardness between them if forced to pass each other closely. But awkwardness reigned regardless, as she stood in the middle of the loft, unsure of how to greet Jen. Jen's exquisite blue eyes had a smile in them, mixed with caution.

"Hi," Jen said, taking extra time to roll the heavy door closed as if unsure how to proceed. While Jen took in the new office space, Kade studied her. Her hair was in a French braid, and she wore a black blazer over a white blouse tucked into faded low-rise jeans.

Black mid-heel boots completed the outfit. It was quintessential Jen—very girl-next-door who doesn't realize how pretty she is even in casual clothes. Kade's desire to embrace her was nearly overpowering, and it took all her self-control not to surrender to it.

"Something to drink? Coffee? Water?" Kade asked.

Jen spied the nearby hooks and hung her purse. "Water, please," she said, still taking in her surroundings. "This is really great, Kade. I love the high ceilings and industrial feel with the exposed pipes and beams." She followed Kade and stopped at the border to the kitchen. "Very un-VC-ish." An unspoken question permeated her tone.

As Kade pulled two water bottles from the refrigerator, she said, "Holly picked it out while we search for a more permanent office, but I like it." She handed a bottle to Jen, and their gazes held as Jen accepted it. Kade wanted to push all talk of work aside and get lost in those dazzling blue pools. Instead she said, "You wished to talk about the term sheet?"

Jen's expression shuttered, and she crossed the room to the far couch. "Tell me about Time Honored Ventures."

Kade schooled her features into business mode as she took a seat on the couch opposite Jen. "Of course. It's a women-centered firm. We partner with and invest in female entrepreneurs in high tech. We want to set the tone for our portfolio companies to create supportive environments for women to succeed without forcing them to choose career over family."

"When you say 'our' and 'we,' who do you mean?"

Kade should have chosen her words more carefully. "Me. My mission. I'm the general partner and am in the process of selecting my limited partners."

"I imagine you've received interest."

Kade nodded. "I've been fortunate. My professional reputation is…" Kade didn't know quite how to phrase what she was about to say.

"Intact? Formidable?" Jen suggested.

Kade shook her head. "I was going to say, 'stronger than my personal one,' but since no one knows that better than you, it seemed moot."

Jen shifted, as if uncomfortable with Kade's admission. "Given your professional reputation, why would you think I'd be interested in taking an investment from you if you won't be on my board or an active partner on my business?"

Kade spun the water bottle in her hands as if it could distract them both from the elephant in the room, her betrayal of Jen's trust. Eye contact was the norm in her work dealings, but she couldn't seem to meet Jen's gaze. In a low voice, she said, "I don't want you to feel I'm forcing you to work with me or make you uncomfortable in any way."

"I have other offers. In large part, thanks to you. I'm not being forced. But for the record, I'm not signing your term sheet unless you're my partner."

Kade stared at Jen. At least Jen had the wherewithal to understand her double entendre. Much to Kade's disappointment, but not surprise, Jen backpedaled. "On the Creative Care team."

"I'm sorry. That's not the offer."

This stance seemed to confuse Jen, as Kade anticipated. Jen said, "It's a simple change."

Whether she was ready for this conversation or not, its time had arrived. Kade stood and began pacing behind the couch, miffed at herself for creating even more of a barricade than the coffee table offered. If anything, she should be on her knees, taking Jen's hand in hers, pleading. Yet terrified that Jen might walk away permanently, Kade opted for the extra wall of defense.

"I've learned a lot about myself these past few weeks. As I've worked with a man I haven't liked for the better part of my life, I've come to believe even he should be surrounded by things that make him happy. And it dawned on me I've been surrounding myself with things that don't make me happy. I also realized it's his home, not a place where he's gone to die, but to live.

"From the moment we met, you reminded me of Cassie. It wasn't merely your physical resemblance. It was how you lived. Live. I've been so scared of hurting the people I love. Debilitatingly so. And as you've pointed out, I hurt them anyway."

"Kade, I was wrong to say that to you."

Kade hadn't brought it up for Jen to berate herself. "No. No." Kade didn't opt for barriers anymore. She crossed to the couch Jen occupied and sat beside her, taking her hands.

"I don't want to bide my time. Cassie didn't. You don't. I want to live. Fully live." She squeezed Jen's hands. "The only way for me to do that is reward myself with what makes me happy instead of punish myself with what doesn't. If Cassie were alive, I could never keep myself away from her because I might hurt her." Kade took an anxious breath. "The same is true with you. You make me happy, and I like who I am when I'm with you. You make me feel alive in ways I haven't allowed myself to feel since Cassie died. And you've taught me to hope…" Kade's voice cracked on the word so full of promise yet seemingly beyond reach. "You've taught me to hope that if a man like my father shouldn't be deprived of love or comfort, then even a woman like me, with all my faults and fears, deserves no less."

Kade raised her chin in defiance of all the self-doubts and reasons she didn't merit what she was about to say. She swallowed the lump in her throat, met Jen's eyes, and said what she hoped Jen still wanted to hear, what she was trying her best to believe.

"I deserve to be loved."

A perfidious tear belied her statement yet found a kindred soul in Jen's suddenly watery eyes. Kade tried to speak with conviction, but she only repeated quietly, "I deserve to be loved. The only way I'll be your partner is in the complete sense. The wake-up-with-me-in-the-morning, fall-asleep-with-me-at-night version. I will hurt you, Jen, but never with malice and never without trying to make it up to you. And you'll hurt me."

Kade brushed a tear from Jen's cheek and offered a tiny smile. "Though I hope to God it's not right now, because it would be a really bad time for you to do it."

Jen laughed despite crying, and somehow Kade's mind registered that Jen hadn't extricated herself from her grasp. Hope, the elusive optimist, peeked out from her heart's shadow.

"You haven't been practicing," Jen said.

And just like that, the same brain that cataloged Jen's touch failed to follow Jen's train of thought.

"The homework I gave you." Jen leaned forward until she was close enough that Kade could feel her breath against her cheek. It felt like coming home on a snowy night and snuggling into cozy blankets in front of a roaring fire. "Say it again," Jen said.

"I deserve to be loved." Kade noticed some strength return to her voice.

"Say it the way you mean it."

Jen hadn't forgotten what Kade uniquely wanted, and she was granting Kade permission to seize it. Nearly overwhelmed with an optimism she'd never before experienced, Kade said, "I deserve to be loved by you."

"Yes, you do," Jen said before capturing Kade's lips with her own.

As they kissed and talked and basked in each other's company, Kade's phone played the notes of Holly's ringtone, interrupting their reconnection. "I have to get this." She kissed the back of Jen's hand and grabbed her phone. "Come on up," she said into the device. She returned to Jen and gave her a quick kiss. "It's Holly. She doesn't know you're here. Do you mind if I tell her about us?"

"Not at all."

"Although she has eyes in the back of her head, I have a surprise for her even she won't see coming."

The heavy door rolled aside, and Holly walked in. She smiled as she spied them on the couch. "I'm sorry. Can someone kindly direct me to the venture-capital firm nearby? It has a distinctly dour vibe, not this…" She circled her palm in their direction. "Jubilant, happy one."

Kade couldn't stop grinning. "Creative Care has a new investor. And I have a new…" Kade turned to Jen.

"Partner," she and Jen said concurrently.

Holly stood across from them and looked at her watch. "As much as I love that you're making your own appointments now, I thought we were meeting about Time Honored Ventures." She placed her hand next to her mouth, pretending to block Kade from seeing her lips move, and mouthed to Jen the words, "Hate that name." She waved her hand to indicate the two of them. "But seeing as how you two have better things to do than talk shop, I'll be on my way."

"I do want to touch base on something first. Do you mind?" Kade asked as she went to the kitchen to retrieve her surprise. She handed a small gift-wrapped box to Holly before retaking her seat by Jen's side and pulling Jen's hand into her lap. "If Jen had made a different choice, it probably would have taken me a little longer to give that to you, seeing as how you'd be picking pieces of me up off the floor, but as it stands, you get it now."

As Holly unwrapped the package, Kade informed Jen, "Holly recently told me the best way to honor Cassie's memory is to care for and nurture the people she loved." As Holly held up a plastic keychain, Kade said, "I couldn't agree more."

Holly read the crossed-out words *Davenport Ventures* written beneath the red circle warning sign with a red slash through its center. She dropped her chin and glared at Kade. "You got me a keychain to memorialize your refusal to change the stodgy name of your new firm? Why, thank you."

Kade smiled and pointed to the box.

"There's more?" Holly asked, removing the white cotton that covered the compartment beneath. She pulled out a rectangular platinum key chain with the letters DKV on the front. "This is pretty," she said, a question in her tone and all traces of sarcasm gone.

"Turn it over," Kade said.

Holly did so, revealing lettering in an elegant font, spelling the words DAVENPORT KELLER VENTURES. Holly's eyes darted to Kade's.

"Only one thing could make me happier than being this woman's partner," Kade said, quickly smiling at Jen before returning her attention to Holly. "Being yours as well."

Holly covered her mouth with her hand and started shaking her head in disbelief.

Kade nodded, as if to counteract Holly's movements. She squatted beside Holly and took her hand. "You're a talented assistant, and you'll be a brilliant fund manager. I'll be beside you every step of the way, as you've been with me all these years. Say yes."

Holly looked at Jen, who tilted her head toward Kade and said, "Anyone who can come out unscathed after dealing with her for so long has my vote."

"You really think I can do this?" Holly asked Kade.

"I know you can."

"Does this mean I don't have to do what you tell me?"

"Did you ever before?"

"There is that." Holly held Kade by the shoulders. "But Kade, have you thought this through? No one's going to want to work with me. I have no experience running companies."

"It so happens I have an idea on that front." Kade returned to Jen's side. "My next investment after Creative Care is in a company I'm starting whose mission is to get stroke victims and those with other brain injuries more immediate access to the rehabilitation tools they need to give them the best chance of a full recovery. Current software applications are severely lacking, and access to hardware is limited. We can do better. I need a CEO." Kade looked pointedly at Holly. "Know anyone?"

"It will take years, and there's no telling if I'll be any good. You should start with Davenport Ventures, then wait and see."

Kade turned to Jen and arched an eyebrow.

Jen said, "Definite CEO material."

Kade said to Holly, "First of all, admirable try, but no. Second, a version of Davenport Keller Ventures has existed for years. Time to make it official."

Holly rose and knelt between Jen and Kade, giving each a one-armed hug. She kissed Kade on the forehead. "In my first move as chief, I'm designating this office a work-free zone for the rest of the day." She headed for the exit and turned to Kade. "And you wondered why I leased a live-work loft." She rolled the door open and called over her shoulder, "Let me know what you think of the mattress."

Epilogue

A curious Jennifer Spencer entered Kade's condo, wondering what was in store. They'd been spending most of their evenings at Jen's place after Kade admitted a growing antipathy toward her own residence. So when Kade had asked her to join her for takeout after work tonight, she speculated Kade had something on her mind.

The door was unlocked, and Jen called out. Hearing Kade's reply, she followed the sound of her voice, leading her to the kitchen. Kade greeted her with an embrace and a kiss. Both were high on her list of favorite things in life, but they had stiff competition from another of her treasures, Kade's smile. It had the ability to transform a mediocre day into a fantastic one, infuse a stressful day with lightness. And ever since they'd gotten back together, Jen had seen it more and more frequently, her new personal balm for life's trials.

Not that Jen had much in the way of complaints. If she didn't have to split nights between Nana and Kade, life would be as close to perfect as possible.

She extended her arms to hold Kade out at enough distance to look her up and down. Kade was barefoot, her toenails a brightly polished, bold red Jen hadn't seen. The fit of the black yoga pants made possible by her exercise regimen showed off Kade's backside and thighs before flaring out at the leg, and a sleeveless hoodie highlighted her toned arms. Her hair was in a loose ponytail, with several strands falling alongside her cheekbones. Jen gently played with some of the ends. "I do love you in classy business attire, but casual Kade is pretty irresistible." Then she moved closer and pinched the hoodie's zipper clasp. She began slowly pulling it lower to get a glimpse of the lingerie beneath. "What's under here?"

Kade slapped her hand out of the way and gave her a swift kiss. "Focus." Then she stepped behind Jen and covered Jen's eyes. "I need your mind tonight, not just your body."

"Boo, hiss." Warm, soft lips trailing along the back of her neck met this complaint. She dipped her head to encourage Kade's exploration. "Are you sure about the mind thing?" Kade encouraged her forward and guided her into one of the chairs. When Kade pulled her hands away, Jen saw a number of photographs and images laid out, covering the table. Kade dragged a chair beside her and riffled through the photos, searching for something. She picked up an image. "What do you think?"

Multiple skylights streamed sunlight into a bright, spacious kitchen. "Wow," Jen said.

Kade handed her another one, this time of a large bedroom with cathedral ceilings, skylights, multiple sets of French doors leading onto a balcony, and a corner fireplace. "Are these from a house you looked at?" Jen asked. Kade had mentioned enlisting a realtor to shed light on the local real estate market while she considered what to do with her condo.

Jen had very specific ideas on the matter, all of which involved moving in together, but two things stood in the way. First, Kade's desire to leave her condo wasn't the same as wanting to live with Jen, and Jen didn't want to wind up under the same roof simply as a matter of convenience. Second, Jen's nerdishly old-fashioned side demanded some sort of formal commitment before cohabitating.

Six weeks into their official relationship, Jen took a step she'd never attempted. It would forever alter her life, yet she advanced without hesitation. From a neglected safe-deposit box, she'd sprung Nana's engagement ring, a gift Nana had given her years ago. Nana had hoped Jen would one day bestow it on her wife-to-be, and the jewel was presently being resized to fulfill its destiny.

Jen had no uncertainty as to what she wanted or when. But she didn't want to pressure Kade, a newcomer to the world of relationships. The entire time they'd known each other, Kade had been two paces behind Jen in terms of acknowledging her feelings. It was part of what made Kade uniquely Kade, and Jen was completely comfortable with it. So she simply listened as Kade worked through various ideas on the housing front.

"No. These are examples from an architect's portfolio he thinks can be utilized in a fixer-upper that's caught my eye. There's a ton of work to do, but the house has what's known as good bones."

Jen studied the pictures again. "Do you have loads of free time and a clandestine longing to install drywall I didn't know about?"

"Don't forget my overalls fetish."

Jen tapped the bedroom image. "I like the idea of you here. It has a kind of casual elegance." Another pile caught her attention, and she picked up the top image. "Why do you have pictures of Nana's house?"

"That's not Edna's house."

Jen turned to Kade, confused, then took another look at the picture. The layout, the furniture, and the color of the walls were similar to Edna's, but with more scrutiny, she could see the interior lacked the artwork and knickknacks her grandmother owned. She picked up another photo, a large two-story house in need of TLC. "What am I looking at?" she asked as she scanned the other photos.

Kade took her hand. "You love your neighborhood and it's close to work."

Jen nodded uncertainly, unable to piece together how this fit with anything she was seeing.

"And Edna loves her house and garden."

Jen offered another hesitant nod.

"And without traffic it's forty to forty-five minutes roundtrip for you to visit her. And me for that matter."

Jen sat back and studied Kade, searching for whatever was at issue. She gently rubbed her thumb along the back of Kade's hand. "You know I don't mind. Plus, you're the one doing most of the driving lately. Is something wrong?" Jen's stomach lurched. Was

Kade feeling taken advantage of because Jen wasn't insisting they spend equal time at their respective homes? Had she missed signals from Kade?

Kade grabbed a few photos of the two-story and set them in front of Jen. "This is the fixer-upper. It's in your neighborhood and coming on the market shortly." She picked up several of the ones that reminded Jen of Nana's. "These are architect renderings of what can be done to the downstairs with several structural changes. As you can see, it can mirror the layout of Edna's house. The backyard gets good sunlight and is a gardener's dream." Kade shifted in her chair and took both of Jen's hands. "Edna wants to stay in her house, and you want to spend more time with her. I've been siphoning you away too much."

Jen shook her head. "No. Kade, that is not true—"

"If we lived here, Edna could stay in the downstairs unit, and hopefully its familiarity would ease the transition for her. We could live above her, and you could see her daily. Plus, there's a detached garage that could be converted into an in-law unit for a live-in caretaker."

Jen weighed Kade's words and took a moment to appreciate the woman behind them. Never one for inaction, Kade was prioritizing Jen's family with an extremely thoughtful approach to their living situations, and her generosity toward Nana never failed to move her. Perhaps Kade was only one pace behind these days. She kissed Kade softly on her mouth. "You're unbelievably sweet to consider such a massive undertaking, and I love you for being so considerate of Nana's wishes. But I can't afford to buy or fix even a small fraction of something of this scale, let alone half. I'm barely keeping my and Edna's finances in the black as it is." She cupped Kade's cheek and smiled regretfully. "I hate to say no when you've given this so much thought, but I can't do it."

Kade pulled Jen's hand from her face and kissed her palm. "Finances aside, what do you think?"

Jen smiled. "I think that's a loaded question, and I refuse to answer on the grounds it may incriminate me."

"It's a good idea, and you know it."

Jen needed to create some distance if they were going to continue this conversation. Kade was an accomplished negotiator and difficult to win arguments against. She pushed her chair back and walked to the fridge, taking time to weigh how to approach the issue. She unscrewed the cap to a bottle of sparkling water and took a sip. Living with Kade and having Nana so close would be wonderful. But moving in with Kade merely to cut down on a commute seemed like a pragmatic solution to what should be a far more romantic question, regardless of how sexy Jen found Kade's consideration of Nana.

Although this conversation was helping move up Jen's vague timetable, it was far too soon to propose. Between their relationship, her new firm, and her surprising continued contact with Gordon, Kade had made a number of significant changes in her life recently. Moving out of her condo would be another biggie. Jen couldn't imagine planning a wedding too.

Kade interrupted her thought process. "Pretend I already live in a duplex walking distance from you."

"You don't."

"Not pursuing this simply because I happen to live here instead of in your neighborhood constitutes geographic discrimination."

"Would you like to lodge a formal complaint?" Jen asked, amused by Kade's tactics.

Kade rose and slid her arms around her. "I'd like to lodge with you." She kissed the corner of Jen's mouth. "Tell me you wouldn't feel better if Edna lived closer to you."

"I'd be lying."

"Then tell me what's really bothering you."

Jen set down the water so she could return Kade's embrace. "Honestly? Very little. I have you, and you're kind of blowing my mind with all of this. In a good way."

"Is it too much, too soon? Living together, I mean?" Kade asked.

"Too much? No. Definitely not." Kade was too astute not to pick up on what Jen wasn't saying, but still Jen circumvented the remark about timing, unprepared to go there.

Kade smiled. "Then what are we waiting for?" She put a finger to her lips as if considering something. "Oh. I think I know. Come." She took Jen by the hand and guided her into the dining room.

The number of clocks on the wall had decreased substantially. Only half a dozen remained. Jen said, "You've been downsizing."

Kade stood behind Jen and rested her chin on her shoulder. "Which one do you like best?"

Jen's eyes immediately went to the only antique among them. Its rim was darker than the cracked stone face, as if it had survived a fire. Full of character with smudges and faded black numbers, it seemed rich with history. But by far its most extraordinary feature was its lack of hands. There didn't appear to be a hole in the center from which a wheel would rotate, though Jen couldn't be sure from this distance. She moved in for a closer inspection. "I can't believe I've never noticed this one before. It's gorgeous."

Kade left the room briefly and returned with a step stool and a screwdriver. She removed the clock from its hook. "I thought you might like it. In fact, I was hoping you could help me with it." She set it on the dining-room table, along with the screwdriver. "The cover that houses the movement is stuck, and I thought together we might have the magic touch."

As she took a seat beside Kade, Jen silently questioned why a clock without hands would have a movement inside. There was nothing mechanical about it.

Kade slid it toward her and asked, "Why did you choose this one?" She held her fingers around a small compartment as if to hold it steady while Jen removed the cover. The entire backing seemed modern and out of place, as if it hadn't been part of the clockmaker's original.

Jen started the strange exercise, wondering why they were handling this timepiece, since her knowledge as to the interworking of clocks could fit on the head of the screw she was removing. "I was kind of hoping there was no movement, because I like what it communicates the way it is. It says, 'Don't waste your time by looking here. Seize the moment you have.'"

All four screws removed, she carefully lifted the cover, which came off readily, unlike Kade had led her to expect. The chamber was empty except for a small, tissue-wrapped item. Confused, she glanced at Kade, who nodded for her to proceed. As she unwrapped the thin paper, her fingers began to detect something hard, though not solid, since the paper gave way in the center.

Kade held her palms out below it, as if to catch whatever was inside in case it fell.

And then Jen saw it: a ring with a swirl of platinum twisted with a swirl of tiny diamonds. She snapped her eyes to Kade's, and Kade dropped to her knees between Jen's legs.

Kade took her hands. "You're right, sweetheart. What I've learned about time is exactly what this clock conveys: all we have is the present. And if we have each other, we're without beginning or end because we've become one. Be timeless with me."

About the Author

Heather Blackmore oversees finance for SF Bay Area technology start-ups. In a seemingly counterintuitive move, she got her MSA and CPA with the goal of one day being able to work part-time so she could write. The right and left sides of her brain have been at war ever since.

Heather was a Goldie Award finalist for debut author and a Rainbow Award finalist in the contemporary lesbian romance and debut author categories for her first novel, *Like Jazz*.

Visit www.heatherblackmore.com and/or drop her a line at heather@heatherblackmore.com.

Books Available from Bold Strokes Books

A Country Girl's Heart by Dena Blake. When Kat Jackson gets a second chance at love, following her heart will prove the hardest decision of all. (978-1-63555-134-1)

Dangerous Waters by Radclyffe. Life, death, and war on the home front. Two women join forces against a powerful opponent, nature itself. (978-1-63555-233-1)

Fury's Death by Brey Willows. When all we hold sacred fails, who will be there to save us? (978-1-63555-063-4)

It's Not a Date by Heather Blackmore. Kade's desire to keep things with Jen on a professional level is in Jen's best interest. Yet what's in Kade's best interest…is Jen. (978-1-63555-149-5)

Killer Winter by Kay Bigelow. Just when she thought things could get no worse, homicide Lieutenant Leah Samuels learns the woman she loves has betrayed her in devastating ways. (978-1-63555-177-8)

Score by MJ Williamz. Will an addiction to pain pills destroy Ronda's chance with the woman she loves or will she come out on top and score a happily ever after? (978-1-62639-807-8)

Spring's Wake by Aurora Rey. When wanderer Willa Lange falls for Provincetown B&B owner Nora Calhoun, will past hurts and a fifteen-year age gap keep them from finding love? (978-1-63555-035-1)

The Lurid Sea by Tom Cardamone. Cursed to spend eternity on his knees, Nerites is having the time of his life. (978-1-62639-911-2)

The Northwoods by Jane Hoppen. When Evelyn Bauer, disguised as her dead husband, George, travels to a Northwoods logging camp to work, she and the camp cook Sarah Bell forge a friendship fraught with both tenderness and turmoil. (978-1-63555-143-3)

Truth or Dare by C. Spencer. For a group of six lesbian friends, life changes course after one long snow-filled weekend. (978-1-63555-148-8)

A Heart to Call Home by Jeannie Levig. When Jessie Weldon returns to her hometown after thirty years, can she and her childhood crush Dakota Scott heal the tragic past that links them? (978-1-63555-059-7)

Children of the Healer by Barbara Ann Wright. Life becomes desperate for ex-soldier Cordelia Ross when the indigenous aliens of her planet are drawn into a civil war and old enemies linger in the shadows. Book Three of the Godfall Series. (978-1-63555-031-3)

Hearts Like Hers by Melissa Brayden. Coffee shop owner Autumn Primm is ready to cut loose and live a little, but is the baggage that comes with out-of-towner Kate Carpenter too heavy for anything long term? (978-1-63555-014-6)

Love at Cooper's Creek by Missouri Vaun. Shaw Daily flees corporate life to find solace in the rural Blue Ridge Mountains, but escapism eludes her when her attentions are captured by small town beauty Kate Elkins. (978-1-62639-960-0)

Somewhere Over Lorain Road by Bud Gundy. Over forty years after murder allegations shattered the Esker family, can Don Esker find the true killer and clear his dying father's name? (978-1-63555-124-2)

Twice in a Lifetime by PJ Trebelhorn. Detective Callie Burke can't deny the growing attraction to her late friend's widow, Taylor Fletcher, who also happens to own the bar where Callie's sister works. (978-1-63555-033-7)

Undiscovered Affinity by Jane Hardee. Will a no strings attached affair be enough to break Olivia's control and convince Cardic that love does exist? (978-1-63555-061-0)

Between Sand and Stardust by Tina Michele. Are the lifelong bonds of love strong enough to conquer time, distance, and heartache when Haven Thorne and Willa Bennette are given another chance at forever? (978-1-62639-940-2)

Charming the Vicar by Jenny Frame. When magician and atheist Finn Kane seeks refuge in an English village after a spiritual crisis, can local vicar Bridget Claremont restore her faith in life and love? (978-1-63555-029-0)

Data Capture by Jesse J. Thoma. Lola Walker is undercover on the hunt for cybercriminals while trying not to notice the woman who might be perfectly wrong for her for all the right reasons. (978-1-62639-985-3)

Epicurean Delights by Renee Roman. Ariana Marks had no idea a leisure swim would lead to being rescued, in more ways than one, by the charismatic Hudson Frost. (978-1-63555-100-6)

Heart of the Devil by Ali Vali. We know most of Cain and Emma Casey's story, but *Heart of the Devil* will take you back to where it began one fateful night with a tray loaded with beer. (978-1-63555-045-0)

Known Threat by Kara A. McLeod. When Special Agent Ryan O'Connor reluctantly questions who protects the Secret Service, she learns courage truly is found in unlikely places. Agent O'Connor Series #3. (978-1-63555-132-7)

Seer and the Shield by D. Jackson Leigh. Time is running out for the Dragon Horse Army while two unlikely heroines struggle to put aside their attraction and find a way to stop a deadly cult. Dragon Horse War, Book 3. (978-1-63555-170-9)

Sinister Justice by Steve Pickens. When a vigilante targets citizens of Jake Finnigan's hometown, Jake and his partner Sam fall under suspicion themselves as they investigate the murders. (978-1-63555-094-8)

The Universe Between Us by Jane C. Esther. Ana Mitchell must make the hardest choice of her life: the promise of new love Jolie Dann on Earth, or a humanity-saving mission to colonize Mars. (978-1-63555-106-8)

Touch by Kris Bryant. Can one touch heal a heart? (978-1-63555-084-9)

Change in Time by Robyn Nyx. Working in the past is hell on your future. The Extractor Series: Book Two. (978-1-62639-880-1)

Love After Hours by Radclyffe. When Gina Antonelli agrees to renovate Carrie Longmire's new house, she doesn't welcome Carrie's overtures at friendship or her own unexpected attraction. A Rivers Community Novel. (978-1-63555-090-0)

Nantucket Rose by CF Frizzell. Maggie Jordan can't wait to convert an historic Nantucket home into a B&B, but doesn't expect to fall for mariner Ellis Chilton, who has more claim to the house than Maggie realizes. (978-1-63555-056-6)

Picture Perfect by Lisa Moreau. Falling in love wasn't supposed to be part of the stakes for Olive and Gabby, rival photographers in the competition of a lifetime. (978-1-62639-975-4)

Set the Stage by Karis Walsh. Actress Emilie Danvers takes the stage again in Ashland, Oregon, little realizing that landscaper Arden Philips is about to offer her a very personal romantic lead role. (978-1-63555-087-0)

Strike a Match by Fiona Riley. When their attempts at matchmaking fizzle out, firefighter Sasha and reluctant millionairess Abby find themselves turning to each other to strike a perfect match. (978-1-62639-999-0)

The Price of Cash by Ashley Bartlett. Cash Braddock is doing her best to keep her business afloat, stay out of jail, and avoid Detective Kallen. It's not working. (978-1-62639-708-8)

Under Her Wing by Ronica Black. At Angel's Wings Rescue, dogs are usually the ones saved, but when quiet Kassandra Haden meets outspoken owner Jayden Beaumont, the two stubborn women just might end up saving each other. (978-1-63555-077-1)

Underwater Vibes by Mickey Brent. When Hélène, a translator in Brussels, Belgium, meets Sylvie, a young Greek photographer and swim coach, unsettling feelings hijack Hélène's mind and body—even her poems. (978-1-63555-002-3)

A More Perfect Union by Carsen Taite. Major Zoey Granger and DC fixer Rook Daniels risk their reputations for a chance at true love while dealing with a scandal that threatens to rock the military. (978-1-62639-754-5)

Arrival by Gun Brooke. The spaceship *Pathfinder* reaches its passengers' new homeworld where danger lurks in the shadows while Pamas Seclan disembarks and finds unexpected love in young science genius Darmiya Do Voy. (978-1-62639-859-7)

Captain's Choice by VK Powell. Architect Kerstin Anthony's life is going to plan until Bennett Carlyle, the first girl she ever kissed, is assigned to her latest and most important project, a police district substation. (978-1-62639-997-6)

Falling Into Her by Erin Zak. Pam Phillips, widow at the age of forty, meets Kathryn Hawthorne, local Chicago celebrity, and it changes her life forever—in ways she hadn't even considered possible. (978-1-63555-092-4)

Hookin' Up by MJ Williamz. Will Leah get what she needs from casual hookups or will she see the love she desires right in front of her? (978-1-63555-051-1)

King of Thieves by Shea Godfrey. When art thief Casey Marinos meets bounty hunter Finnegan Starkweather, the crimes of the past just might set the stage for a payoff worth more than she ever dreamed possible. (978-1-63555-007-8)

Lucy's Chance by Jackie D. As a serial killer haunts the streets, Lucy tries to stitch up old wounds with her first love in the wake of a small town's rapid descent into chaos. (978-1-63555-027-6)

Right Here, Right Now by Georgia Beers. When Alicia Wright moves into the office next door to Lacey Chamberlain's accounting firm, Lacey is about to find out that sometimes the last person you want is exactly the person you need. (978-1-63555-154-9)

Strictly Need to Know by MB Austin. Covert operator Maji Rios will do whatever she must to complete her mission, but saving a gorgeous stranger from Russian mobsters was not in her plans. (978-1-63555-114-3)

Tailor-Made by Yolanda Wallace. Tailor Grace Henderson doesn't date clients, but when she meets gender-bending model Dakota Lane, she's tempted to throw all the rules out the window. (978-1-63555-081-8)

Time Will Tell by M. Ullrich. With the ability to time travel, Eva Caldwell will have to decide between having it all and erasing it all. (978-1-63555-088-7)